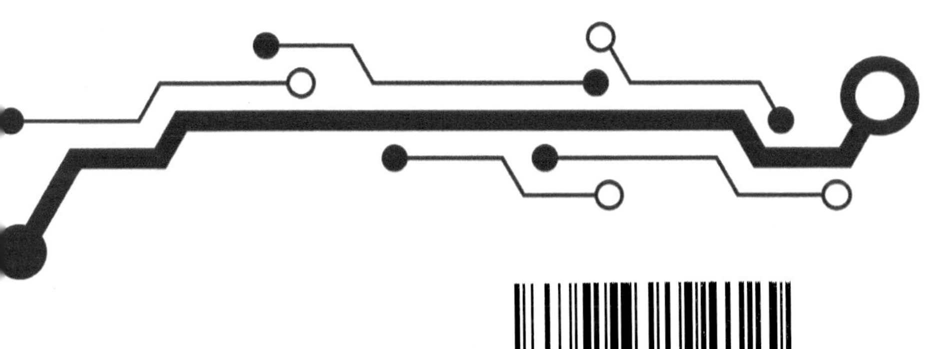

COLLECT THE KEY.

REACH THE END.

DEFEAT THE GOD.

Books by P. J. Hoover

Game of the Gods Series
A Broken Truce
A Ruined Land
A Buried Spark

The Hidden Code

The Dying Earth Series
Solstice

The Demigod Chronicles
Furiously Awesome

Tut: My Immortal Life Series
Tut: The Story of My Immortal Life
Tut: My Epic Battle to Save the World

The Forgotten Worlds Trilogy
The Emerald Tablet
The Navel of the World
The Necropolis

Camp Hercules Series
The Curse of Hera

A BURIED SPARK

GAME OF THE GODS
BOOK 3

P. J. Hoover

ROOTS IN MYTH, AUSTIN, TX

For my readers,
thank you!

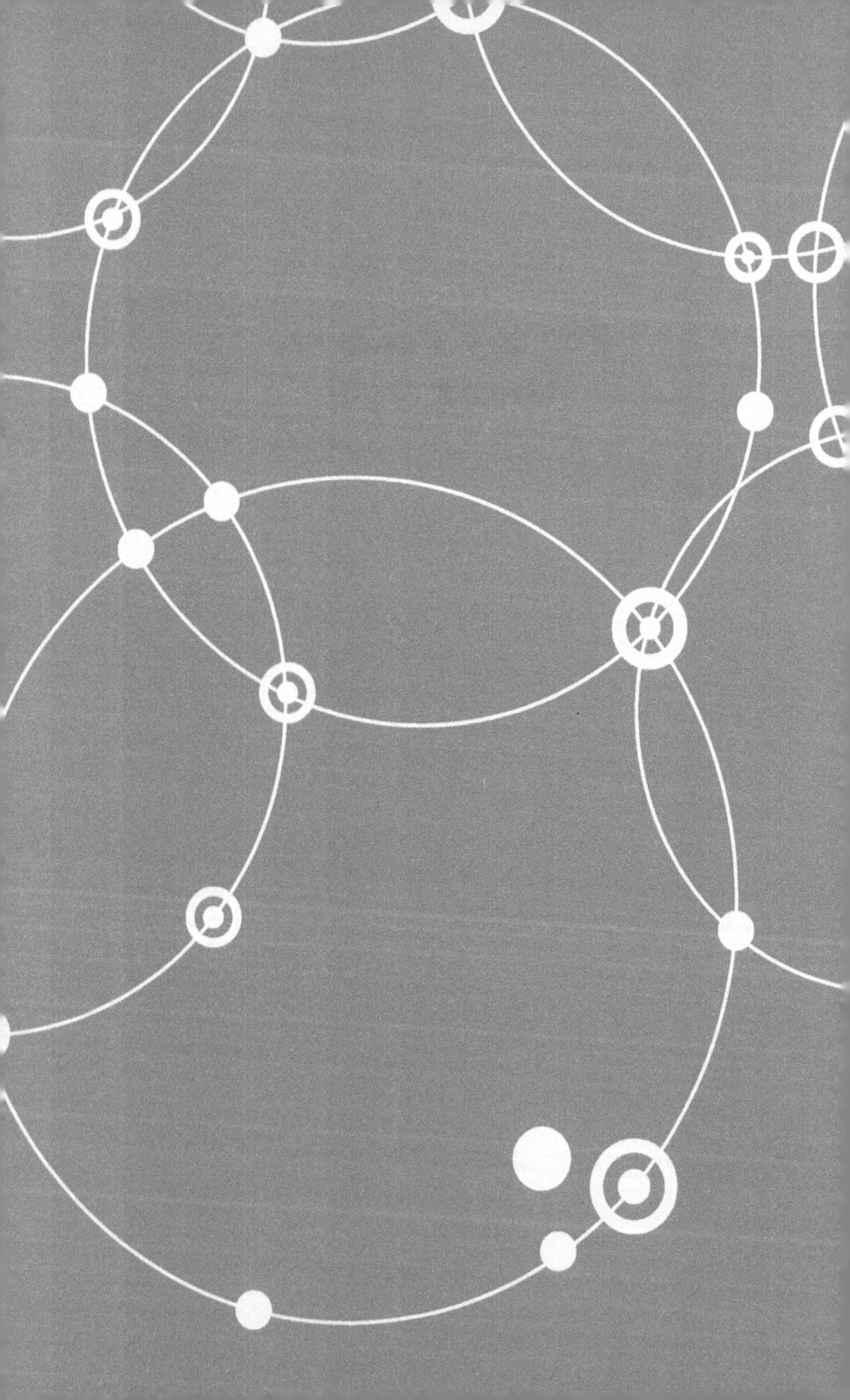

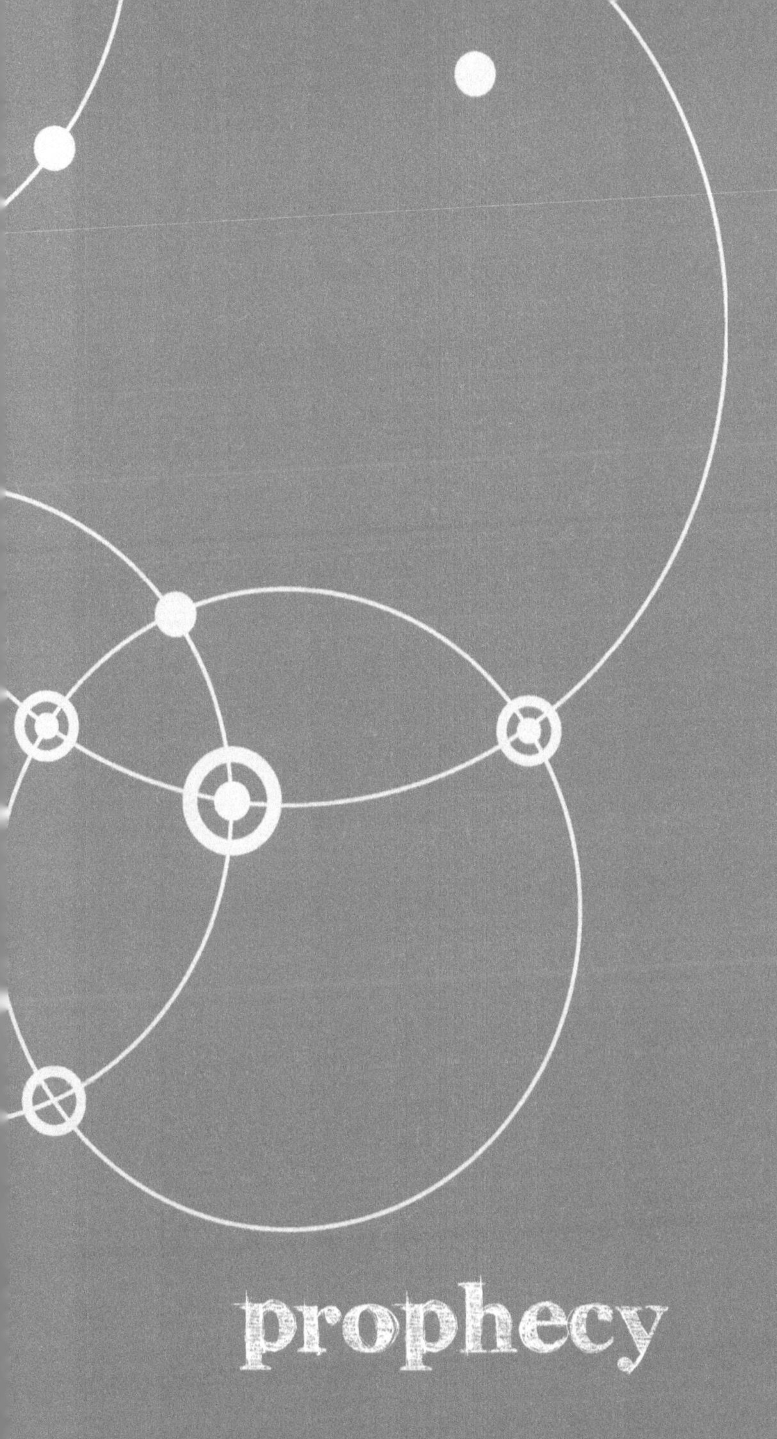
prophecy

i

TAYLOR AND I WATCH AS COLE AND
Pia get farther away on the glowing river. The lava bubbles beneath them, threatening to reach the floating platform where
they stand, but the platform moves with it, lifting gently to keep
them safe.

To keep Pia safe.

I ball my hands into fists. I knew it. I hadn't trusted her from the
start. I'd wanted to, once Cole told me what she'd been through,
but from the second we'd seen her in the simulation, my sensors
had gone on high alert. My instincts had been trying to tell me,
but I'd pushed them away. Still I'd never thought she'd manage to
turn Cole against me. It's one more horrible reminder of what we
face in this game.

Trust no one.

I swallow the hurt that builds inside me. I'd never thought
Cole was included in that statement. Above everyone else, Cole
was my rock. Now he's gone.

His voice echoes in my mind. *We weren't meant to be together. I see that now.*

Except we were meant to be together. I'd known it from the moment I met him, back in Louisiana, when this whole disaster started. How could I have been so wrong?

Taylor grabs something from the dark ground we stand on and throws it hard toward the river of lava. It's discarded code formed together into a huge flat chunk of metal. Based on its size, I have no idea where she gets the strength to do this, unless physical rules don't apply the same way here in the Nether Zone as they do in the other zones we've been in. It spins through the air like a Frisbee, nearly reaching Cole and Pia, but falls short before reaching the floating platform they ride on.

"Get back here!" Taylor shouts. She grits her teeth together and punches the air. "Don't you leave us here!"

Cole doesn't look our way. But Pia . . . She turns to look, and the edges of her lips lift into a smile I hate more than the gods who placed us in this game in the first place. If I ever see her again—no, scratch that. I will see her again, and when I do, I'll . . . what? Would I kill her?

I don't know. I'm not a killer . . . not deep down. But this goes beyond anything that has happened so far.

"Edie, they're leaving," Taylor says, as if she thinks I don't notice.

"Maybe there's . . ." My words trail off. There's what? A mistake? There is no mistaking what is going on. Cole's words had been clear. No matter how much I want them to be something else, they repeat over in my mind. Cole has turned against me.

"There's nothing except a bullseye painted on them when I see them," Taylor says. "Now how do we get across this stupid river?"

I squeeze my fist and force away the rejection that flares in my mind. I am stronger than this. I am not going to give in to it. Cole is gone. I have to accept that and move on. Move forward. And moving forward means doing what we came here to do. We have a key to find, hidden here in the Nether Zone. The only difference is now instead of just having Owen and Abigail looking for the key, Cole and Pia are also on an opposing side. I am not letting any of them stand in my way. I'll fight them with everything I can.

"We need payment," I say, hardening my face. I make a pocket in my mind, and I file away my feelings for Cole. There is no room for them if I want to get the key first. I have to pretend that Cole is no one except one more competitor. And sure, maybe our number of opponents has dwindled, but that only means the ones that are left are the strongest. Owen. Abigail. Cole. Pia. Taylor. Me.

And Hudson. He'd followed Owen and Abigail. And hopefully he can stop them. Or at least slow them down.

"Where do we get payment?" Taylor says.

So vividly I see Cole collecting the prize. "Cole got the coin in the gaming zone."

Taylor's scowl is filled with distaste. "The gaming zone. Hell no we're going back there." The gaming zone had nearly kept all of us. There are still plenty of kids trapped there. Plenty of kids we can free once we get the key and gain entry to Main Control Room Alpha. It's where we'd found Pia. I'd freed her. And that's when everything had changed.

I can't go back to the gaming zone either. If I did that, I could be lost forever. Even thinking about it, remembering how good I was, makes me want to delve back in and see if I can make it to the next level. There was such a bliss in it. No worries. Only the game. But that is not going to happen.

I turn back to where we came from. The world gate I'd created is gone, blended back into the code that makes up the Nether Zone. Even now, when I focus, I see the bits of code streaming everywhere, making up everything that exists in the virtual world around us. I'd seen more when I'd had the Oculus. It had heightened my ability. Now Taylor has the Oculus—inside her eye socket, so there is no way I'm getting another chance to look through it.

"Do you see anything with it?" I ask. For me, I'd seen through the layers of the virtual world and back into the real world. I was able to see some of the destruction being caused outside. It almost felt like I could pass right through. And then there was Elise. She'd looked through the Oculus, and she almost hadn't been able to resist its power . . . as if there is more to it than I was able to see.

Taylor finally shifts her face away from her anger at our current situation. "Anything? More like everything. Edie, it's crazy." She opens and closes her eyes, alternating which is open. "I don't even know what all this stuff is. It's like layers upon layers of colors and images and . . . I don't know. There are flickering pictures, but I don't know what they are. What's it supposed to be showing me?"

Raven had desperately wanted the Oculus. But even though it was there, in her simulation, it was like she was afraid to take it from Amos herself. Afraid or unable to. That was why she tried to trick me into getting it for her. But after seeing how badly she wanted it and how much it tempted Elise, I knew I could never give it to her.

"The layers of the worlds," I say. "At least that's what it looked like to me."

Taylor closes her right eye and keeps only the left one open, the one with the Oculus. Still so fresh in my mind is Amos cutting her eyeball from her head and devouring it. But I don't bring this up for obvious reasons.

"Yeah, well, it's kind of hard to focus on any one thing," Taylor says. "There's just so much stuff."

We don't need to focus on all the layers, only the one we're in right now. We need to find a way across the river of lava.

"Try to pull back your focus," I say. "Think only about the Nether Zone. Can you see it?"

"What? Are you an expert?" Taylor snaps.

Same old Taylor. Instead of annoying me, it actually helps me calm down.

I can't help the grin that slips onto my face.

"What?"

"Nothing," I say. "I'm just glad you're here." I don't know what I would do without Taylor. She is without a doubt the strongest of us all.

"Yeah, well anyway. I'm doing the best I can here." She pulls her head back as if that will help her focus. "This layer is really dark. And all this shit around here . . ." She kicks one of the many bones that litter the ground. "It's getting in the way."

"Is there anything we can use?" I say. "Some kind of payment?" I pull on my powers and try to bring the bits of the world together into a coin like Cole had, but the zone seems to be working against me. It won't let the object manifest.

Taylor shakes her head. "Give me a second."

While she tries to focus through the Oculus, I tap the wristband that I still wear. I hope for the green concentric circles to appear. For Zachary Gomez to pipe through on my heads-up display. The tiny screen flickers, turning solid green for two full seconds, then back to black and stays that way. I tap it a few more times trying to get some response, but there's nothing. It's dead, like everything else around us. Like my powers.

No, I can't jump to conclusions. It could be that my powers need time to recharge or something.

"Okay, wait a second," Taylor says. "I'm starting to see things." She nods toward the river of lava. "Like out there. I can't see the other side. But there's an invisible path, kind of, floating above the river. Like a road made out of computer code. Do you see it?

Maybe you can yank it over toward us."

I focus again on the code of this world, but instead of trying to create a coin for payment, I grasp in the air for the path she's talking about. My mind gets hold of a tiny piece of it. A small spark forms in my brain, and I almost have it. This is progress. I grab for more of it, but the second I do, it slips away.

I shake my head. "Almost."

"Yeah, well, almost won't get us across," Taylor says.

This is true. I try again, but it's worse this second time. It's like the simulation knows what I'm hoping to accomplish and is actually stopping me. Like someone besides Pia and Cole doesn't want me to get across. Still I try a third time. This time, the moment I attempt to grab hold of the code, a spark shoots into me, throwing me backward.

I land hard on my butt. Okay, fine. I get the hint. Going about this the straightforward way isn't going to work.

I unhook the compass from my belt and flip open the cover. The needle spins around one full time and then settles on the river ahead. There is no doubt that it's the direction we need to go. But maybe there is another way. I spin around slowly. I want the compass needle to point somewhere else. A secret passage. A different path I haven't noticed. But the needle always points the same way that Cole and Pia went.

"That's unhelpful," I say, and I hook it back to my belt. I don't want to lose it, especially not after Elise fixed it. Without knowing what is ahead or where to go, I can't be without it.

Taylor grabs a piece of metal from the ground. It's covered with grime, but she wipes it on her shirt to make a more solid grip.

"I'm getting a bad feeling about being here, Edie," Taylor says.

The hairs on my arm stand up, almost like at her words, the bad feeling becomes contagious. "What kind of bad feeling?"

She holds the piece of metal like a weapon. The sheered edge looks sharp enough to slice off my forearm. She circles me, as if she's guarding me. "Something is going to happen."

The hot air presses in on me from all sides. "What?"

Taylor circles again, listening to the crackle of lava and the shifting of junk that surrounds us. "I don't know," she finally says. Then she closes her right eye and looks straight out at the lava. "Something from there."

The river of lava is the same as far as I can see. Bubbles lift and pop. Streams of darkness and light blend together like a giant mixing bowl. The platform that Cole and Pia disappeared on does not return.

We need to get out of here.

We need to get across.

The two thoughts conflict. Across the river is the key, and we need to get the key. But my gut also tells me that staying here any longer is not a good thing.

I squat back down to the ground, and I scramble through trash until I find a small piece of metal. I flip it over in my palm, looking at the sharp edges where it's been severed from a larger piece. It almost looks like a bracket, the kind that would be used to hold a computer board. But when I pull my focus back, it turns from the cruddy piece of metal into a stream of data. There are bits and pieces to describe the color, the edges, the type of metal used. Now to use my powers to shift it.

"Edie, we need to go," Taylor says.

I shake my head. It will work this time. "I got this." I start with the base metal: aluminum. All I have to do is make the smallest change. A change so tiny that whatever is trying to keep my powers from working won't even notice.

The spark flares inside me. The power is mine. I shift the code around, making the change, turning it to solid gold. But it still looks like a piece of junk. I reshape it, forming a circle. A coin, like Cole had. Then I change the color, making it shine so brightly that I have to look away.

I hold it up for Taylor to see. "What do you think?"

Taylor shakes her head. "I think we need to leave."

I stand up. "We need to cross."

She clenches her teeth together. "I don't think that's a good idea."

But it is a good idea. We have to get across the river, and now we have a coin as payment.

I take the coin back and flip it up in the air. Only then do I realize it doesn't have a heads or a tails. I delve back in, just for a moment, and form Alpha on one side and Omega on the other. The beginning and the end. I only hope we're reaching the end of our journey.

"Let's go," I say, clenching the coin in my fist.

Taylor doesn't move.

"Come on." I take a step back toward the lava river. My heavy boots crunch bits and pieces of the junk below.

"No, Edie." Taylor grabs at my hand.

But the platform appears, almost as if it can sense the gold. The tall silhouette is there, pure darkness with nothing to distinguish fingers from hand from arm.

I yank my hand away from her. "Come on, Taylor. They already have a huge head start."

Taylor doesn't move. Her eyes are locked on the river of lava. Her left eye shows no emotion, but her right eye is filled with fear.

Taylor is never afraid. It's enough to give me pause.

"What?" I say.

"Someone is out there," Taylor says.

Cole? Or Pia? The cloaked silhouette? Or someone worse?

My steps pause. "Who?"

"They're watching us. They're waiting . . ."

Watching us. Waiting. And the second Taylor says it, Elise's words return to me. *Don't cross the first river. You'll die if you do.*

This has to be what she was talking about. This is the first river we've come to since she told me. But we have to get across. The key is on the other side, and we need the key.

My foot lifts and hovers, ready to move forward.

"Edie—"

But she never gets the chance to finish what she's saying. Something flies through the air and hits the figure on the platform which is almost to the shore of the river. The silhouetted figure explodes in a mass of fire. He raises his arms. The fabric of his dark cloak bursts into flames. He's covered from head to toe.

He falls backward, into the river of lava. Slowly he sinks in, but no sooner is he under the lava, it begins to rise, stretching upward inch by inch until it forms a wall of lava instead of a river. It blocks everything.

Taylor and I scramble backward. I trip on something and fall flat on my back. Taylor grabs my arm and drags me to my feet. I can't pull my eyes away from the wall of lava. If we'd gotten on the floating platform, the fireball would have hit us. We'd have been trapped on it, burning alive. That would have been us. And now there's no way to cross. But in case I thought the wall of lava would block our attacker from us, I would be wrong. Before I can process what is happening, another ball of fire punches through the lava and lands two feet away. We may not be able to see through the lava, but whoever is firing at us is able to.

"Run!" I shout, and we take off. But the world behind us is dark and full of ruin. There is nowhere to hide.

TAYLOR AND I RUN ALONG THE BANK

of the river of lava, trying to get away. Fireballs come at us, bursting through the living, glowing wall, landing at our feet. The lava that gets sprayed splatters on the ground, barely missing us. The entire zone is a wasteland of nothing with nowhere to hide. We keep running, but unless we find somewhere to go, we will die.

I yank on Taylor's arm, pulling her back from the river. Then, without thinking about what I'm doing, I grab the bits of computer code around us with my mind and pull them together, forming a solid barrier in front of us. I hardly have time to register that my power has worked flawlessly.

It's not a second too soon. A fireball smacks into the barrier. I almost lose the hold on it. Fire covers the entire thing, but it stays together . . . barely.

"I saw this happen," Taylor says. "I knew it."

"How?"

Another fireball hits.

She points to the Oculus. "I saw it with this thing. It

showed me."

Her words twist into the truth in my mind even as another fireball smacks into our makeshift barrier. "You saw the future?"

"Maybe."

If that's true, then it makes more sense why Raven wanted the Oculus so badly. Seeing through the layers of virtual worlds is one thing. Seeing the future is totally different.

"Who's firing at us?" I ask.

Taylor shakes her head. "No idea. I mean I see them. It's one person. No one else around. But I can't see who it is."

"What do you see?" There could be some sort of clue.

She narrows her left eye just as another fireball slams into the barricade. It holds, but I'm not sure for how much longer.

"Their face is covered," she says. "I can't see who it is."

Whoever it is most definitely is trying to kill us. I'd think it was Owen, but even with his dad helping him out, I don't see how he would have the power for this. And if it were lightning I would assume it was Abigail. But this is straight-up fire.

An enormous fireball hits the barrier, and this time a small crack appears. I try to repair it, diving into the code I formed, but it's spreading too fast. I grab for it again, but now that I'm actually focusing on using my power, it doesn't work. Then the entire thing comes down and shatters at our feet.

Someone grabs my arm from behind.

I whip around and raise my fists, ready to fight. Standing there is Zachary Gomez. His face is charred with smoke from the burning zone around us. His dark hair sticks out in five different directions. An entire sleeve is torn off his plaid shirt. Whatever he's been through, it can't have been any easier than it's been for us.

"Come with me," he says.

There is no time for questions. He takes off away from the lava waterfall, and Taylor and I follow. Fireballs continue to pummel us from behind, but they're getting farther away. We run into the darkness and come to a metal barrier. The end of the line, I think. But Zachary taps some kind of pattern on the barrier. Small lights illuminate where his fingers touch, and the barrier splits apart, revealing a path. No sooner are we inside, the panel closes behind us. I jump as a fireball smacks into it, lighting the entire thing up bright orange. I think it will melt, but it holds. We don't stick around to watch any longer.

The path winds around in the darkness and has walls that seem to be made of pure darkness, like the silhouette on the floating platform.

Zachary leads the way to the end of the path. We come to another wall, but he does the same thing, tapping some kind of keypad. He uses a different pattern this time. A panel slides open and he rushes inside. As soon as Taylor and I are in also, the panel slides closed.

"What are you doing here?" I say, trying to grasp the fact that Zachary is really here, standing in front of me. I push him on the arm to see if he's real. Well, at least as real as I am.

"I'm—" Zachary starts.

"Who is this?" Taylor says. She glares at Zachary, like she'll rip his throat out if he sneezes wrong.

That's right. They've never met. Zachary met me and Cole back in at the end of the labyrinth, and he communicated with me through the heads-up display. But besides Cole, my friends have not met him.

Zachary backs up and put his hands up in defense. "I'm a friend of Edie's."

I let the words settle in my mind. A friend. Yeah, that's true. In a weird sort of way. Zachary has helped save my butt any number of times. I guess I have to add this one to the list. But with him being a minor god, I wonder how much of this he's responsible for in the first place.

"This is Zachary Gomez," I say. "He was the one who gave me the KLAM STEW cheat code back in the labyrinth."

"You're one of the programmers?" Taylor says, and she narrows her eyes even more. I think if she had her bow and arrows right now, she would put an arrow through his heart and never give it another thought. In all fairness, the programmers of these simulations are sadistic, Zachary included.

"Just of a couple zones," Zachary says. "They weren't bad, I swear."

Taylor only glares in response. But what defense can Zachary have? Adam, Taylor's twin brother, had died back in the labyrinth, and Zachary had been one of the main programmers for that simulation.

"What are you doing here?" I ask.

Zachary's face flushes and he points to my wrist. "I got your message."

The wristband. I tap it again, but it remains inactive. "I didn't think it worked."

"It gave me your location," he says. "I thought you might need help."

"Edie doesn't need your help," Taylor says before I can say a word. "Edie could kick your ass if she wanted to."

I kind of love how she's sticking up for me. Like she's totally on my side. Part of the team. So much of our past has been tenuous, and sure, having Cole run off with Pia completely sucks, but it's also cemented Taylor's loyalty.

"Well, yeah, that's true," Zachary says. "But I can program things. I can do things to help."

"Edie can program," Taylor says. "She doesn't need you to program anything. Got it?"

"What?" Zachary says. "You want me to put you back out there so you can get killed by a flaming projectile? Does that sound good?"

Taylor crosses her arms. "Maybe."

I step between them, hoping to diffuse the tension. "It's okay, Taylor. He helped me get through the other simulation."

"Simulations," Zachary says, emphasizing the plural.

"Simulations," I say. "And we're happy for any help you can give us now."

Zachary runs a hand through his messy dark hair. It looks like he's never owned a hairbrush. "This zone . . . This isn't how it's supposed to be."

"What? We aren't supposed to get killed before we've even started?" Taylor says. "Because that would be a pretty shitty simulation."

But the fact that Zachary is confused at this zone worries me. "What do you mean?" I ask.

He gestures back out toward where we came from. "I mean that the Nether Zone was just a dumping ground for us. For the programmers to stick pieces of code we didn't need. Or didn't want."

"Okay. And . . . ?" As far as I can tell, that's what it looked like out there.

"And there was never any lava river. Never any cloaked figure to take people across. None of that was there."

"So you think we're just making it up?" Taylor says. She still has the piece of metal in her hand, her grip tight on it.

Zachary looks to the metal weapon like he's worried if he says the wrong thing, she'll split him open. It is a valid concern.

"You guys aren't making it up," Zachary says. "But the thing is that those elements shouldn't exist. The river. The ferryman. The fireballs. The programmers never put them there."

"But they do exist," I say. They exist and they're able to kill us.

Zachary leans against the dark circular wall around us. The room is a solid dome, all perfectly black. Low light glows from the ceiling, casting shadows everywhere. There's no way to tell where the panel we came through is.

"Now I see that," Zachary says. "I'd heard rumors, but I wasn't sure they were true."

"What rumors?" Taylor asks.

He blows out a deep breath. "Here's what I heard. Raven was supposed to have the key. She did have the key. And then . . . I don't know. Someone took it. Or tricked her. Or maybe she gave it away. With Raven, you just don't know. Her motives are always a little unclear. So is her loyalty, for that matter, but that could be said for any of the gods. Anyway, whoever it was got the key. They brought it here. And then they created that lava river and built up a simulation on the other side of it, outside the Nether Zone. A new simulation. Unsanctioned."

"Who?" Taylor says.

He grits his teeth and lowers his voice. "One of the gods."

"Like you?" I say.

Taylor scowls. "This guy's no god."

It might be my imagination, but Zachary seems to stand a little taller. "Well, technically, I am."

Taylor rolls her eyes. "You don't look like a god."

"And you know what the gods look like how?" Zachary says in what may be the most godly act I've ever seen of him. At least he's willing to stand up to her. Maybe that's what finally softens her toward him.

She shrugs. "I just know that the gods don't look like you. You're a kid."

Zachary pats down his hair like he's trying to straighten it. "Looks can be deceiving. You should remember that."

"You should remember—" Taylor starts, but I put up a hand

to stop her. Now isn't the time to argue about how gods are supposed to look. From what I've seen, gods can look however they want. Iva and Elise are proof of that.

"Which god is it?" I say, cutting her off.

He glances around, like someone might overhear, then whispers once again. "One of the old gods. Gods of the second age. This one . . . Chaos is the best way to think of him."

At the words, I'm back in the labyrinth simulation, in Zone Omega. I fight the old god in the golden throne. I watch the snakes cover him. Watch his body shrivel away to nothing. I kill him. But that's not the god we're talking about. That god is dead. The god Zachary is talking about, Chaos, is not.

"I thought the old gods were dead," I say. "Aren't they?" I wish the answer was no. I know it's not. It had taken every bit of my strength to kill the old god in the throne room. Even with as ancient and decrepit as he was, he'd gained control over me, Cole, and Zachary for that matter.

"We're pretty sure they're all dead except for one," Zachary says. "But—"

Taylor puts up a hand. "Don't say something like 'He's the worst of the bunch' or anything like that."

"But he's—" Zachary starts again.

She points at him. "Don't say it."

Zachary puts up his hands. "Okay. I won't. But we're pretty sure Chaos is the one who took the key from Raven. He knows he's dying. But he doesn't want to die. He wants to get his power back."

"Nobody wants to die," Taylor says.

"True," Zachary says. "But the rumors say that Chaos has a plan. He created this new simulation. Simulation Omega. Hid the key here. He set it up like a game to see who could find it. Who could get to the end. But it's got to be a trap. He needs to figure out who the strongest of you are—which ones of you are able to get the key—so he can steal your power."

The words swish around in my mind. "So we need to get this key, but it's all a trap."

"Exactly," Zachary says. "But the worst part is that we minor gods don't know anything about this place beyond the lava river."

"You and Iva?" I say.

He nods. "And Elise. Raven. A few others. We don't know the rules. We don't know the structure."

"What do you know?" Taylor asks.

"Not much," Zachary says. "But I do know that someone out there is trying to kill you. Someone who most likely works for Chaos."

That's reassuring. In the off chance I thought it was only a co-incidence that someone was shooting fireballs at us, now I know it's definitely personal.

"So what do we do?" I ask.

Zachary looks around as if something finally dawns on him. "Where's . . . Cole?"

A hard ball forms in my stomach. "He's gone."

"Gone where?"

I open my mouth and try to figure out what to say, but Taylor gets up in Zachary's face. "Just don't mention it, okay?"

Zachary slowly nods, barely meeting my eye. "Okay. Consider it not mentioned."

I wish so much in that moment that things were not how they are. That Cole hadn't left me. I still can't believe it. Just thinking about it . . . I force him out of my mind. He has no place there now. All that matters is finding the key.

"How do we get across the river?" I ask.

Zachary glances back from where we just came. "I don't think you should try. Someone is trying to keep you out."

"I noticed. But why? If this old god wants the power, why would he want to keep me out?" I'm not trying to brag here, but Cole and I got the power from the labyrinth simulation. Chaos would want that power the same way the other god had.

"Elise has a theory on that," Zachary says.

"Which is what?"

"A prophecy," he says. "She claims that prophecies travel on the wind, and that she can catch them. So she caught this prophecy. And she told it to Chaos as he was dying. She didn't think it would matter."

So Elise is not perfect. She makes mistakes. Which means any of the gods, Chaos included, can make mistakes. I file this information away for future use.

"What prophecy?" At the word, my heart rate speeds up. Memories of gods and prophecies swim around in my mind. Of things I've heard that gods will do to keep prophecies from coming true. "Was it about the river?"

"What about the river?"

"Elise told me that if I tried to cross the river, I would die," I say. "Was that the prophecy you're talking about?"

He shakes his head. "A different one. One with Chaos. She told him as he was dying that his time as a god was over anyway. She claimed that even if he lived, the prophecy showed that he would came face to face with the one who had the power of the gods, and when that happened, he would be defeated."

A mixture of nervous chills run through me. The power of the gods. I have that power now. Cole and I both do.

"That's absurd," I hear myself say. And yet I want to believe it. I want to defeat this god and make the world right again.

"Is it?" Zachary says.

I swallow as I process the thought. I don't know. The power in me is real. I can do things with it. And I've only just started. What if it could be more than I ever knew was possible?

"Are Elise's prophecies normally right?" I ask. I'd almost crossed the river, and I'd almost died. If the payment had worked and I had crossed, I would be dead.

"Normally yes," Zachary says, so matter-of-fact. "She's chatty and annoying, but she's normally right."

Chatty and annoying. That had been Elise. She hadn't told me about Chaos or the prophecy, but she had gone out of her way to mention how Zachary was always talking about me. But no way does he like me more than as a friend.

I push thoughts of Elise and the prophecy to the back of my mind. I can worry about that later. "So how do we get out of here? How do we get across the river? We need to get into this simulation."

"Can't either of you two make a world gate?" Taylor says.

"A world gate can't get us there," Zachary says. "This is one simulation. Chaos's Simulation Omega is completely another."

Taylor waves her fingers like she's a magician. "Fine. What about some other powerful godly thing? Can't you do that?"

Zachary blushes and looks quickly to me like he's embarrassed. But his face is layered with a thin mask of confidence. "A powerful godly thing? Well, sure, I guess I can do that." Then he pushes both hands forward, palms out.

A holographic globe forms in the air, directly in front of him. It pulses slowly, but Zachary reaches out and spins it, causing the pulses to come closer together. Then he presses a hand to it, resting it on the hologram.

I try to focus on it, to figure it out, but it spins faster and faster.

"You two ready?" he says.

It's just a blur now, and it's flashing like there's some sort of countdown going on, similar to a world gate and yet a different type of model. "Where's it taking us?" I ask.

Zachary actually smiles, like this is some moment of levity. It's annoying and kind of cute all at the same time.

"Don't you trust me?" he says. His eyes meet mine, and there is something almost boyish in them. Something hopeful and vulnerable.

The thing is that of all the minor gods and people we've met so far, I do trust Zachary. I don't know why, but deep down, I don't feel like he's trying to lead us astray. Yet I'd trusted Cole, too, and look where that had gotten me. Still, Cole and Zachary are not the same person, and just because Cole betrayed me does not mean Zachary will.

I place my hand on the flashing blue globe. Even though it's a hologram, it's solid against my palm. I look at Taylor and raise an eyebrow.

"Hell no, you're not leaving me here," she says, and she puts her hand on the globe also.

Then the flashing stops and the spinning globe sucks us in.

When it spits us back out, I know immediately where we are. We're home. Really home. My house is there in front of us. Except it's fallen into ruins. But it's not just my house. It's the entire world.

We're too late.

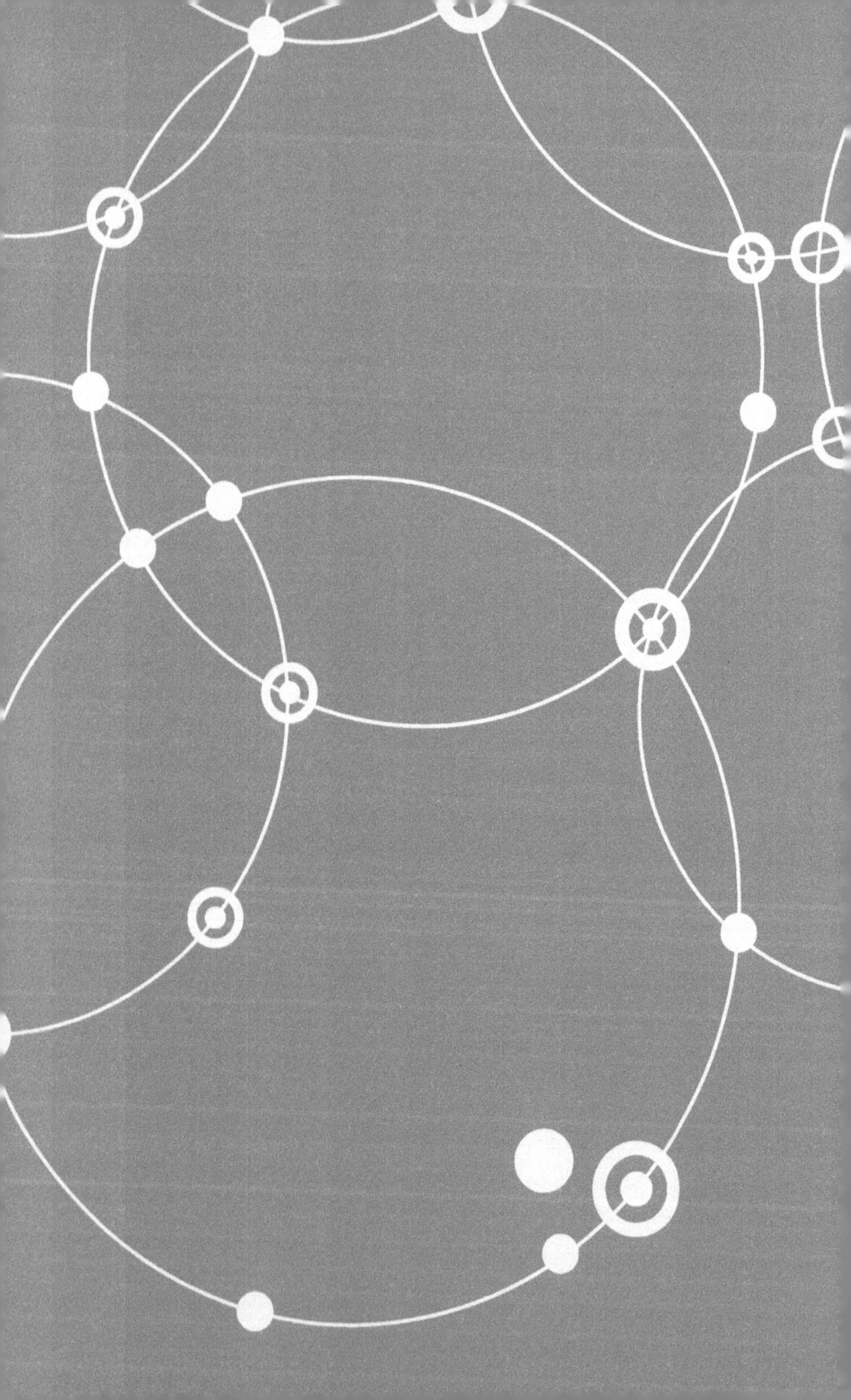

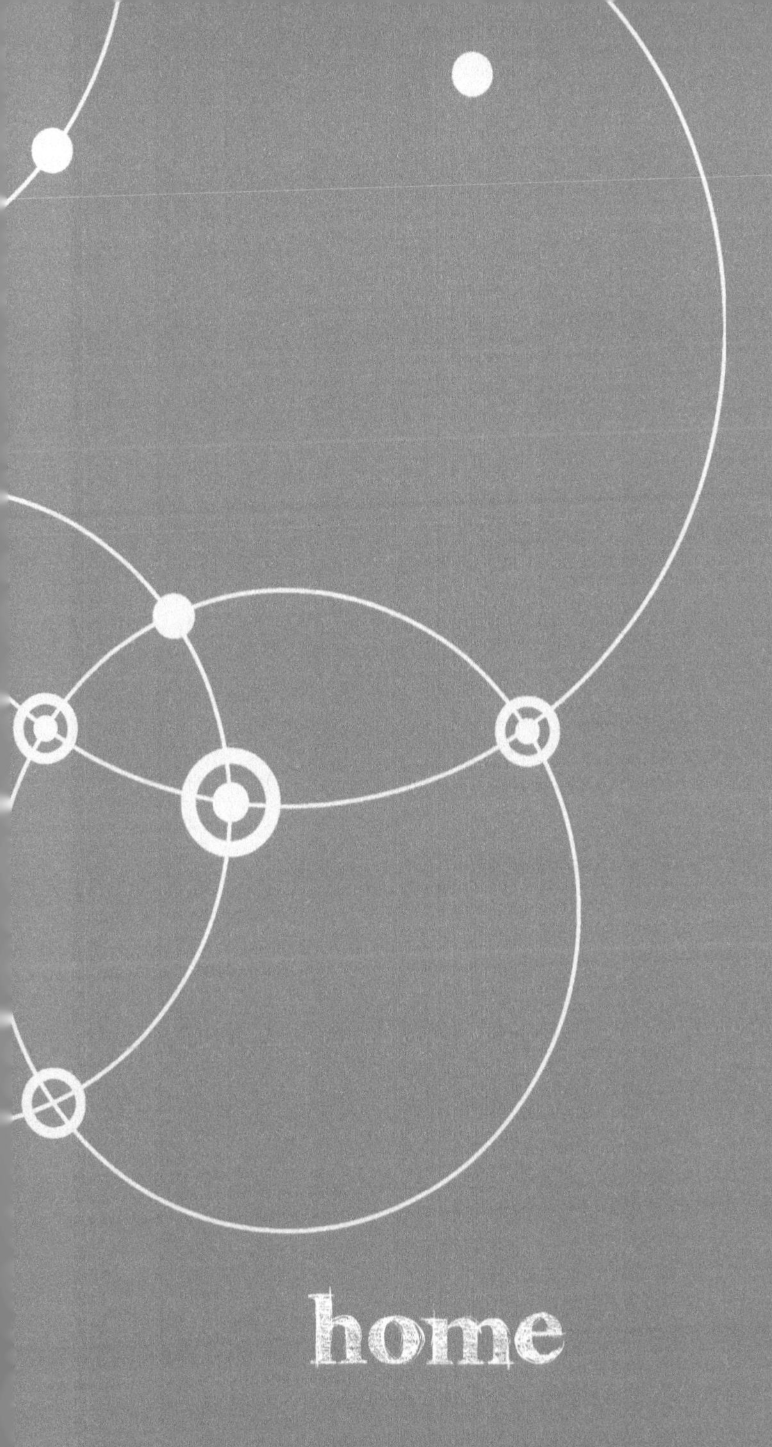
home

MY HOUSE IS RUINED. THE APPLE TREE

out front has fallen over and broken through the front bay window. Part of the roof has been torn away, like a giant hurricane
ripped through Florida and destroyed whatever was in its path.
The garage door lies in the middle of the driveway.

The street we stand on has giant chunks of asphalt torn from it
and tossed around everywhere. I live—lived—in a cul-de-sac, and
of the four houses around me, mine isn't even in the worst shape.
Next door, the Prall's house looks like a giant has come along and
smashed half of it flat with a titan-sized baseball bat. All around
us, trees have been ripped from the ground, shrubs are dead. Two
cars sit abandoned in the street, doors open, occupants long gone.

"I saw this," Taylor says. She points to the Oculus. "When I
looked through, I saw this layer of the world."

I'd seen it, too. Not my house, but other parts of the world. But
seeing it through the lens of the Oculus and seeing the reality of
it are two very different things.

Zachary whips around to face Taylor. "You got the Oculus?"

He reaches out, almost like he wants to touch it.

Taylor swats his hand away. "You can't try it out."

"How did you get it?" Zachary says. His face is filled with awe.

"None of your business, god boy."

"This is my house," I say, pointing to the ruin ahead of me. My voice sounds really funny, and I realize that I'm shaking all over. I wrap my arms around myself to try to keep it together, but while we've been inside the simulations, fighting for our lives, trying to gain the power, the very world that we've been trying to save has been destroyed.

"What happened?" Taylor asks, fixing her uneven gaze on Zachary. The piece of metal she'd grabbed in the Nether Zone is gone, left behind when we moved through the transporter. But the look she gives Zachary conveys enough emotion to be a weapon itself.

Her words sound far away. They break the silence of the world. Aside from us, there is nothing around. No birds. No planes. No cars. Only a faint rumbling in the distance.

"It's like this all over," Zachary says. He puts his hand on my arm, in an awkward attempt to comfort me. But I'm numb. I want to blink and make it go away. I can't believe this has happened.

"Not all over. It can't be all over." I turn slowly and try to accept what I'm seeing. But the level of destruction is beyond hurricane damage. I step forward, toward my house, stopping at the fallen apple tree. The last time I'd seen this tree, it had died in front of me. "How long have I been gone?"

Zachary shrugs, trying to make it sound not so bad. "A couple years maybe."

I shake my head. I'm no older. Neither is Taylor, Hudson, Cole. We're all the same. "That's not possible."

"Edie, don't you get it?" Taylor says. "None of this is possible. But it's still reality."

Reality? After the simulations, is it possible that we're really back? "So this is the real world?" I ask.

"The globe," Zachary says. "It's what brings us back here. Out of the simulation. It's hidden in the simulations, like a secret escape code. A way to break out."

I try to process the words, but they don't add up. So many things. There was an escape code? All that time and we could have gotten out of the simulation that way? And if Simulation Avine had an escape code, then the labyrinth simulation must have also.

Now we're back. We've left the simulation. But letters still float in front of my vision. My heads-up display is still active. Taylor still has the Oculus. It all confirms one thing.

"Everything really is a simulation," I say. "The world where we grew up. It's nothing but a simulation."

Zachary brushes a hand along the bark of the fallen tree, picking a piece of it off and rubbing it between two fingers. "It's easiest to think of it that way. This is reality—the original reality—but it can also be changed and affected by the programming team. Except it's been locked away forever. That's why getting the key and getting into Main Control Room Alpha is such a big deal. Whoever gets in there gets control of not just the other simulations but of everything. That's why Chaos doesn't want to give up control."

Control of everything. "And if I get this key, I can fix this," I say.

"*When* you get this key," Zachary correct. "Yes, then you'll be able to fix this. Or start over. Or make changes. You can do whatever you want."

"Yeah, but who did this?" Taylor asks. "Chaos?"

"Not Chaos," Zachary says. "It's—"

"The Creators," I say before Zachary can finish. We'd visited their zone and I'd seen the destruction they'd caused when

I looked through the Oculus. "But I stopped them. I added the game subroutine. They should all be trapped in it, not worrying about destroying or creating or whatever they do."

"You only slowed them down," Zachary says. "And they're not the only ones. It's why places like the Nether Zone exist. The Creators take bits of code and make new things out of it. Like you with the power. You create also, just like them. But in order to create, you need to destroy."

"I haven't destroyed anything," I say. Yet his words make perfect sense. Like the world gate. To create it, I pulled bits and pieces of everything around it. Am I really no better than the creatures who'd tried to devour us?

"Not intentionally," Zachary says. "But when you make new things, you have to tear down old ones. That's all simulations are except on a bigger scale. Creating and destroyed bits and pieces."

"Does it matter?" Taylor says. "I mean, yeah, this is really messed up, but talking about it isn't helping anything. Why are we here?"

I blink a few times. She's completely right. We need to get back on track. Seeing the destroyed world only makes that more evident.

"Yeah, how do we get into Simulation Omega?" I ask. "Because all we're doing now is wasting more time."

"I have a plan," Zachary says. He points off toward the bay, away from my house. "We need to go that way."

"Why?" Taylor asks. "Where are we going?"

Zachary tries to hide the proud look that crosses his face. "I work that way. That's where we need to go."

Sometimes it's hard to remember that Zachary is not really a teenager like me and Taylor. He's a god.

"We're going to your office building?" Taylor says. "What? Do you need a coffee break?"

"Maybe," Zachary says. "But I'm thinking more that if we go there, I'm pretty sure I can get you guys into Chaos's simulation."

Pretty sure isn't one hundred percent confident, but if it's our only chance, then we have to take it.

"Where do you work?" I'd seen Zachary here in Florida before everything changed. He'd said he'd been assigned to watch me. Creepy, yes, but what this implies is that maybe he was close by. He'd also been one of the lead programmers on the labyrinth simulation.

"Ocular Technologies," Zachary says.

It's like someone punches me in the stomach. Ocular Technologies is the gaming company where Owen's dad worked. It's the place with the cutting edge VR goggles. The ones that put us into the entire simulation, or at least triggered my entry.

"Oh," I say.

"Yeah. I think you can get in from there," he says.

"So what are we waiting for?" Taylor asks.

A horrible sucking sound stops my next words. The noise has been there, low and in the distance, but it amps up, making the hair on my arms stand on end. I immediately place it. Or place what it's supposed to be.

"What's wrong with the ocean?" I ask. I've heard the ocean my entire life, its smooth regular tidal pattern. This is different. Worse. It's like something is fighting against it, trying to suck it up through a giant straw.

Taylor gazes toward the sound, angling her head so the Oculus is forefront. Her lips curl up as she listens to the mockery of what has always been such an integral part of my world.

She doesn't speak for a long moment as she sees whatever Zachary and I don't through the Oculus. Then finally she replies. "It's being drained."

iv

"DRAINED HOW?" I ASK. THE OCEAN IS vast and limitless. There is nowhere for the water to go.

She narrows her eyes and leans forward, in the direction of the sound. "I can see the level going down. And there's something coming out of the water. Something growing from a crack in the ground. Like a mountain."

A mountain. Or . . .

"A volcano?" I ask.

Her eyes widen. "Yeah. That's it. A volcano. There's lava. But the volcano isn't what's draining the ocean. It's something else, underwater."

I think of the simulation with my parents, of their last moments. *We dug too deep.* The hook from their research ship had embedded itself in the glossy egg beneath the surface of the water, cracking the layer between our world and the world of the gods.

"Are my parents responsible for this?" I ask.

Zachary considers my questions. "Not exactly. I mean, yeah, sure, they were messing around in places that were dangerous.

But that could have been said for any of your parents."

"Not mine," Taylor says.

"Yep, your parents, too," Zachary says. "But the point is that it was all fated to be that way. Even if they'd known what was going to happen when they went out on their ship, it still would have happened."

Over and over again it had happened, back when I'd visited their ship via the compass rose. I'd tried to stop them. I'd tried to warn them. Even when I thought they were listening, events had still played out the same. It was like a game simulation that ended the same way no matter what I did.

"We have to repair the crack," I say. If we don't repair it, it will suck down everything until there is nothing left.

"Definitely," Zachary says. "And the only place it can be done is in Main Control Room Alpha."

"But Chaos is there," I say. "Why can't he do it?"

Zachary laughs. "He's not going to try to fix the world. But even if he wanted to, I don't think he currently has the power. He's weak. That's why he set up the simulation. He needs to steal the power back. Doing something like repairing a layer of the world takes immense power, power I don't think he has. So yeah, the layer between the world of the gods and the human world was torn away. The only thing to do is to create a new layer and keep the worlds separate."

"It's draining fast," Taylor says. Her voice wavers the tiniest amount. She's always so strong. But even this, seeing our world destroyed, is too much.

"We'll get the key," I say. "We'll fix it."

But even if the layer is fixed, that doesn't answer the biggest concern. It's the thing I haven't wanted to address. It's right there in front of me. There is no ignoring it.

There are no people around.

V

"WHERE IS EVERYONE?" I ASK ZACHARY.
"Are they dead?"

"They aren't dead," Taylor says.

"How do you know?" Zachary asks.

"If they're dead, where are the bodies?"

She's right. We've seen destruction of houses, cars, trees. But we haven't seen a single body. It's like everyone has vanished.

Zachary scuffs his feet against the side of a giant pothole. "It is a little weird." He's intentionally keeping the emotion out of his voice.

I stare at him, trying to get him to look me in the eye. "A little weird. That's all you can say about it? There should be thousands of people around, and them not being here is a little weird?"

"More than a little weird?" he says.

I grasp both his arms with my hands and look him right in the face. "It's impossible, Zachary. There has to be some other explanation."

He nods slowly as he tries to process my words. "They could

have been taken by the Creators and repurposed," he says.

I shake my head. I'm not willing to accept that. That would mean that everyone was erased. "Or . . . ?"

"Or . . . ," he starts. "I guess they could have been stored."

Stored. Like in racks and racks of data. Like the data racks that Cole and I found. Maybe they were everyone, everywhere. And when someone had pulled the racks out and smashed them, they could have killed people. Real people. Kids I went to school with. My neighbors.

Thomas.

No. Thomas is okay. I have to make sure he's okay. We need to make things right.

I try to hold my voice steady, but it wavers as I talk. "When Cole and I escaped the labyrinth, we found this room with a bunch of circuit boards. Someone had come in and ripped some of them from their racks. They'd tossed them onto the floor and crushed them."

Zachary's eyes go wide. "Where?"

So I tell him about the whole thing, escaping from the volcano. And what we'd found. His face darkens with every second.

"You're sure?" he says.

"Definitely."

"Oh."

I clench my hands into fists to keep them from shaking. "Is that what's stored there? All the people?"

He bites his lip like he's trying to figure it out also. "It has to be, Edie. I mean, I didn't store them there. But it could have been Iva. Or Elise. Or one of the others."

Or Chaos. He could have done it as some unknown part of his plan. Some motive not clear to us.

I take a deep breath and think it through. "Okay, so let's say that the people got stored. That's good, right?"

"Not if someone's going around smashing them," Taylor says. "Because unless I'm missing some vital information about computers, if the memory is destroyed so is whatever is stored on it."

She got to have people she's worried about also.

"No, you're right," I say. "But I mean good in that they aren't out here. Look, I'm not saying it's a great thing that people could have been destroyed. Trust me. I can't even think about that." A lump catches in my throat, but I go on. "But if everyone wasn't stored away, then pretty much they'd all be dead."

"Pretty much," Zachary says.

It makes me think that maybe it wasn't Chaos. That instead it really was Iva or Elise, protecting the people of the world, even if in secret. I focus on what our choices are. "So let's say that Chaos learned about it and found a way inside and is responsible for the destruction. Is there anything we can do to keep him out?"

He pauses as he thinks over my question. "Like security? Yeah, we could do that. I mean, maybe only a short term solution, but something could be done."

Short term or long term, anything is better than nothing, because if people are dying, we need to stop it.

"So we go back to the volcano," I say. When we'd originally gone to the volcano, it was way out west. And though there is no part of me that wants to make that trip again, if it's what we have to do, then I'll do my best to have a good attitude. But it had taken weeks, and that was with Cole hot-wiring the Jeep. Weeks is too long.

He runs a hand through his hair. "What about the simulation? The key?"

I glance at Taylor and unspoken words pass between us. She nods. Then I look back to Zachary.

"Getting the key won't matter if everyone is dead," I say. "We have to make sure the data storage is secure. Then we can go into the simulation."

"You're sure?" Zachary says.

I've never been more sure of anything in my life. If I can't protect Thomas, my parents, my friends, then I might as well quit right now.

"Definitely."

vi

TAYLOR SAYS, "CAN YOU GET US TO THE volcano, god boy. Maybe you can snap your fingers and transport us there."

Zachary laughs. I'm not sure if it's at the god boy comment or at him snapping his fingers. I'm hoping the former, because if there is some magical way he can transport us across the country, I am all for it.

"God boy?" he says.

Taylor fixes her eyes on him. "You got a problem with that?"

"Kind of," Zachary says. "And just to be clear, I'm a minor god. Not a god boy. God boy makes me sound like a child,"

"A god is a god," Taylor says. "You all act like children, and you're all full of bullshit."

"Maybe," Zachary says. "But let's just say that my level of bull-shit is less that the average."

This is a conversation that is going nowhere. We need to stay on track. "Can you snap your fingers?"

"Sure." Zachary holds up his hand and snaps.

I rolls my eyes.

"Oh, you mean can I snap my fingers and magically transport somewhere? Sure." He snaps again, and this time he vanishes.

"No way," Taylor says.

I stare at the spot where Zachary was. Even after everything we've been through and everything we've seen, it is still almost impossible to believe. I count the seconds as they go by.

Taylor clears her throat. "Is he coming back?"

A horrible thought passes through my mind. What if he doesn't come back? What if this has all been part of a trick to keep us out of the simulation and we've fallen completely for it? Now, not only are we out of the Nether Zone, we have no hope of getting into Simulation Omega.

But no. This is Zachary we're talking about. He's given me no reason to doubt him.

"Yes," I say, hoping I sound confident.

Sure enough, less than thirty seconds later Zachary reappears. He's in the exact same spot where he started.

"Did you miss me?" he asks.

"No." Taylor is blunt and honest.

"Great," I say. "So you're taking us to the volcano."

"Well," Zachary says. "That's where it gets a little tricky. I can move myself around between layers, but I can't move you guys around."

"Have you ever tried?" Taylor asks.

Zachary's eyes flash my way. "Maybe."

Taylor's right eye widens. "You tried to move Edie?"

"When?" If this is true, then I was totally unaware of it.

He gives his head a small shake. "Long time ago. When you were about to fall into that pit back in Louisiana. Do you remember that?"

Of course I remember that. The world had split in half and

dead things had crawled from the ground. It was impossible, and yet I'm sure if Cole hadn't pulled me out, I would have died.

"You were watching me then?" I ask.

He won't meet my eye. "I told you. It was my job to watch you."

"Watching people is creepy," Taylor says. "You shouldn't do it."

"Maybe," Zachary says. "Unless the people that you're assigned to watch are more important than they know."

Important in that we were needed to go into the labyrinth simulation. If we'd died before then, the gods would have been short contestants. It's halfway amusing that they watched out for us only to put us in life-threatening danger shortly thereafter.

I cross my arms. "So you can't transport us around. That means it'll take us forever to get across the country."

Humor I don't understand lights up his eyes. "Oh, right. I keep forgetting that you don't think like a god."

I find this insulting and reassuring at the same time. This means there might be an easier option.

Neither Taylor nor I say a word. We wait.

"Okay, fine," Zachary says, and he puts up his hand. "Remember what you said about the ocean?" he asks Taylor.

"It's draining?"

"Not that part. The part about the volcano."

Taylor frowns. "That's a different one."

He laughs. "You guys really need to think more like gods. You can't limit the way you view things. The volcanos . . . they're all the same one."

All the same one. I don't try to figure out the physics behind that because I'm sure that no matter how much sense I try to make of it, it will never come together. Maybe that's what thinking like a god comes down to. I need to eliminate common sense from everything.

"So we visit this volcano," I say. That our journey could be so short fills me with hope. "It's off the coast of Cape Canaveral. That's where my parents went."

"Right you are, Eden Monk," Zachary says.

Taylor points to the right. "Ocean is that way."

Even if I didn't hear it, I'd know which direction it was. I also know that it's not far. Even walking, it's only a couple miles.

We hurry along toward the cape. Taylor leads the way, using the Oculus to navigate a safe path. I try to ignore the damage around me, but mentally I begin to make a list. I list out all the things that need to change. Things that need to be fixed in order to get the world back on track. With this much damage, it's a huge job. It needs to be done in layers. Fixing the core of the earth . . . that has to be a starting point. If earthquakes are going to destroy anything we repair, then the earthquakes need to be eliminated. Fixing the weather and atmosphere. Recycling the debris for future use. I piece through them, partially to help bring sanity to the situation and partially to distract myself. I'm so much in my own world, I haven't even noticed that Taylor is far ahead of us.

"What happened with Cole?" Zachary asks. Taylor can't hear. Otherwise I think she'd knock him upside the head for asking.

I shrug and try to act like it's no big deal even though it rips a fresh hole in my chest to think about it. "He left me."

"Maybe he had something to do," Zachary says. He holds his voice steady, as if he's offering up the words to help me feel better.

"No. He chose Pia over me. They left together. Went across that lava river and into Simulation Omega without me and Taylor. That's all there is to it."

He narrows his eyes. "That doesn't make sense."

"It's fine," I say, though it's not.

"Not just about him being crazy for leaving you," Zachary says. "Though anyone who would leave you is nuts. But it's the whole thing with the power you two got back in the labyrinth."

"What about it?"

"That's the reason that Chaos cut off access for you. Why you couldn't get into the simulation. The prophecy said that whoever had that power would have the ability to defeat him. You weren't the only one with the power. Cole has it, too."

I parse through his words. "But he got in. He paid with the coin and got across the river."

"And that never should have been able to happen," Zachary says.

"Maybe Pia had something to do with it." After all, Cole wasn't alone. He could have slid through security that way.

"Pia . . . ," Zachary says, rolling her name around. "You know I did some digging around after you inserted yourself into Simulation Avine. It was when I was trying to hook into the heads-up display. She wasn't part of the original simulation."

I stop walking and face him. "What do you mean?" A horrible feeling begins to form inside me, like rotten food sitting in my stomach.

"I mean that she was inserted into the simulation later," Zachary says. "Just before you guys placed yourselves in there."

Not in the original simulation . . .

I think back to when I'd been trying to locate the signatures for Owen and Abigail. I'd hacked into the system. There had been the four of us, me, Taylor, Cole, and Hudson. We were the last to enter. There had also been Owen and Abigail. But between our groups there had been one single person. I'd wondered about it at the time, but I hadn't had time to look into it.

"Why?" I say. "Who put her there?" My stomach twists. Something is wrong. Very wrong. I hadn't trusted her, and maybe there was a very good reason I shouldn't.

"I don't know," Zachary says as we start walking again, hurrying to catch up with Taylor. "But I do know that she was not part of the original plan. And changes like that have to come from the gods.”

“Like Chaos,” I say, barely able to fathom the thought. But the reality that Chaos could have inserted Pia into the simulation is unsettling to say the least. “She can read minds.”

Taylor has stopped, giving us time to catch up. “Yeah, well I can see the future, and in every future I see, next time Pia comes across my path she’s going down.”

It sounds like a good plan to me. But it also ignores the fact that Cole is with her right now.

“Can you see Cole?” I ask Taylor.

She glances to Zachary, like she wants to check out his reaction. He holds his face so steady it’s obvious he’s trying not to move, as if maybe he wants to see the Oculus in action.

She shrugs. “No idea.” Then she focuses her eyes ahead, almost like she’s looking at her heads-up display. But her eyes don’t flicker as they would if she was reading data. Instead they narrow.

“What?” I say.

“He’s alone.”

Alone.

“You’re sure?”

Taylor nods. “No sign of Pia.” She looks through the Oculus for another moment. “I can’t see her anywhere. It’s like she’s been removed.

How nice that would be if Pia simply vanished. I know it’s a horrible thought, but I don’t care. Regardless, Cole alone means something has changed, and when we finally get into the simulation, we’ll find out what. But for now, we need to get to the memory banks.

“Come on,” I say, and I start walking again, quickening my pace. One thing at a time, but that doesn’t mean I should waste a second of it.

Before long the beach comes into view, and alongside it, a marina. If we're going to get to the volcano, we're going to need a boat. But because of the lower water level and the damage resulting, most of them are a wreck. The only one far enough out that looks halfway usable of course needs a key to start. A key we don't have.

I kick the boat. "Stupid thing. Would it be too much to ask for something to go our way just once?"

Taylor jumps back onto the dock and stares out at the water, but Zachary places his hand on my arm. "Edie, come on. You're not thinking like a god again. Remember? You need to think this through logically."

"How would a god think?" I ask, jumping onto the dock also. "No key. No boat. That's pretty logical to me. Unless you can hot-wire this thing for us."

He shakes his head. "Not that part. Didn't you decide this was all a simulation?"

A stupid simulation that is falling more into ruin with every second that goes by. But simulation or not, it's the world I lived in. The world I need to save. "So what?"

"So look at the boat," he says.

I do. I look at it. It's a useless boat unless we want to row. That's looking more and more like our only option. Except then my vision flickers and the heads-up display comes to life.

SELECT ITEM TO INTERACT

I look to Zachary, eyes wide. A simulation like the others. And that means we have the ability to execute commands through the heads-up display.

"Really?" I say.

He smiles. "Really. See? Logic. It always works."

I turn back to the boat and select it using my heads-up display. The boat turns in the water and faces out toward the ocean.

On my heads-up display are the words BOARD SHIP. I'm not sure it's a ship. Maybe that's a flaw in the programming. But regardless, I step aboard and the motor roars to life.

"Now that's what I'm talking about," Taylor says, and she steps on after me.

vii

ZACHARY IS THE LAST TO BOARD. I
expect the simulation to recognize this and launch the boat, but
it doesn't move.

I look to him, but he only shrugs.

"Oh, I get it," Taylor says. "You want us to move it."

"Well . . . ," he says. "Maybe not you, Taylor."

I have never seen Taylor move so quickly. She is up in his face
in a second. "Why not me?"

He pushes her back gently. "Because your heads-up display
isn't working right. Is it?"

She waits a few seconds before responding. "And that matters why?"

"Because that's how you control things in the simulation. Until
you find another way, that's how you guys interact."

I roll my eyes and access my heads-up display. Zachary and
Taylor could make an Olympic sport out of bickering, but that
won't get us to the volcano. In a couple quick commands, the boat
begins to move.

Taylor sits back and crosses her arms. "I could do that, too."

"Good," Zachary says. "Keep me updated on your progress."

I take hold of the steering control even though the boat seems to be guiding itself. I don't have the coordinates of where my parents' ship went down, but that doesn't seem to matter. The boat glides through the water, evading debris, like a pre-programmed transportation item in a video game. It moves quickly, too. Way faster than it should.

The next thing I know, Taylor shouts, "There it is."

On the horizon, set against the blue water of the ocean, is a black mountain with smoke curling out of the top of it. I focus my heads-up display on it to see if any commands come on-screen, but the display remains blank. But with every second, the volcano gets larger as we approach. I can't look away from it.

The same volcano. Here. In New Mexico. Possibly all over the world. In New Mexico, a garden had surrounded the volcano, protected by a nest of sirens. And within moments, I realize that though there doesn't seem to be a garden, the security is the same.

Music drifts to my ears. Music I've heard before.

"Cover your ears," I shout, and then I press my hands on either side of my head, blocking out the sound.

Taylor and Zachary immediately do the same. I look to Zachary and raise my eyebrows. He mouths something in reply, but I can't hear what with my ears covered. Maybe even the gods aren't immune to the song of the sirens.

As we approach the shore, I see them. Three women sit on the rocks, basking in the brilliant sun. They're barely dressed. Their long hair covers their chests. Their mouths move with the song they sing. And their eyes, piercing blue, are focused directly on us.

They beckon us. We have no choice but to move closer to them. I can only hope that without us hearing their song, they are powerless.

Taylor watches them. With the Oculus, maybe she can see more. Her eyes never leave them. Our boat glides by, avoiding landing near them. Instead it continues around until they are out of sight.

I dare to pull a hand from my ear. The music is nothing but a whisper. Far enough away that it has no power over me. I drop both hands from my ears. Then I look to Zachary.

Almost like he knows what I'm thinking, he says, "I have nothing to do with them."

"Then where do they come from?" Taylor asks.

He shrugs. "They're an element of mythology from the era of the ancient gods. Not just the old gods. The ones even before that. They still exist, though before the barrier was ripped open, they were kept at bay. But they and others like them shouldn't be here. They should be contained."

His words form layers in my mind like a pyramid built from the ground up, one level at a time. "The ancient gods. And the old gods? Was there a struggle for power before this?" It's hard to believe that thousands of years ago the same struggle among the gods could have happened. Hard to believe and yet it fits together logically.

"There's always a struggle for power," Zachary says. "We're at the brink of a new era now, but down the line, there will be another challenge after this. The new gods now will be the old gods. And other gods will take their place. It's the way of things."

An eternal struggle for power. A way to put the gods in place. And when the gods begin to slip, they get replaced.

"Wait, so you're telling me that thousands of years ago the gods did this same virtual reality thing?" Taylor says. "I don't believe it."

Zachary actually laughs. "Not virtual reality. They didn't even have computers back then."

"Really?" I say. Sarcasm drips off my voice. But does he think we're idiots?

He puts his hands up in surrender. "Yeah, I know you know that. What I'm saying is that there was no concept of computers. Your generation has the concept of computers. Gaming. Virtual reality is what made the most sense."

"So what did the old gods have then?" Taylor says.

"I wasn't there," Zachary says. "But from what I've heard, it fit in with the times. Olympic games. Gladiator-type fighting. Mythical beasts. Actual labyrinths. Stuff like that."

Given that technology has helped us so far, I'm glad to have the added advantage of computers and coding.

Our boat has pulled up against a wooden dock built into the side of the volcano. Dark water slaps against the wooden supports that disappear beneath the surface. The wood of the dock is weathered but solid. That said, I still test it before putting my full weight on it. The last thing I want is to disappear beneath the waves. If sirens exist out here, I can only imagine what hides in the water. If Hudson was here, I'm sure he'd be more than happy to explain every potential mythological threat. But Hudson's not here. I hope by now he's managed to subdue Owen and Abigail.

I hope he's alive.

Where we've docked, the flow of lava is minimal. A staircase is carved into the side of the volcano, and though I can't see all the way to the top, from here it looks safe.

Safe. It's a ridiculous word to use. Nothing we've been through could ever be considered safe.

"I'll go first," Taylor says, and before I can disagree one way or the other, she's five steps up. She grabs a rock and holds it in her hand like a weapon. I reach for one myself, but then I hear Zachary's word in my mind. *You're not thinking like a god.*

As soon as the thought is there, an idea forms. I reach out with my powers and search the materials around me. There's lots of soft stone, from the cooled lava, but there's also obsidian. I pull bits and pieces of it apart with my powers, and I reshape it. When I'm done, a shiny black knife waits for me.

I reach to pick it up.

"Not bad, Eden Monk," Zachary says. A small smile creeps onto his face.

I flip it over in my hand. It's seamless and so perfect that my silhouette reflection shines back at me with the sun behind me.

"You want one?" I ask Zachary. He's the only one of us with no weapon.

He shakes his head. "I don't need anything."

Doesn't need anything? Or doesn't want anything?

"Your call," I say.

We continue up the stairs. They curve around flows of lava. They work their way into the clouds. All the while we follow them. And when they finally come to a stop, we are on a shelf with nowhere else to go. But unlike the first time we'd entered the volcano, there are no symbols noting the home of the gods. No bloody handprints. There is only a control panel.

I tap the panel and a holographic keypad appears.

"What's the password?" I ask Zachary.

"There is no password," he says. "Or at least there isn't supposed to be. We all have access to the volcano. It's shared ground among the gods."

I jab my finger at the panel, and it buzzes in response. "Yeah, well someone locked us out."

We need a password, and we don't have one.

viii

MY FINGERS HOVER OVER THE HOLO-
graphic keypad. A password . . . and one that Zachary doesn't
know about. The last time I'd needed a password was in the control substation back in the Garden of the Gods. I'd hacked into
the system, run a subroutine, and gotten it. And though I don't
want to spend the time to do that now, I don't see much other
choice.

"We can figure it out," Zachary says, and he steps forward,
ready to run the same subroutines as me I'm sure.

I almost step to the side. But first, I type the same password
from the Garden of the Gods.

```
pHaSM47$A
```

The keypad disappears and giant metal doors appear and begin
to separate. The sound they make could be heard across the world.
I cringe as they grind apart until finally they come to a stop.

"How'd you know what it was?" Zachary asks.

I tell him quickly about hacking the system back at the Garden of the Gods. His eyes widen as I explain.

But when I finish, he says, "There shouldn't have been a password back there either."

Not a password here. Not back there. Which means that it is very likely the same person who put them in place. It would have to be a person who's pretty good with programming. Also someone with a reason to keep me—or others like me—out.

"When we hacked in back at the substation, someone detected us and shut it down," I say. "I thought it was Iva, because that's who's voice it was, but—"

He shakes his head. "Iva wouldn't bother with that. If she doesn't want you in somewhere, she keeps you out, no passwords required."

I hope I never have to get in anywhere Iva doesn't want me.

"Then who?" I ask.

Taylor holds a finger to her lips, telling us to be quiet, and points ahead. "Someone's inside," she whispers.

"Can you see them?" I ask. I strain to hear, but there is only the hum of machines from deep inside the volcano.

"Vaguely. Like a shadow moving around, trying not to be seen."

Yet the power of the Oculus lets us see them.

We move into the volcano. Before I can think to do anything about it, the metal doors grind shut behind us, making an equally awful racket as when they opened. If someone is inside here with us, then they know we've arrived.

The second the door is fully closed, the inside of the volcano is cast into darkness. Slowly green LEDs appear on the floors and ceiling. Unlike the rocky area outside, we're back in something more like a warehouse, with smooth walls and a hard concrete floor. None of us says a word. We've lost the element of surprise, but that doesn't mean we have to run forward without knowing what's ahead.

Taylor takes the lead. I'm hoping the Oculus lets her see more than Zachary or I can. Or maybe Zachary can see better than me. He is a minor god after all.

We walk for well over two minutes before we hear the next sound. Like a switch being flipped. If I weren't listening for something I might have missed it. But it's definitely there. Taylor stops walking. Listens. Looks back to me and Zachary. Then we continue on.

The hallway widens. This has to be the same path Cole and I took, though we weren't in the dark. The LEDs only light up enough for me to see five steps ahead. But then, in the distance, white light appears, as if at the end of a tunnel. My stomach clenches. Whoever is responsible is up there. They're waiting for us.

ix

I PRESS AGAINST THE SMOOTH WALL
as we get closer to the light. But when the wall comes to an end,
there is no one there. Instead are the rows and rows of data banks
that stretch on as far as I can see. It is definitely the same place
Cole and I saw. I nod to Taylor and Zachary and motion that we
should continue ahead.

Silently we move. I clutch the black knife. The first row of data
storage is untouched, as is the second. But at the third, halfway
down from the main aisle where we walk, scathes of computer
boards have been pulled from the racks. They lay smashed on the
ground. I'd seen them before and not thought much about them,
but now, all I can see are people. People like Thomas. My best
friend Emily. My parents. People that had been stored in memory
but are not coming back.

The hum of cooling fans is dull white noise at the edge of my
hearing, but it's disrupted by something smashing to the ground.

"Come on," Taylor says, and we take off running toward the
noise. Staying quiet doesn't matter any longer. All that matters

is stopping more people from being destroyed. Our heavy boots slap on the concrete. Zachary keeps up no problem. My knife is poised. Ready.

Another board smashes on the ground. Then another. We're getting closer. Finally we reach an aisle and movement registers in my peripheral vision. A person holding a board high over their head.

"Stop!" I shout. But it's too late.

The man slams the board in the hard concrete ground. Components fly everywhere, ricocheting off the racks of storage. Destroying lives.

Once the damage is done, the man looks at us and smiles. And yes, I've seen him before, at games, in the stands. It's Owen's dad. He reaches for another board, but Taylor is on him so fast, she's like a blur across my vision. She tackles him, knocking him off balance. He staggers but doesn't fall, and he struggles to reach another board.

"What are you doing?" she shouts. But before he can answer, she swings the rock she carries. He moves at the last minute and it clips him in the shoulder rather than hitting him in the head.

He staggers back, out of her reach. "I'm cleaning the world," Owen's dad says so calmly, it's almost like he's practiced saying it a hundred times. Like he's been waiting for us to show up.

"You're killing people," I shout. I want to lunge at him with the knife, but I need to wait for the right time. I hold it out in front of me and edge forward.

"Hardly," Owen's dad says. "These aren't real people."

Aren't real people? He's insane. Stored in these memory banks are our families, our neighbors, kids that went to school with me and Owen.

"They are, you asshole," Taylor says.

He waves his hands dismissively. "They aren't. You aren't. We cleanse the world, and then we redesign it."

He must mean Chaos. But I don't get the chance to ask. Before I can move, he reaches for a board. Taylor swings out again, but Owen's dad moves out of the way, barely holding onto the board. Still, he gets it, and he slams it down.

I watch pieces of the world being destroyed. How many people are stored on each one? I can't take anymore. My grip is sweaty from the tight hold I have on the knife, but unless I get close enough to him, all I'll do is scratch him.

Unless . . .

I throw the knife. I probably do it horribly wrong, but I will it to fly through the air, to spin over and over like I've seen in movies. I think of it as an object in a video game, meant to perform how I want it to. The knife is sleek and makes a whooshing sound as it moves. Then it hits Owen's dad directly in the chest, sinking deep beneath the surface of his skin.

It's a perfect hit.

"You got him, Edie," Zachary says.

But instead of Owen's dad collapsing to the ground, he doesn't move. His image begins to flicker, like a hologram being disrupted.

Taylor maybe doesn't get what this means because she takes the distraction of my knife and swipes out again. This time the rock connects where his head is. But he's flickering and shifting, and the weapon passes right through him.

"Not good," I say.

"I got this," Zachary says, and he rushes to the end of the row. A holographic keyboard appears and Zachary begins typing commands into it. Owen's dad is stabilizing. The obsidian must have interfered with the communication to wherever he physically is. He's getting it under control.

He spots Zachary working away at the keyboard, and the calculated smile slips from his face. He ignores both me and Taylor and runs for the racks of circuit boards. Ten feet. Five feet. He's almost there. When he's less than two feet away, his holographic image begins to flicker, but he's close enough. He reaches out and yanks a circuit board from the rack, tucking it under his arm.

"I can't forget the most important one," he says with a huge grin. It fills me with dread. Why would this board be so important? Then his image freezes and vanishes along with the circuit board.

My knife clatters to the ground.

"Where'd he go?" Taylor asks.

But Zachary doesn't answer. Instead he keeps typing and programming. I hurry over to him and look over his shoulder.

"You're blocking him from coming back here, right?" I ask. His fingers are moving fast, and there are symbols and keys I don't understand, but the universal laws of programming still apply.

He nods and keeps typing. And only when he hits the enter button on the keyboard and steps back does he answer.

"He shouldn't be able to get in here anymore," Zachary says.

I glance back at the smashed circuit boards. Tens of thousands of people dead possibly. And even though it is completely selfish of me, I don't want them to be my parents or Thomas. Not my family. Not after everything I've been through to save them.

Taylor comes up next to me. "Doesn't matter who they are," she says almost like she can read my mind.

I bite my lip. It does matter, and yet she's right. It also doesn't matter. We have to continue on no matter who might have been stored in the memory.

I move to the keyboard and press a few keys, trying to figure out the system. My heads-up display kicks in and overlays images to help me understand.

"I programmed it so he can't get back in here," Zachary says.

I tap keys until I stumble upon a menu, and then I test out

options until I find security. "We can't let anyone back in here," I say. "Not just Owen's dad. He might not be the only one we need to keep out. There might be others like him working for Chaos. We don't know."

With Owen and Abigail out there, he's definitely not the only person who might cause damage.

"True," Zachary says. "But the only way to set the security to this place is from here." He points to the screen to show me what he's talking about. "So that means if we ever want to get back in here we have to leave open the permissions."

I shake my head. "Not for everyone. Just for the three of us."

Taylor laughs, but it's tinged with sarcasm. "What if all three of us die?"

I shrug. "Then no one ever gets in here again, and all these people are safe." It's not my real answer. If we die—which I have no intention of doing—then someone else will eventually find a way in here. People always learn to get past any new security system put up. It just takes creative thinking.

"This is good," Zachary says. "I like us not dying."

I stop typing and look to him. "Can you die?"

He looks at me like I've forgotten some major details. "Eden Monk, you've seen a god die. We die just like anyone else. Not quite as easily as humans. But we aren't immune to danger."

Taylor steps to him and holds up the rock. "So if I hit you in the head with this, you'll die?"

He gently presses it down, out of the way. "Let's not test it out, okay?"

"Don't give me a reason to, god boy," she says. And she lowers it to her side.

He mutters something under his breath about "god boy" but Taylor acts like she doesn't hear it.

Zachary and I work through the specifics of the security

algorithm while Taylor cleans up and patrols the area looking for any more issues. When we're done, we leave the data storage unit and start back down the long hallway toward the exit. As we leave, we engage the security program. It kicks in as we seal the door. Only the three of us are allowed back in.

We have to survive.

That boat is where we left it, but before it sets out across the water, I ask Taylor, "Can you see anything beneath the surface?" The water is black here by the volcano, and my vision doesn't go more than a foot or so down.

She angles her head and nods. "The rift is there. Sucking in water."

"Anything else?" I ask. "Any wreckage? Bodies?" I force the last word out. Rationally I know there wouldn't be bodies down there under the water. But I have to ask.

She shakes her head. "Just the tear in the world, Edie. It's hungry. Like a monster."

A monster we need to stop. And now that we've secured the data storage area, we can do that.

X

THE BOAT CARRIES US BACK TO THE mainland, and it only takes us about a half hour to get back on track. We walk by my high school. They sky overhead is bright blue. The sun beats down. There isn't a cloud in the sky, as if they've all been ripped away, too. But the school looks like someone has walked on it with giant feet. The bleachers around the football field have been pulled apart and scattered. Every light on the scoreboard blinks slowly, as if in a permanent state of error.

I look away. Everything I see is worse than anything before it. It reminds me of a post-apocalyptic video game, as bad as it can possibly be.

We come to the cul-de-sac where Owen lived. Where my best friend Emily lived. And even though I should keep walking, I stop. I have to see if there is any sign of her.

I walk up the steps to Owen's door first. There, carved on the wood, is the labyrinth symbol. The same symbol we all had carved into our doors.

"Owen lived here," Taylor says before I even need to say a word.

I nod, forcing the rage that runs through me to settle down. Owen's dad had been trying to destroy everyone. If we hadn't stopped him, he would still be doing it.

"So if that was only a holographic projection of Owen's dad, do you have any ideas where he actually is?" I ask Zachary.

A small smile crosses his face, like he has some secret he's keeping to himself. "No chance he's at the game company. I secured it so only I can get in and out. But there are other programming locations. He could have made his way to one of those. He could be operating from there. If I get to my workstation, I might be able to find him."

Might is at least a chance. We may have locked him out of the data storage, but he's still out there. It's a small amount of justice that he is nothing more than a pawn in this game of the gods, just like the rest of us. The only difference may be that we are now aware of it, and he may not be.

Emily's house, unlike Owen's, is almost perfect. The front window is shattered, and the door is ajar, but otherwise, it is untouched.

"Hello?" I call despite myself. I know she's not home. And even if she were home, I'm not sure she'd be able to see me. That's how it had been the last time I'd seen her. She'd been unable to see me. I was already in the virtual reality simulation at the time, though that fact was unknown to me.

From deep in her house, a phone rings, a startling sound that makes me jump.

I glance back at Zachary and Taylor. They've heard it, too.

I lean forward, unsure whether I should call out once more. The phone rings again, then again, consistent. My feet feel rooted to the ground. Two voices battle inside my head.

Answer the phone.

Don't answer the phone.

Answer the phone.

Don't answer the phone.

I have to answer the phone. If I don't, it will only follow me. It will find me no matter where I am.

I push the green door the rest of the way open. It creaks on the hinges, as if it hasn't been oiled in years. It confirms Zachary's assessment of how much time has gone by. I'm trying to be quiet, but the first step I take, I crunch broken glass under my heavy boot.

I stand still, waiting . . . for what? I'm not sure. The phone continues to ring. I've been to Emily's house more times than I can count. I cut through the entryway and into her dad's office where the ancient green phone is still plugged into a wall jack. I reach down and unplug it.

It continues to ring. Even though I know each ring is coming, I jump every time. The phone has no place in this dead world. It had no place in my world either, after my parents died. And I know with certainty who it is on the other end.

I look to Zachary.

"You should get it," he says.

I slowly lift the receiver and put the phone to my ear. Before I say a word, Iva speaks to me.

"I have something I need you to do," Iva says. Her voice is high and cute, almost happy. Like the entire world is a game and she's one of the players.

"Are you a god?" I ask her. Iva had told us all that she was the power, but if Elise can be believed, then Iva is so much more.

"Of course," Iva says. "How else do you think I have so much power?"

Power. "But you said . . . ," I start.

Iva cuts me off. "I said what I had to say in order to get you to play the game."

Anger brims below the surface of my skin. People are dying, and she acts like it's no big deal. Like maybe she and the other gods can just get some replacements. That's not good enough for me. I want my old world back, flawed though it may be. I want it back, and I plan to get it back. But I also know that in order to do that, I have to get into the simulation. I have to find the key and get control of everything.

"What do you need me to do?" I ask Iva. Zachary and Taylor watch me, but neither says a word. Zachary, for being a minor god, looks as clueless as Taylor and I. But that could be an act. Nothing the gods do can be trusted.

Iva giggles into the phone. "I knew you'd see things my way, Eden," she says. "You were my favorite, you know that, right?"

I glance to Zachary. He's watching me, and he smiles when our eyes meet. Was I his favorite, too? And what about Elise? Had I had an advantage all along?

"Hmm . . ." It's the best thing I can say to acknowledge her words.

"I need you to recover something for me," Iva says.

Immediately my mind goes to the Oculus, and like always, it's as if she can read my mind.

"Not that," Iva says, giggling. "We don't all want that. Elise said you let her try it out. I can't believe she didn't keep it."

After seeing how much Raven wanted it, I can't believe it either.

"Anyway, the Oculus wouldn't work for me," Iva says. "Remember? I don't have eyes."

Taylor lost an eye and it still worked for her, so I'm not sure what that has to do with anything. But I decide to drop it. The Oculus is not something anyone can have at this point besides Taylor.

"What do you need?" I ask.

"I like you, Eden," Iva says.

I don't respond. I only wait.

"The simulation is locked to you," Iva says. "You won't be able to get in."

I open my mouth, about to explain that Zachary is going to get us in.

"He can't," Iva says. "Chaos has it locked. He's scared of you."

"Because of the prophecy?" I say aloud before I can stop myself.

"That's right," Iva says. "You have the power. If he lets you into his simulation, you'll defeat him."

"But Cole has the power," I say. "And he's in the simulation."

"He's not in the simulation," Iva says. "He never made it in."

Never made it in. My stomach tenses at the words. Taylor saw him alone. He betrayed me. I shouldn't care what happened to him. And yet I can't help but hope, deep inside, that maybe there is more to the story.

"I have to get in," I say, putting Cole out of my head. "Zachary knows how to do it."

I glance over to Zachary who actually beams at my words. But I'm not just saying them to flatter him. He's one of the designers. He has to be able to figure this out.

"He can only do it with my help," Iva says. "Elise and I found a backdoor in. And I'm willing to share it with you if you do something for me. So here's where we get to make a deal. You recover a small item for me, and I create a crack in the simulation, allowing you to sneak inside."

I cover the receiver with my hand and tell Zachary and Taylor what Iva just said.

"I can hear you," Iva says in my earpiece. "And are you seriously doubting me? I already told you that you're my favorite."

"I told you I can get you in," Zachary says. "Iva has to be wrong."

"Tell him I'm not wrong," Iva says. "And tell him that we all know he likes you. It's so obvious." Then she giggles.

My face gets really hot and I look away from Zachary.

"Here's what you need to do," Iva says. "There's a place in New Orleans, in a cemetery."

Like the cemetery from Cole's vision. He'd seen all our parents there on a tour. They'd come to a crypt, and when it had opened, Iva had been there. I hadn't seen the vision, but that's what Cole had told me.

"Right," Iva says, again, like she can read my mind. It makes me wish for a way to shield it. Pia had been able to read my mind. Read all our minds. An image of the crypt appears in my heads-up display. "Go to the crypt. You have to go first, Eden. I unlocked it for you. Step through the root of the largest. When the flower is red, look for the yellow umbrella. It's the fourteenth monument. There you'll find the symbol that I made for you."

"What?" None of her words make sense.

"You open the crypt, Eden," Iva continues, as if I haven't said a word. "And inside you're going to find something. It looks a lot like a black pearl. I need you to get it for me and give it to me. It's hidden, so it won't be easy to find, but if you follow the pattern, you'll find it."

"What pattern?" I ask.

"You'll figure it out," Iva says. "Bring it to me. I'll be waiting at the gaming company. I'll get you into the simulation."

"But New Orleans is really far away," I say. Even to my own ears it sounds like I'm complaining. But come on.

Iva giggles again. "Not if you know how to get there, Eden."

Then before I can ask anything else, the calls goes dead. There is an impossible dial tone that shouldn't be. I unplugged the phone. This world is no more real than the labyrinth or Simulation Avine. But it's also the world where I belong. It's the world

I need to save.

"What'd she say?" Taylor asks.

I relay as much as I can remember. Aside from the crypt, Iva's words had only confused me more.

Zachary shakes his head. "She's wrong. If she and Elise found a backdoor, I can find it, too."

He believes his words, but I also wonder if Chaos and his programming skills could be a match for Zachary.

"We need to go to New Orleans," I say though it's the last thing I want to do.

"We don't have time," Taylor says.

I motion outside the window at the destroyed world. "We have time. The world is already being destroyed. How much worse is it going to get? We can't just move on from here. We need to fix this."

Taylor clenches her teeth. "Edie, sometimes you just need to move on. You can't fix everything."

I don't want to listen to her words. They try to worm their way inside my head, but I push them away.

"I'm going to New Orleans," I say, starting for the front door. "Are you guys coming with me?"

Zachary immediately follows. "I really think I can get you guys into the simulation."

The story of the crypt from Cole's vision won't leave my mind. There was a reason Iva was there. A reason all our parents went there before we were born. Somehow it all ties together.

"Even if you can, I'm still going." The front door has closed most of the way, but I pull it open and walk outside. The sky, previously blue, is now solid gray. A layer of clouds sits in front of the sun. It's like a warning of the storm that lies ahead.

"Then I'm going," Taylor says and turns to Zachary. "What about you, god boy? You coming?"

He rolls his eyes. "Of course I'm coming."

It's settled . . . except that the only way we have to get there is by walking.

Not if you know how to get there, Iva's voice echoes in my mind.

How to get there.

I've never been there. But Cole's been there. Lived there. And Iva had shown me the image.

No, not shown me the image. Given me the image. It's there in my heads-up display, stored away with the pieces of other data I've collected. I zoom in on the image of the crypt. When I select it, iron gates appear and block the entrance, but we'll worry about that once we get there.

A menu pops up.

Crypt 505
» Interact
» Transport
» Destroy
» Relocate

The last two options are grayed out. I can't relocate the crypt here, but I can transport us to it.

"Hold on," I say, and both Taylor and Zachary grab one of my arms.

For effect, I look to Zachary, smile, and snap at the same time I select Transport.

xi

"YOU DID THAT HOW?" ZACHARY ASKS.
His voice is filled with awe.

I shrug. "Guess I'm not the only one that can transport around from place to place." I act like I'm not as surprised as him. Like I've expected it all along. But if this really is something I can do . . . well, once I'm back in the real world permanently, it's going to come in amazingly handy.

New Orleans looks like someone has come along with a giant pick and dragged it through the entire city. We stand at the edge of a crevasse so deep I can't see the bottom. The sides are muddy and brown and covered in trash and debris. But that's not the worst of it. The worst part are the things crawling from that pit. Coming for us. I've seen them before, with Cole. Dead things.

As soon as we appear, the dead spot us. Their heads, barely hanging on, swivel in our direction. Their rotting fingers claw at the mud, trying to find a grip. They want to reach us. And if they reach us . . .

No. We can't wait around to find out.

"We need to get out of here," Taylor says.

We back up and run far from the edge of the crevasse. This is not what we came for. Once we're out of reach of the creatures in the pit, I scan the area, looking for the crypt. The iron gates of the cemetery are easy to find. The only problem is that they're across the giant ditch.

I point across the way. "We need to get over there." The Transport command had brought us maybe as close to the crypt as it could. But the ditch is keeping us from getting any closer. I'm sure it's intentional. Someone trying to keep us out. Someone trying to keep Iva from getting what she needs.

This has to be why she sent me. She must have tried to get here and been unable to. I'm not sure our luck will be any better.

The dead moan as they claw at the earth. Some of them reach the top of the crevasse. Their decaying fingers grasp the edge and they pull themselves out. They stumble as they walk, but there is no denying it. They are coming for us.

I look around for anything that will help. Something we can use as a bridge. The gap is at least twenty feet across. It's too far. One misstep and we're doomed.

Then Zachary steps forward. I pull on his arm, trying to get him to stay back. But instead, he holds his hand up, palm out. A breeze blows out of nowhere, whipping his already messy hair around in every direction. He closes his eyes and mutters something under his breath.

The dead stop moving.

I have no idea how he's doing it, but he's able to control them. He puts up his other hand, palm out, and almost like there is invisible power coming from it, the dead begin to back up. They scramble over each other in their efforts to get back into the pit from where they came. And only when the last one is finally over the edge and deep inside does Zachary turn around.

He grins, like he's half embarrassed that he's just saved our asses.

"How'd you do that?" Taylor asks. Her hands are clenched into fists like she was ready to tear them limb from limb if she needed to.

Zachary lowers his hands. The wind dies down. "I'm a god," he says. "Remember?"

God doesn't explain it. There has to be more of a reason.

He shrugs. "All the minor gods have different abilities. Power over the dead happens to be one of mine."

The image of him standing with the dead at the edge of the compass rose comes back to me. The dead had chased us. They'd forced us forward, toward the garden and the volcano. Toward the labyrinth. And when we'd finally reached where we'd needed to go, Zachary had stood there among them, watching. Almost like he'd been the one controlling them, pushing us forward, making sure we got to the labyrinth.

I don't know why this surprises me. Of course he'd been involved. He was one of the programmers. And also maybe one of the architects behind the entire game.

"Yeah, well, let's not give them time to come at us again," Taylor says. "I don't want to see what happens if your power fails."

Zachary pretends to look hurt. "It never fails."

"There's a first time for everything," Taylor says.

Without the threat of being pulled apart by zombies, getting across the crevasse seems a lot less treacherous. We search around and find a telephone pole that's fallen over. The thing weighs a ton, but Taylor's strength seems to have doubled. We roll it and push it. Zachary and I help, but she does the bulk of the work. When it's close enough, we're able to raise it up, turn it, and then let it fall across the ditch.

I go first, picking my steps carefully because the last thing I want is to slip. Zachary may have sent the dead people back into the ditch, but they're still down there. If I fall, I'm sure they'll feast on my body.

I shudder as my feet touch the solid ground once again. Taylor and Zachary are right behind me. Then we cover the distance to the iron gates.

I tug on one, but they're closed tight. It doesn't want to open. Rust covers the latch. Two years of the elements have secured it in place.

"I got it," Taylor says, and she grabs hold of one of the gates and yanks hard. It makes a sound like a cat dying, but then it snaps and screeches open.

"Nice work," I say, again impressed with her strength.

She smirks. "Don't thank me. Now we have to go inside."

"You're scared?" Zachary says to Taylor. "I didn't think you got scared."

"Not scared," Taylor says. "And also not stupid." Parts of the gate have broken off, and Taylor reaches down and picks up a bar of rusty metal. She clenches it in her fist. "Now where's this crypt?"

I pull up the image of it on my heads-up display. Light pulses from it, like it's alive. Like it's the heart of the place.

"The center," I say, setting out down the path ahead. Bricks have lifted from the path, making each step a challenge. Around us, graves, mostly above-ground crypts that look like coffins, have shifted, in some cases knocking the lids aside. I don't look in any of them. I can't be distracted, and I also don't want to see more of the dead, even if Zachary does have some sort of power over them. Whereas in Florida, the world was silent, moans fill the air around us here. New Orleans is an ancient place filled with dark mystery, much of it buried beneath this soft ground.

"Cole grew up here?" Taylor asks.

I nod. "His dad gave cemetery tours."

She shakes her head. "I don't get that fascination with dead people. Why do people want to see where they're buried?"

"It's a human thing," Zachary says, like that's some normal kind of response. "Humans want to know what happens after death."

"And gods don't?" I ask.

He stops walking and looks me directly in the eye. And in that moment, I know exactly what he's thinking about. It's like we're back in the throne room, reliving the moment before I killed the old god. And even though he was a horrible god and was destroying the world, before now, I've never really thought about the fact that I ended his life.

"Gods think about it all the time," Zachary says.

I open my mouth, trying to come up with something to say. But Taylor saves me from needing to.

"I think I found it," she says.

I spin around, back the way we were heading. And there, at the end of the path is the crypt Iva had shown me.

I take a step toward it. I don't want to be here. I want to be in the simulation, finding the key, finding Thomas. But I have to be here. This is part of my journey. Taylor and Zachary flank me as I walk forward, and soon we stand in front of it.

It's made entirely of stone, with four columns out front, like a miniature Greek temple. It's not tall. Maybe five feet at the most, but it's bigger than any of the other monuments around it.

As we stand there, the sky darkens, turning from gray into a blue the color of dusk. Stars twinkle in the sky above, and a crescent moon shines down on us, casting light directly on the crypt. It almost glows, eerie purple, as if it's alive.

A solid stone door seals it away from the rest of the world. We need to get inside. I cover the remaining distance to the door and pull on the handle that's been bolted in place. No sooner do my fingers touch the handle, it lights up, glowing like an ember in a fire though not any warmer to the touch than normal. I release the handle and the light goes out.

"Open it," Taylor says.

I shake my head and step back. "You try." I need to know if it will act that way for any of us.

Taylor places her hand on the handle, and but it doesn't light up. She pulls hard, but the door doesn't open. So she pulls again. It still doesn't budge, not even with all her strength.

"It's stuck," she says, letting go.

I grab hold of the handle once more. It glows again, and I pull gently. The door swings open.

Taylor scowls. "I loosened it for you."

Maybe, I think. Or maybe not.

"It's because Iva gave Edie access," Zachary says. "That's why she was able to open it. I wouldn't have been able to open it either."

Remote access from wherever Iva is. Maybe she's being kept out, but she's still able to control this place.

Blue light shines from inside the crypt, exposing stairs that lead downward. The light coming from inside is so bright, I can't see anything but the first five steps.

"You sure about this?" Zachary says. He glances at the entrance then looks away.

"We have to," I say. "Why?"

He shakes his head. "Gods aren't really supposed to go in the domain of other gods. It's kind of a rule."

I narrow my eyes at him. "This is Iva's domain?"

"Well, yeah," he says. "What'd you think?"

To be honest, I hadn't thought about gods and domains.

"Where's your domain, god boy?" Taylor says.

"Not here," Zachary says, which is no answer at all.

"Then where?" Taylor asks, raising an eyebrow.

He meets her gaze. "Somewhere else. Okay? I don't need to tell you."

Taylor doesn't say a word. She only holds his gaze, like she's staring him down. But the last thing we have time for is an argument.

"Let's go," I say. I don't wait to see if they follow. I start down the steps.

There are forty-four steps leading down. I count them as I walk. Halfway down I look back up, but I can't see the entrance we came through. It's masked by the brilliant light. When I reach the bottom, I step to the side, making room for Taylor and Zachary to join me. Zachary is ten steps behind but at least he's following. He acts like he wants to turn back. Like he thinks Iva is going to jump out and smite him.

"Elise said how much she liked you," I say, hoping to calm his nerves. I need him at one hundred percent if we're going to get through this. Having him worry about some other god attacking him isn't helping.

Zachary lets out a small laugh that is way more sarcastic than funny. "Elise has ulterior motives."

"And you don't?" Taylor says. She's reached the bottom of the steps and stands in front of a closed door. She turns back to Zachary.

"What's that supposed to mean?" he asks.

She rolls her eyes. "You gods all have your own motives. We're just pawns playing along."

"Not true," Zachary says, hurrying down the rest of the steps so the three of us all stand together.

"You don't have anything you're angling for?" Taylor says.

He glances to me then back to Taylor. "I'm trying to help you guys get the key. That's it."

"I call bullshit," Taylor says.

I turn to the door, because I don't really care about ulterior motives right now. All I want is to get the black pearl for Iva and get into Simulation Omega. And if Cole really isn't in the simulation, I need to find him. I can figure out everything else later on.

"How do we open it?" I ask. The door is a glowing blue panel. There's no handle, no knob. No way that I can tell to operate it. The outline of a blue square starts at the edges and pulses and hums as it gets smaller. One. Two. Three. Four. One. Two. Three. Four.

Taylor holds her hand over it. "Pretty sure it's electrified."

I look to Zachary, but he backs up and puts his hands in the air. "Don't ask me. It's not my domain. Remember? And no way am I going in first anyway. Iva would be furious."

I almost can't imagine Iva mad, but then I remember Elise's transformation when she'd had the Oculus. She'd become a different person entirely. She'd transformed from a friendly little girl to a full-on god with destructive powers that could wipe out the world with a thought. I don't want to see any of the gods like that.

Except that's exactly what I'm trying to do. I need to get to Chaos and defeat him whether I want to or not.

"Right." I turn back and study it. The light pulses at the same rate. One. Two. Three. Four. Over and over again. "Taylor, you see anything?"

She angles her head as she focuses on the door with the Oculus. I try to find the code that makes it up, to see if I can twist it around and reshape it so we can pass through. But the thing is solid. Whatever power I have, it's not going to get me through this door. I access my heads-up display next to see if I can interact with the thing, but no luck there either.

"Nothing," Taylor says. She traces her finger over the door, holding it a couple inches away so it doesn't shock her. "Just the squares."

Squares. Four of them. Iva's clue returns to me. *Step through the root of the largest. You have to go first, Eden. I unlocked it for you.* This has to be the same as the crypt door. It only opened for me.

Root of the largest. The largest is a four-by-four square, making it sixteen squared. The square root of that is four, meaning it would be the two-by-two square. The second from the smallest.

"Maybe . . . ," I say, and I explain the logic.

Taylor eyes me skeptically. "You're saying we just step through the second to last square?"

I shrug, hoping I'm not making a huge mistake. "Well, yeah. But we have to get the timing right. And I have to go first."

"And if you're wrong, we all get electrocuted?" She shakes her head, her short bleached braids slapping against her neck. "I don't know about that."

"Do you have a better idea?" I ask. To me it makes perfect sense. Logical sense. This has to be what Iva had meant.

"No." She crosses her arms.

Zachary gives me a conspiratorial grin. "It makes perfect sense to me."

Taylor rolls her eyes. "Of course it does."

"You guys ready?" I ask.

They both nod. I reach out and grab onto both their hands. Then I wait. When the three-by-three square pulses, I take a breath. When it changes to the two-by-two square, I step through.

I hold my breath, waiting to get shocked. For me to be wrong. But instead we pass through. The only effect I feel is the hairs on my bare arms and the back of my neck raising. I turn. The blue glowing door is now behind us. We've made it in.

"So that worked," Taylor says. "Now what?"

That worked. Now we look for the next part of the clue.

I study the room. With the humming of machinery and the

pulsating of lights, I would have expected computer equipment everywhere. But there is none of that. Instead we stand on a ground made of sand. The ocean is far ahead, waves rolling in and out.

"I've been here before," I say.

"Yep," Taylor echoes.

When we'd first reached the volcano after the garden with the sirens, Iva had brought me here, to the beach, to tell me about the power and the simulation. That wasn't part of the volcano. She'd brought me to her domain.

"I really shouldn't be here," Zachary says.

"It's fine." I go through Iva's clue in my mind, trying to piece out what is next. "A red flower. A yellow umbrella. Fourteen monuments."

"There's a yellow umbrella," Zachary says. He points off to the left where ten different umbrellas decorate the sand.

"Yeah, there's one, too." Taylor points the complete opposite way. All told, from where we stand, at least five yellow umbrellas are visible.

"Don't move yet," I say. "Look for a red flower." Since it came first in the clue, it has to somehow tie in to the umbrella.

"It's a beach," Taylor says. "There are no flowers."

"Except those," Zachary says. He points to a bar where a bartender stands watching us. He's got an assortment of glasses ready for us to drink, some with umbrellas, some with pieces of orange and melon staked with small swords, and some with . . .

"Flowers!" I say. "Zachary, you are a genius."

"Yeah, I know."

"Also humble," Taylor says. But we're all happy to go to the bar. Just seeing the drinks makes me realize how parched I am.

The bartender grins as we walk up, but it's so calculated that I'm sure he's an NPC of some kind.

"A Shirley Temple on a hot day?" he asks.

Sweat drips down my face at his words. The sun overhead is baking hot, and a Shirley Temple has never sounded so good.

"Anything stronger?" Taylor asks.

"Afraid not," the bartender says. "We're happy to serve up the best Shirley Temples around." Rather that seeming upset that he can't fill Taylor's request, he beams with pride at his words. Then he slides over a bowl of figs.

Zachary grabs a fig and pops it into his mouth in a single bite.

I point to one of the glasses with the red flower. "I'll take a Shirley Temple in that glass."

"A perfect choice," the bartender says, and he mixes the drink and slides it over to me.

I drain the glass without even planning to. And the second I set the glass down on the bar, everything around me vanishes.

xii

WHEN MY SURROUNDINGS REAPPEAR, Zachary and Taylor are nowhere to be found. Neither is the bartender or the bar. Instead I sit under a cabana, my drink freshly refilled and resting on the table next to me. There are two chairs. I am sitting in one, but the other is empty.

I've been here before, except the last time I was here, Iva was in the other chair.

Root of the largest. Red flower. I've followed her clues so far. I need to figure out the rest of it.

I stand and step out from under the cabana. The ocean water is blue like a sapphire, and waves gently roll in and out, lapping against the white sand. I'm alone on the beach, though umbrellas decorate the sand every so often. Red. Green. Blue. Yellow.

There is only one yellow umbrella.

I walk toward it. My heavy boots sink deep into the sand, making each step feel like I have ankle weights on. It figures that the yellow umbrella is farthest away. It's staked into the ground, near the edge of the sand. I slog through the sand until I reach it.

Under the umbrella, a plump golden apple sits on a table. I reach down and lift it to my lips, smelling the sweetness. Then I take a huge bite out of it. Energy runs through me as juice drips down my chin. Energy that refuels the power inside me. This is the same type of apple that Iva had placed in the simulation. Possibly the same apple? It's hard to know. Time and space don't seem to matter where the gods are concerned. Under the umbrella, I devour the entire apple until there is nothing left except five brown seeds. I tuck them into one of the pockets of my cargo pants, then lift my head to figure out what's next.

Beyond the beach and the yellow umbrella a path extends into darkness. It's filled with mist and a faint blue light, like a haunted pathway through a graveyard.

Graveyard. That's it! Lining the right side of the path are grave markers. No, not grave markers. Memorials. I move close to the nearest one and try to read the letters, but they're all ancient symbols, like the symbols at the entrance to the volcano. Like names of those who are memorialized here. There's also a line with an angle drawn on it. The ancient way to write the number one. The next one has different symbols and the ancient symbol for number two. On top of each one is a small bowl containing a single black pearl like I am looking for. But not these. I need a specific one.

The fourteenth memorial. I look at each one as I walk down the path. Three. Four. Five. The path gets darker with each step I take. Ten. Eleven. Twelve. Thirteen.

I move to the fourteenth memorial, ready for the end of this clue hunt. But my eyes find and register the number symbol. Fifteen. There is no fourteenth memorial. It's another trick.

No. Iva specifically sent me here to find and retrieve the black pearl. The fourteenth memorial is hidden to make it more secure.

I push through the thirteenth and fifteenth memorial stones, leaving the path behind. There is only darkness and fog ahead. I'm swallowed by the darkness. But it has to be here. It's the reason I'm here. But one wrong step and I could get lost. I squeeze my eyes closed and try to picture it there in my mind. I try to build it with my power. And when I open my eyes, directly ahead of me is a small hill. On top of the hill is the fourteenth memorial.

I don't need to see the number marking to confirm it, but all the same it's there. The ancient way to write fourteen. The memorial also has four symbols. Greek letters.

My name in Greek letters.

There you'll find the symbol that I made for you, Iva had said.

The symbol made for me. My name.

Sitting on top of the memorial is a small bowl. I can't see in it, but I reach my hand up and feel around, finding the black pearl. I grasp it with my thumb and forefinger. As soon as I do, the symbols of my name vanish from the memorial.

The pearl is warm to the touch, and even in the fog, it shines like it's made of gloss. Whatever it's made of, whatever it's made for, this is what Iva wants.

xiii

I STEP BACK FROM THE MEMORIAL.
The world around me shifts again, and I'm back at the bar. Taylor and Zachary are still there, holding their Shirley Temples in their hands as if nothing has changed.

"I got it," I say, holding up the shiny black pearl.

Zachary cocks his head as he studies it. "I wonder what she wants with that."

"You don't know?" I ask, thinking of all the other memorials, each with their own pearl. Maybe it's her secret. Maybe none of the other minor gods are aware.

"No idea," he says. "But with Iva, you never know."

"When did you get that?" Taylor says.

I shrug. "Just now." And I give them the very brief overview of what happened, leaving out the part about my name being on the memorial.

Taylor holds her hand out and even though I want to keep it safe, I hand the black pearl over to her. She flips it around, like she's looking for something. The entire surface appears the same

to me. Solid black with no markings or imperfections or anything that makes it look like anything other than a decoration. Then Taylor holds it up to the Oculus.

Immediately she pulls it back. "Oh . . . I get it."

"Get what?"

She puts it to the Oculus again, then flips it around. And around again. Over and over she does this as if she's trying to look at it from every possible angle.

"What do you see?" I ask.

She holds it close then far away, and her mouth drops open slightly, like she's about to say something.

"I see possibilities," Taylor says, finally handing it back to me.

"Possibilities of what?" I ask.

Taylor runs her fingers along the scars on her cheeks, something I notice she does when she's thinking. "At least twelve things that might happen with this."

I roll the pearl around in my palm. All I see is the black surface, but with the Oculus, Taylor must see possible futures.

"Can we talk about this once we're out of here?" Zachary says, glancing around. "I don't like being in Iva's domain."

My guess is that Iva doesn't like Zachary here any more than he likes being here.

I nod slowly, placing the small sphere in one of my pockets. Now that we have it, it's time to leave.

We backtrack from the beach to the doorway we came through. There's no lock from the inside. We simply step through. Then we're up the stairs and outside the crypt door. While we've been gone, the dead have had a chance to regroup. They wait for us, only steps away. Zachary steps forward with his palm raised, and they hold their position. Their eyes are filled with the desire to get to us, to pull us apart limb by limb, but he keeps them back.

I draw up the image of Florida, of Emily's front door. It appears in my mind perfectly, and I create an inventory item of it. Then I select Transport, grabbing hold of Zachary and Taylor before I do. The dead, seeing their chance, lunge after us, but we're gone just in time. We're free from them, safe . . . at least for the time being. But before I can take a step, I fall to the ground as a vision fills my mind.

I'm standing on a shiny black surface with vines reaching down from above, supported by a ceiling that isn't there. The sky above is orange and yellow, like it's alive with fire. In front of me is a building that seems to be made of pink and black glass. In front of it, huge spiky rocks jut up from the ground, blocking my path.

"Save me, Edie," a voice calls. It's thin and weak, like it's been calling for me for ages and I haven't come.

"Thomas?" I shout across the distance. I can't see him. The rocks are blocking everything.

"I'm holding on as long as I can," he says. "But if you don't make it here soon, he's going to reprogram me."

"I'm coming!" I shout, and I begin to run forward, toward the black jutting rocks and the pink building. But arrows fly out from the rocks and I fall to the ground. I've been hit by at least ten of them. I try to stand, but my knees buckle out from underneath me.

"Hurry, Edie!" Thomas says.

I try to hurry. I really do. But another wave of arrows comes, burying themselves inside me.

I try to call out to him, to tell him I'm sorry, but words take too much energy. My mouth won't listen to my brain. My fingers claw at the ground as I try to pull myself forward, but the black surface is like glass, and there is nothing to get a hold of.

Then the vision fades.

I'm on the ground, back in Florida. Taylor stands guard, but Zachary squats next to me.

"Are you okay?" he asks.

Not, I'm not okay, I want to shout. My brother needs me, and I can't get to him. But then I remember that Zachary is trying to help me. He can get me to Thomas. He can help me save him.

Slowly I pull myself to my feet, Zachary trying to help but not quite sure what to do. "Can Chaos reprogram people?" I ask.

The logic goes through my mind. *IF-THEN-ELSE.* If the gods can place people in storage and reprogram worlds and simulations, then they are bound to have the power to reprogram individuals.

Zachary looks me right in the eye. "Yes."

Hatred flows through me. Hatred for these gods. For the game we are now caught in. For the fate of the world resting in our hands.

"But it's really hard to do, and it almost never happens," Zachary adds. "It's easier to erase people and start over. Not that either of those things are supposed to ever happen. They're against the rules of the gods."

"Rules of the gods?" Taylor scoffs. "And what rules are those?"

I've never mocked the gods like Taylor, but in this case, she is absolutely right. Thus far, the gods have all seemed to play by their own rules.

"We should get moving," Zachary says. The gray sky has darkened like a blanket placed over everything.

"You're avoiding the question," Taylor says. "What rules?"

We walk in the center of the street, stepping around debris, but staying as much out in the open as we can.

"The gods operate by rules," Zachary says. "We have to."

Taylor kicks at a piece of metal that's fallen into the street. "Tell me one rule."

"There are lots of them," Zachary says.

"One rule."

He blows out a breath. "Fine. We don't go into the domain of other gods."

"A rule you just violated," Taylor says. "Am I right?"

He shakes his head. "I didn't have much choice if I was going to keep the dead away from you two. Not to mention Iva basically gave me permission."

I don't point out that Iva told me to go into her domain, not Zachary. Not even Taylor for that matter.

"Not good enough," Taylor says. "What's another rule?"

We keep walking. Ten seconds go by before Zachary answers. "Fine. We aren't allowed to outright kill humans."

I can almost see the anger building up inside Taylor, so I hurry to respond first. "That's why you have the simulations," I say.

He nods. "We can program the events and the world, but killing humans directly isn't allowed."

"So what you're saying is that you're not going to stab us while we're sleeping," Taylor says. "But if you happen to push over a building and it happens to fall on us and kill us, your hands are clean? Right?"

"Taylor," Zachary says. "Why are you seriously thinking the worst of me? I'm risking my butt by helping you out in the first place. You don't understand the old gods. They freaked out when one of us minor gods broke the rules. There were consequences."

"What kind of consequences?" Taylor asks.

He shrugs, trying to act like he's not bothered by the conversation, but his muscles are tight around his mouth, and he won't look either of us in the eye. "I've always been a rule follower. You know that. But one time . . . well, it's just rumor. I didn't see it myself. But Iva and Elise . . . you know they're sisters, right?"

I nod. Elise had told me that when Cole and I had visited her.

"So their father was one of the old gods," Zachary says. "One you've met actually."

I suck in a breath. That's right. Elise had told me that the old god I'd killed back in the throne room at the end of the labyrinth simulation had been their father. I'd worried that she would be upset with me. But if anything she'd seemed relieved that he was dead.

"You do know that," Zachary says. "Okay. Yeah. So what I heard was that one time he caught them interfering with his work, and he'd punished them."

"What work?" I ask.

"Probably just the usual," Zachary says. "Wars. Famine. Whatever he felt like doing to amuse himself. And Iva and Elise tried to stop him."

"So what'd he do to them?" Taylor asks.

Zachary stops walking and faces us, finally meeting my eyes. "Well, for starters, he had Iva's eyes pulled out."

My stomach twists into a horrid knot. The blindfold. But what kind of father would do that?

"And Elise?" I ask, barely in a whisper.

"Yeah, Elise," Zachary says. "He made it so she was always thirsty and could never quench her thirst. And the more she drank, the thirstier she got. I tried to help her. We all did. But nobody's been able to do anything about it."

Wow. Just wow. It's unbelievable that a father—even if he is, or was, a god—could do something like that.

A ball of hatred forms in my stomach. I watch him die over in my mind. The image gives me a sense of peace. "I'm glad I killed him."

Zachary laughs. "Yeah. Lots of us are, especially Iva and Elise. Let's just say no one really shed a tear. Well, no one except . . ."

Immediately I know who he's talking about. "Chaos."

He nods. "Yep. His brother. You definitely made an enemy."

I straighten my shoulders. I'd kill him over again if I had to. But now, if anything, I have more reason to.

"So what happens to you if Chaos finds out that you're helping us?" Taylor asks.

It's a really valid question.

"Well," Zachary says, "I hope I never find out."

I swallow as I process his words. He's always seemed so casual about helping us, but if what he says is true, he won't just be killed if his part in this is discovered.

"Thanks for helping us," I say.

He shrugs. "Yeah, let's just pick up the pace. I don't like the dark."

Night comes as we walk through the streets of Florida toward Ocular Technologies. It's across the bay, not far from the sporting goods store where I got my bicycle when I first set out on the journey. Part of me wants to make a stop inside. To see if they have another jacket like the one I'd gotten there. But the smarter part of me knows that I will never find another jacket like that one. Zachary had placed it there, so long ago. A way to help me, even back then. An advantage. But him being with us is a much bigger advantage.

The crescent moon has long since set when we finally reach Ocular Technologies. If not for the sign out front, I would never know there was anything special about the place. It's a typical office building with glass windows and glass doors out front. Shrubs line the sidewalk to the main door, but they are shriveled and dead, like they haven't been watered in decades.

Zachary walks up and places his hand on the rusty handle. It lights up at his touch. When he pulls on it, I expect it to squeak like rusty old metal, but it doesn't make a sound, almost as if it's been opened recently. He raises his eyebrows and puts a finger to his lips, telling us to be quiet.

The door closes as soundlessly behind us as when it opened. Inside, the main lights are out, but small LEDs decorate monitors, pictures on the walls, signs above doors and elevators.

"Fifth floor," Zachary says. "That's where I work."

I nod and we hurry to the stairwell. No way am I getting in an elevator in this place. The emergency lights are still on in the stairwell, casting red light everywhere. We climb quickly, trying to walk lightly so our heavy boots don't alert the world to our presence. And when we reach the fifth floor, Zachary opens the door and steps through.

It's a room full of desks facing each other with all sorts of high tech equipment laying around. VR goggles and monitors and haptic gloves and arm bands. If none of this had ever happened, I would have killed for a tour of this place. I'd almost asked Owen if his dad could get me a tour. Almost. Then Homecoming had come.

"Where did Owen's dad work?" I ask.

Zachary points over to one of the corners. A row of offices lines the wall, blocking most of the windows. "Corner office. He got promoted pretty quickly."

"And why was that?" Taylor asks.

Zachary shrugs. "He was smart. And good at his job."

"And maybe he had help?" Taylor says.

An image forms in my mind then. Owen's dad may have been excellent at his job. But was he excellent enough to dig deep enough to find out about the gods? Or was he nudged in the right direction?

"Chaos had to have helped him get started," I say. Sure, there is the small chance that he found out about the world of the gods all on his own, but if I had to bet one way or the other, I would be willing to bet a pair of VR goggles that someone gave him inside assistance.

Zachary stops walking. "That's my guess, too. Chaos must have fed him information. Just enough for him to hack into Raven's simulation and help Owen."

"But why him?" Taylor says. "Why Owen?"

It's a good question. Chaos is trying to keep me out because he's scared of the prophecy. Scared of me. And the power that now runs through me.

"He wanted Owen to kill me," I say as the truth settles in. "Chaos couldn't kill me himself, so he enlisted the help of Owen's dad and Owen, knowing Owen would be going into the simulation along with me."

Zachary nods. "Which means when you finally find Owen again, you need to be extra careful."

Maybe. Yet Owen didn't kill me. He had multiple chances, but he never did. He'd even suggested we were meant to work together. I can't see that as being part of Chaos's plan. Owen's dad might still be a pawn, but I wonder if Owen may be something more.

XIV

ZACHARY WALKS TO THE OTHER SIDE of the aisle where doors line a wall. He pulls open one of the doors. Immediately lights inside flicker on.

"Your lab," I say. I've been here, back before the labyrinth.

"Yep," Zachary says. "This is where I do all my work."

The chair in front of the desk is turned away from us, but slowly it rotates until it faces us. There, sitting in it, is Iva, blindfold on. Ponytails sprouting out to the side. Blue sequin shirt and checked Vans. A god in the permanent form of a little girl.

She crosses her arms like she's pouting. "You guys took so long. I was about to give up on you."

I highly doubt that. More likely she was tracing our every move.

Zachary takes two steps toward her, and his entire posture changes. He stands straighter. His shoulder go back. He becomes a god.

"What are you doing here?" he asks. There's a harsh tone to his voice that I've never heard before. I wouldn't have believed it possible given his casual attitude thus far.

Iva stands and skips over to him, navigating the lab like she can see despite the blindfold. "Oh, Zachary, don't get so upset. You went into my domain. I thought you realized that meant I'd be able to come into yours."

He crosses his arms. "It meant nothing of the sort."

His domain. That makes perfect sense. This lab. Maybe even the entire office building, is Zachary's domain.

I step forward, hoping to diffuse the situation. Gods and their domains is the least of our concerns right now. I pull the black pearl from my pocket. Placing it on my palm, I hold it out for her. "I got it."

Iva immediately takes the small sphere, not even pretending to act like she's not interested. Before I know what she's doing, she shoves it into her mouth and swallows it. Though it's small, I watch it go down her throat. I try not to gag, but it reminds me of a snake. Once it's all the way down she smiles.

"Thanks, Eden. I owe you one." She acts like I haven't just ful-filled my part of the bargain.

"The simulation," I say. "You're going to get us in."

Iva giggles. "You still want to go?"

Her childish games drive me crazy. "We still want to go," I say evenly.

Iva grins. "Okay. But first . . ." She angles her head toward Taylor. "What do you see with it?"

Iva's non-seeing gaze is so intense, if I were under her scrutiny, I feel like I would step back. But Taylor holds her ground. "You can't have it."

"I don't want it. I just want to know what you see."

Taylor shrugs, though Iva can't see her do it. "All sorts of things."

The smile falls from Iva's face replaced by a stone-cold look of intense concentration. "Do we have a chance?" she asks. "Can we defeat him?"

Him is Chaos. Our enemy. Her enemy. The true enemy of everyone on Earth.

Taylor crosses her arms and acts bothered, like she's been asked this question a million times already and is so over it. "I see fifteen possible endings."

"Fifteen," Zachary says. "That's all?"

"That's all," Taylor says.

"And of those . . . ?" Iva asks.

Taylor's eyes are focused on something else, not in this room. Something only she can see. "In two we succeed," she says. "In the other thirteen, we all die."

We all die. Her words hang there in the air. I can't let one of those thirteen options happen. Not for me or for selfish reasons, but because if we fail, there won't be anyone left to save the world. We are the last chance for this round in the game of the gods.

Iva clasps her hands together and the smile returns to her face. "Two chances is good."

Her statistics skills leave a bit to be desired, but two chances is certainly better than zero.

Iva steps back, leaning against the white board. "Now to get you guys into that stupid simulation," she says.

"I told you I can get Edie and Taylor in," Zachary says, and he sits in the chair where Iva just was. He starts tapping away at the keyboard. Bits of code fly across the screen. Then they pull from the screen and fly through the air, landing on the whiteboard where they mesh together into mini-programs.

Iva crosses her arms. "Let's see." And she waits.

Zachary shakes his head, like he's had about as much of this game as he can take. Then he keeps typing. The algorithms erase from the whiteboard and are replaced by others. Over and over again.

"The thing is that even though Chaos runs the simulation, it's still a simulation," Zachary says. "And like any simulation, there are back door algorithms in place to allow programmers to test computer code out."

"Cheats," I say.

He nods, typing the whole time he talks. "Exactly. This should be no different, especially if he had Owen's dad helping him with it. I've seen how he codes. I know his work."

I glance to Taylor. She's scowling at both Zachary and Iva.

"If we just enter a couple decoder commands, it should . . ." His voice trails off as the whiteboard is erased. He taps a few more keys and new code appears there. Then he waits. Types some more. And waits again.

Nothing happens.

"Well . . . ?" Iva says.

"It's possible that . . ." Zachary gets lost in his words, trying to get the simulation to open up to let me and Taylor in. But minute by minute the confidence is deleted from his face.

"Do you believe me yet?" Iva says once he's tried and failed five different times.

He shoves his chair away from the desk and stands. "What did you do to it?"

"Nothing," Iva says. "I told you. You can't get Eden in. Chaos has blocked her identification code from entering."

Understanding dawns on Zachary's face, and he sits again. "Okay, so we change her code."

"You can't change her code enough," Iva says. "Chaos isn't stupid. You do remember he's been ruling for thousands of years."

"I can do it," Zachary says. And he goes to work, hacking away at the keys. But the look of frustration grows on his face until he finally lifts his hands and pushes back from the computer. "Fine, what do you suggest?"

Iva giggles. "I told you so."

Zachary grumbles something that I can't understand. It almost sounds like "little brat know-it-all" but I don't ask him to clarify.

Iva turns to face Zachary. If she didn't have a blindfold on, I'd say she was fixing her eyes on him. But instead, it's more like she's fixing her intent on him.

"You missed a perfect backdoor solution," Iva says. "We get someone else into the simulation and they make the coding changes to open it up to everyone."

Zachary's eyes narrow as he tries to process Iva's words. But he gives a small shake of his head. "If the simulation is blocked, Edie can't get there to make the changes."

"Uh huh," Iva says. "But I'm not suggesting Edie make the coding changes. She's not the only coder around here."

"So put me in," Taylor says. "Tell me what to do."

Iva places a hand on Taylor's arm. "Oh, Taylor. You're so brave. Were you always so brave?"

Taylor says nothing.

"But the problem with that is—" Iva starts.

"You wouldn't know what to do," Zachary says slowly. "Which means . . ."

The smile on Iva's face grows.

"Which means what?" I ask.

Zachary blows out a long breath and stands. "Which means that I have to go into the simulation. I have to make the changes."

Iva claps her hands together in applause. "Exactly! Zachary goes in first, and from there, he opens the simulation up wide. Then Taylor and Eden can get in. Chaos will have no idea. It's perfect."

I'm not sure it's perfect, but it is a solution.

XV

"FOLLOW ME," IVA SAYS, AND SHE SKIPS
out the door we came through earlier, leaving Zachary's lab. Darkness fills the empty workstations around the interior of the office building. Though Iva can't see, she moves forward with confidence, not even so much as stubbing her toe. She leads us right to Owen's dad's office. There's a nameplate on the door, but someone has sprayed over it with red paint making it unreadable. Iva lifts her hand, palm out, and the door flies opens. Then she steps inside.

Lights come on as we enter. The office is a lot like Zachary's office in that it's more of a lab with all sorts of equipment laying around on tables. There are at least five pairs of VR goggles, haptic gloves and suits, spinning trampoline treadmills that simulate a full range of motion. Pretty much every state-of-the-art piece of VR equipment I ever knew existed before the labyrinth. Off to the side of the room are three pods, inclined at an angle like glass coffins.

"Nope," Taylor says, shaking her head as soon as she sees them.

"I am not getting back in one of those."

I have zero desire to get into another VR pod either. But I am also determined to get into the simulation.

"We have to," I say, starting for the pods.

"Oh, Edie," Iva says. "Those are just for show. Haven't you figured that out yet?"

I've been inserted into two VR stasis pods thus far. I've come out of one. "We're still in the other pods," I say.

Iva nods. "Exactly. You never left, so logic says that you're still there."

Logic. It's almost escaped me with everything that's been going on, and yet here it is, right when I need it.

"Well," Iva says. "That's if you were ever really in one in the first place."

Iva and her games are getting old faster than day-old cheese left out in the Florida sun.

"So what do we do?" Taylor asks.

Iva picks up a pair of the goggles and passes them over to me. "I've programmed these for each of you. I'll activate Zachary's first, and once he's opened the simulation, yours should come online. Then, with the heads-up display options, you should be able to enter the simulation."

"That's it?" Taylor says.

It does sound pretty simple when Iva puts it like that.

"That's it!" She hands Taylor a pair of the goggles also. Taylor flips them around, looking for wires or buttons, but the goggles seem to be self-contained.

Zachary grabs the third set of goggles. "Just for the record though, I'm going in, but then I'm getting out. I'm not staying in the simulation."

"Whatever you say," Iva says, then she skips over to one of the computer terminals. "Now can we stop wasting time?"

Time that Owen can use to find the key and reach Main Control Room Alpha. Time that Chaos can use to steal power from anyone who happens to make it all the way to the end.

I slip the goggles over my head, making sure the strap in the back is snug but not too tight. Instantly the lab becomes a sketch of itself, almost like a doodle. I move my hand on front of my face. It looks like a drawing also, and where it moves, motion lines blur across the screen. It's like we've been inserted into a comic book.

"Why is it all black and white?" Taylor asks.

"Just hang tight," Iva says. I can't see her even when I turn to face where I know she should be. But I hear typing, like she's clicking away at some kind of keyboard. I don't know how she can see what she's typing. "Okay, you guys ready?"

"No," Zachary says. "But I don't think that's an option. So I guess I'm ready."

He better be if we need him to get into the simulation.

"I'm sending Zachary in now," Iva says.

I'm looking right at him, and he vanishes. It's impossible just like everything else.

Iva keeps tapping keys on the terminal, counting down, muttering things that range from "access point" to "stop complaining." I'm guessing from this last one that she's in direct communication with Zachary.

Then the heads-up display in front of me comes to life, flashing a range of icons instead of just words. Symbols. Greek letters. It only takes me a second to spot the logical choice.

"Select the Omega," I say to Taylor.

With my eyes I select it, and new icons appear, choices. There is a green check mark that highlights when my eyes move over it. I select it.

The background of the lab and its comic sketch vanishes and everything around me turns gray.

XVI

CLICKING. SCRAPING, LIKE SOMETHING being dragged over metal. More clicks. And endless gray.

"Taylor? You still there?" I say.

There's no response. Only the scraping and the clicking. Then there's a snap, and everything goes black.

I step back, and the edges of my vision begin to fill in.

The lava river flows in front of me, but it's different than before. It takes me a moment to figure out why. I must be on the other side because far in the distance is the wall of lava, still blocking entry. On top of the lava, black platforms float, like some sort of ferry system. Above me is a gray sky, devoid of clouds, birds, anything. Everything. Only gray. I turn slowly, counterclockwise, spinning until I'm looking the opposite way. Ahead of me is a solid sheet of silver, starting at the ground and extending upward far into the gray sky. I can't see the top of it. For all I know there is no top of it.

"Edie," someone says, off to my left.

I turn to see Taylor and Zachary standing twenty yards away

near a white column that also extends up into the sky. It must be some kind of interface, because symbols scroll all over it. Zachary's messing with them like a control panel. Whatever he and Iva did, Taylor and I now seem to be across the river.

"You did it," I say, hurrying over to join them.

But Zachary shakes his head. "You're not in yet." He points to the wall of silver. "This is like the prep room. The actual simulation is inside there."

Dread fills me as I turn back toward the silver barrier. It ripples and moves, like a sheet of mercury that is alive. Once I pass through it, there will be no turning back. I know that. But I also know that I have to. We have to.

"You guys ready?" I ask.

"Not me," Zachary says. "I need to get back."

Taylor laughs. "Get back. Why? You scared?"

Zachary scowls. "I'm not scared. But I opened the simulation. You guys should be able to get in no problem."

"What if we can't?" Taylor says. "What if you messed up?"

"Please," Zachary says. "I don't mess up."

"Why not come with us then?" Taylor says.

I can't tell if she really wants him to come into the simulation with us or if she's testing him. Either way, the muscles in his face gets tighter with every second that goes by.

"Gee, I'd love to," Zachary says. "But I have simulations running. I need to get back to them."

"Simulations running!" Taylor says. "What? Like the labyrinth? More kids you're deciding to torment?"

He shakes his head. "No. But things I'm testing. And if I'm not there to monitor them, we're going to have some serious problems."

"What kind of problems?" I ask.

He raises a lip, as if the thought torments him. "Well, here's the thing about the simulations. When I'm there, I control them. When I'm not there . . . they control themselves."

"Like what?" I ask. "They become . . ."

"Sentient," Zachary finished. "They do what they want."

The last thing we need—or the world needs for that matter—is simulations coming to life. The world is already in enough trouble.

"Sounds like an excuse to me," Taylor says.

I'm not so sure. If Zachary is telling the truth, then he has done his part. We're across the river. Taylor and I can go into the simulation.

"It's okay," I say. "You can go. But thank you for your help."

"Help," Taylor says, scoffing. "Let's not be too generous with our thanks."

Maybe. Maybe not.

"Is this where you snap your fingers and leave?" I say.

"I guess so," Zachary says. He shuffles on his feet, and for a second I think he's going to hug me. Instead he says, "Be safe, you guys." Then he snaps his fingers.

Nothing happens.

Nobody speaks for a moment. Zachary snaps his fingers again. But still he remains right there with us, at the space between the wall of silver and the lava river.

"Okay, this is ridiculous," Zachary says, and he turns back to the white column. I come around so I'm standing behind him. From there, through my heads-up display, a screen becomes visible. He taps through a bunch of commands and menu choices. "All I have to do is find the . . . okay there it is."

The screen lists four choices.

The only problem is that all four of the menu choices are grayed out. Zachary presses EXTRACT, but each time, it buzzes in response. After five times, a male voice I don't recognize says, "Extraction from Simulation Omega not permitted."

"Not permitted," Zachary says. "But we're not in the simulation yet."

The voice doesn't respond to him. But the options remain grayed out. Simulations to babysit or not, Zachary seems to have only the same choices as Taylor and me.

I place a hand on his arm. "You could come with us."

He shakes his head. "That's not the plan."

"The plan," Taylor says. "And what plan is that? Iva's plan? Don't you think she knew this would happen? Don't you think this was part of her plan all along?"

Understanding dawns on Zachary's face, and he narrows his eyes. "Next time I see her, she is seriously going to be sorry."

I pull him away from the column, toward the wall of silver. "Yeah, well let's just make sure there is a next time, okay?"

"Oh, there will be," Zachary says. "Trust me."

"Not a chance," Taylor says. "Now let's go."

She grabs his arm like she's going to drag him forward, but Zachary pulls back.

"Do you have any idea all the things beyond that barrier that are going to try to kill us?" he says.

I don't, which is probably a good thing. If I'd known ahead of time what was waiting for me in the labyrinth and in Simulation

Avine, I never would have gone. Or at least I wouldn't have been so eager.

"Do you?" I ask, a small bit of hope creeping into my voice. Maybe Zachary knows more than he's told us. Anything to give us an advantage.

He shakes his head. "No. Not a stupid thing. Chaos created it, and all I know is that we better be prepared for the worst."

If as in prepared he means that we have no weapons, then I guess he's right. I realize now that my knife is gone, my compass is gone. Taylor is equally empty-handed. I almost pull on my power and create something from the materials around us, but I stop at the last second. I can't use the power. Not yet. If I do, it might alert Chaos to the fact that I'm here. I'll save it for when I really need it.

We trudge across the uneven ground to the wall of silver and stop about a foot away. The thick liquid moves like a metallic waterfall, except it flows upward. It comes out of the ground. There is no seam under it. No way to see through it. I tap it lightly with my finger. It depresses slightly and bounces back, but it stays solid. I press harder, using the palm of my hand. I push as hard as I can, trying to make a dent, but it doesn't separate.

"We aren't breaking through," Taylor says, kicking at the wall. "This thing is solid."

I press harder on the wall. For only having VR goggles on, everything feels as real as if I were really here. But the VR goggles are only a layer over the stasis pod. Or is that a layer over a different set of VR goggles? Instantly my mind wants to piece out the logic of what came first, of the layers of virtual reality. But it doesn't really matter. All that matters is moving forward.

I press my hand flat on the wall of silver, barely touching it. My heads-up display flickers and words appear.

I look quickly to Taylor and Zachary. This was not part of the plan. The plan was for the simulation to be open.

Zachary puts up a hand. "It's okay. There's a code."

"What code?" I ask. I try to keep my breathing under control, but we can't fail here. Not now. We aren't even in. Not really.

"A generic code I created," Zachary says. "Like a guest log-in account. If the simulation is open, then it should work to let us in."

On the top of my tongue is the opposite option. What if it doesn't work? But no. I'm not going to assume failure. We are getting into this simulation one way or the other.

"What's the code?" Taylor asks.

"0m1cr0n5," Zachary says, spelling it out in letters and numbers.

I input it through my heads-up display once he's told me the whole thing. A single option appears when I'm done.

Enter Simulation

I select it.

Instantly the wall of silver begins to morph. Instead of flowing upward in front of me, it moves like water around my feet, so fast that by the time I think to look over to Taylor and Zachary, the silver has blocked them from view. Then it's over my head, and I'm solely inside it, silver on all sides of me like a cocoon. There is no sign of Zachary or Taylor. There's no sign of anything. Only me now encased in the silver.

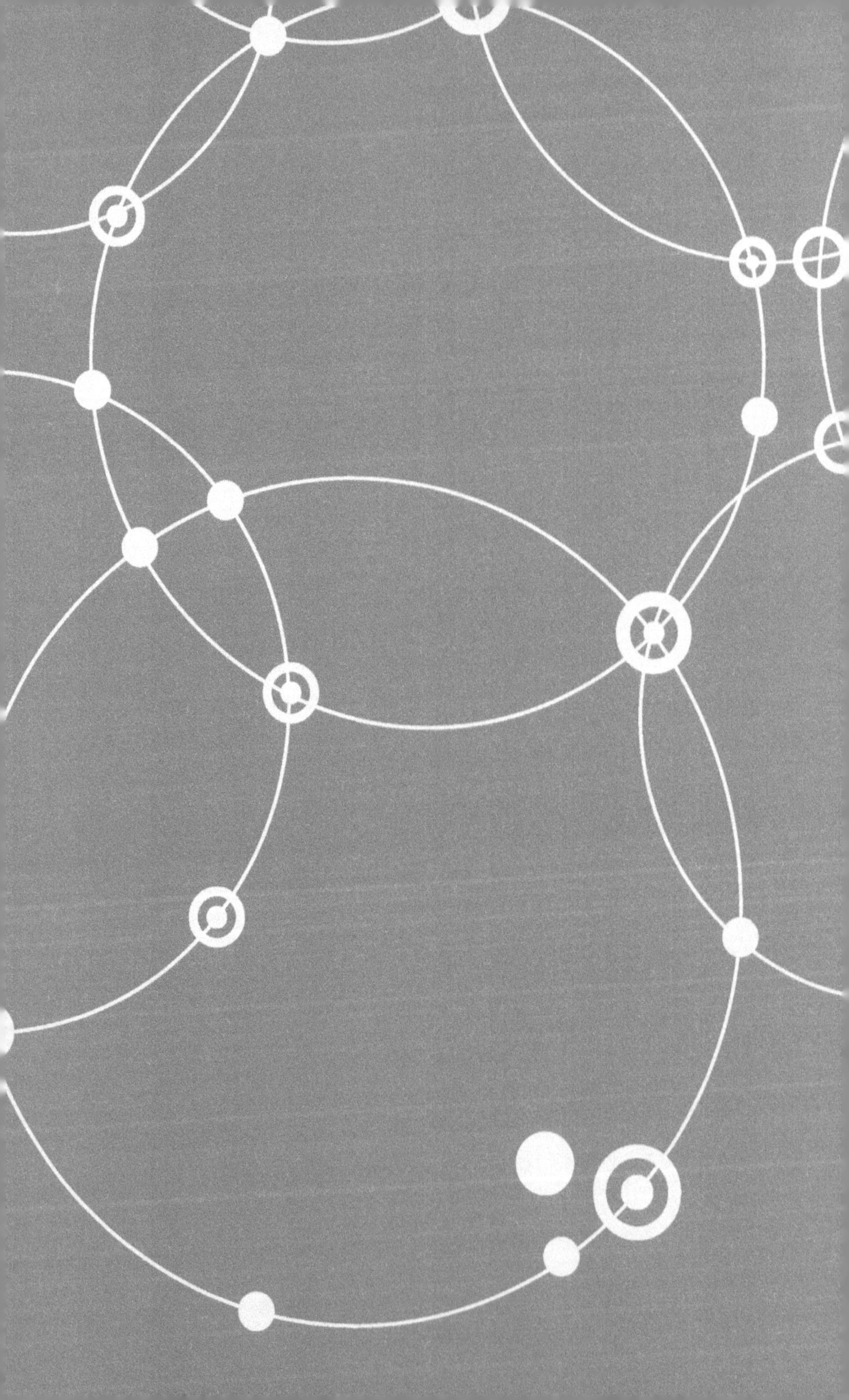

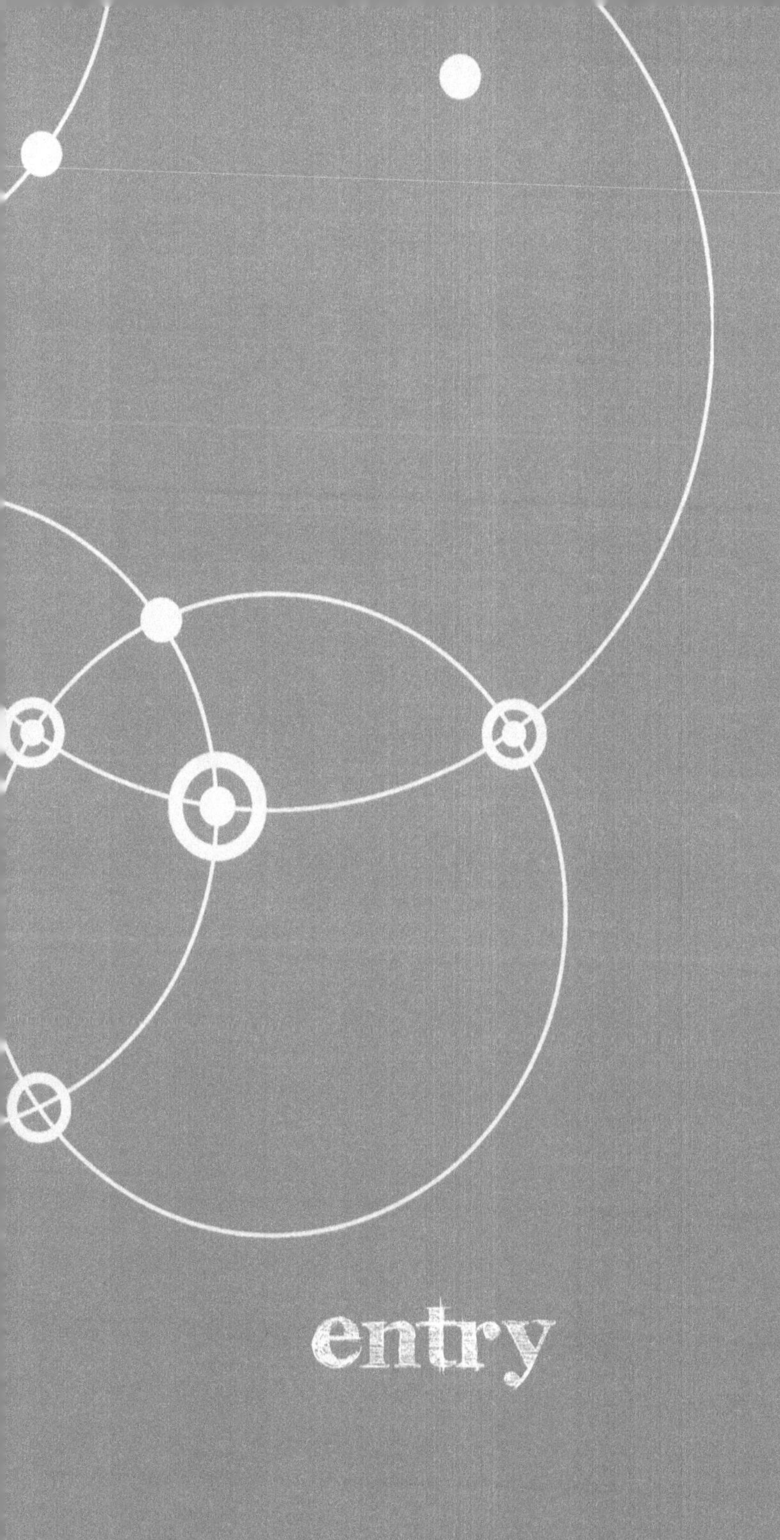

entry

XVII

I PRESS ON THE BARRIER AROUND ME.
It molds to me but doesn't break. I hit it with my fists and shoulders, but it doesn't budge. There is no sign of where I came from. No obvious way out.

"Taylor!" I shout. "Zachary!"

There is no answer. I am alone. I need to figure out what to do next.

The silver is like an eggshell around me. Over my head. Under my feet. Wide enough for me to extend my hands around in all directions.

I'm dressed in fresh clothes, identical to the ones I wore before. Gunmetal gray tank top and cargo pants. Heavy black boots. But there is no belt around my waist. No weapons. No wristband that I'd used to communicate with Zachary Gomez. No supplies. My curly hair is tied back in a ponytail at the base of my neck.

I flex my fingers, feeling for the simulation connections. I press my hands to my eyes. The simulation, as with the others, is perfect. Precise. And now that I'm here, I need to move on.

I take a step forward, and the silver morphs and flows, keeping my boundary secure. I step backward, and once again it follows me. But I can't just stay here. I need to get into Simulation Omega.

Logic. I fall back on it. I got in here by pressing my palm on the silver. In Simulation Avine, we pressed our palms on the world gates. It must be the method of contact. A means of communication.

I press my palm flat on the barrier in front of me. Instantly my heads-up display comes to life.

It flickers and shifts and all sorts of code and images scroll across my vision. Then it finally resettles. Against the backdrop of the silver barrier, blue words appear.

IDENTIFICATION CODE VALIDATED.
ARE YOU READY TO ENTER SIMULATION OMEGA?

Upon seeing the words, my stomach tenses. This is it. Simulation Omega. Whatever happens inside this place, it will be the final simulation. And it's where I need to go.

There are two options below the words.

» YES
» NO

There is no chance in hell that I would say no. I've sacrificed too much to get here. Been through too much. I need to find Thomas. I need to defeat Chaos. And then . . . I'll figure out what comes next after that. But until then, I have a plan.

I take a deep breath and select YES with my eyes. The words fade away and new ones appear.

My biggest strength has always been my mind. My logic.
At the thought, the words fade away and are replaced.

I am not weak. I have never been weak. There is nothing I can't use logic to solve. That's why it's my biggest strength. But if logic were to fade into the background and no longer work . . . that's when I'd run into a problem. Still, in a simulation, logic has to prevail.

The words fade away. Whatever my answer, the simulation has recorded it.

New words appear.

I look around my cocoon of silver, sure I'm being watched. There is no one here but me. Still, it's like I'm a rat in a cage and an entire room full of gods sit watching me. Wondering what my fear will be. Thinking up ways to use it against me. There had been the spider, the trees, the monster at the end of the labyrinth. But I've faced all those. There had even been Owen. After Homecoming, I would have sworn he was my biggest fear. Even the thought of visiting my best friend Emily who lived on his street was enough to send me into a near panic attack. But I'd faced Owen, too. Multiple times. And sure, Owen is a monster in his own right, but he's not my biggest fear.

Instead images come to me. My parents on their ship as it sinks beneath the black water. Thomas taken from me and brought to this place. Cole, leaving me.

The words fade away. I know they will. I can't stand the idea of losing someone I love. Even remembering the cops telling me that my parents were dead . . . The thought is enough to bring tears to my eyes.

New words appear on the screen.

CALIBRATION COMPLETE

That's it. Simulation Omega has been calibrated for me.

A silhouette appears to the side of the heads-up display. Small defined features with shoulder length hair. I can't tell if it's a man or a woman. Then a man's voice pipes through.

"My name is Chaos, the last of the old gods. As with all things, my time has come to pass on my reign to the next generation. Congratulations. That's why you're here. You've been invited to participate in Simulation Omega. Being here means that you have faced the worst in the other simulations and survived. You are among the best. This simulation will determine if you are the best of the best."

The best of the best, which means whoever has made it inside has survived everything else so far, whether that be the labyrinth or Simulation Avine. But Chaos doesn't know who I really am. If he did, I wouldn't be allowed inside.

"The best of the best will take my place as the supreme entity," Chaos says. "All others will be terminated."

Of course he's lying. Not about terminating those who are not the best. But about the best of the best taking his place. Iva and Zachary already told me that Chaos plans to take the power from whoever makes it to the end. Maybe from everyone inside the simulation. And me, with the power of the other old god . . . I

118

can't let him find me. I can't risk him getting that power.

The silhouette disappears and an image appears, six concentric circles, each a different shade of blue. They are labeled with Greek letters: Alpha, Beta, Gamma, Delta, Epsilon, Digamma. My breath catches at the last one. Digamma was the hidden zone from the labyrinth. It was the symbol Mom always used to draw. The Greek W. It can't be a coincidence. It had been the last zone in the labyrinth, and it is the last zone here. It had also been the hardest zone to get through before, with a monster at the end. I have every reason to believe the same will be true here in Simulation Omega.

The circles pop inward, three-dimensional. I reach forward to touch them even though they aren't there. They're coming through the heads-up display. They almost seem to vibrate with electricity.

"Simulation Omega is a series of zones, one after another," Chaos says, shaking me back to the reality of the situation ahead. What I'm looking at is not a set of circles. It is a set of death traps, one after another. "Each contestant must move from one zone to the next."

"What about the key?" I ask.

"The key has been divided into five segments," Chaos says. "Each segment is located in a different zone. Complete the quest in each zone in order for the location of the segment to be revealed. Collect all the segments and reach the center zone of the simulation for victory."

He makes it sounds so simple, like all I have to do is stroll from one zone to the next, picking up Easter eggs as I go.

"How many contestants are there?" I ask. I haven't thought of myself as a contestant before now. The labyrinth and Simulation Avine had felt more like horrible nightmares I needed to escape from. But when it comes right down to it, they'd been games also, just like this simulation ahead. Games of the gods, designed to suit their needs.

"That information will not be provided," Chaos says. The outermost circle lights up, then the one inside it, then the next, one after another as he speaks. "Each zone will provide new and exciting challenges. Only the contestant who adapts will be able to survive."

This is nothing new. But in the past there have been rules to go by. Items to help us. The water bottle. The jacket. A knife.

"What about supplies?" I ask. "Do I get anything to help me?"

"One item from the list," Chaos says. "That's all you may take."

At his words, the circles disappear and a scrolling list of items appears on my heads-up display. I'm hoping for my compass or maybe a knife, but the items on the list aren't even tangible.

- » MEMORY
- » STRENGTH
- » EXTRA LIFE
- » RESET
- » STAMINA
- » ENERGY BOOST

There are a handful of others. Maybe twenty total. But I can only pick one. Energy is always a solid choice. We'd nearly died when we'd run out of energy back in Simulation Avine. But with added Stamina, I would be able to use what energy I had for longer. Still, if I die in the simulation, neither of those choices will help me. What I need is a second chance.

When I play video games, reset is what I use when death is imminent, so it seems like a good decision. But when I do reset a game, I lose all my progress. Extra Life may mean I get the same second chance but my progress won't be lost. Still, if for some reason I have just died and I use my extra life, then whatever killed me could immediately kill me again.

"Reset," I say as I select it with my eyes.

The scrolling list of choices vanishes, and the concentric circles of Simulation Omega appear once more.

"Your choice may not be changed," Chaos says. "Once used it will be removed from your inventory. Before leaving a zone, make sure to collect the segment of the key. Once a zone is exited, it may not be re-entered for any reason. No exceptions will be allowed. In addition, without the segment of the key, the next zone will remain closed, leaving the contestant in a stasis situation. Contestants in stasis will be terminated at the completion of the simulation."

It's pretty straightforward. I can only move forward through the zones. I have to collect the pieces of the key. If I don't, I will die.

With that, the voice cuts out, leaving me in silence. The concentric circles on the display change color, the outermost one turning blue, the others fading to gray. Four menu choices appear.

» ENTER ZONE ALPHA AND BEGIN SIMULATION
» ABORT SIMULATION AND TRANSPORT TO STORAGE
» TRANSFER INVENTORY TO ANOTHER CONTESTANT
» HELP

I can never imagine choosing Abort. Even if I wanted to be transported back to the storage banks, I don't believe Chaos would actually follow through on that. The odds are much more likely that termination would occur.

And transfer inventory to another contestant? What? Like I'd give my Reset to Owen?

Or Cole?

At the thought, an image flashes through my mind. Cole is held in place by blue bonds that crackle with electricity. His shirt is torn. His skin is smeared with black grime. The scar on his face is bright red as if it's inflamed. His prosthetic is missing.

"Cole?" I say. The vision is so real. It's like he's standing in front of me. And like he can hear me, his head snaps up.

"Edie?" he says. His eyes don't focus. "Edie, I tried. It didn't work."

"Cole, where are you?"

I forget I'm in the vision and I take a step forward, trying to get closer to him. But the vision moves with me, keeping him out of reach. I want so badly in that moment to be able to turn back time. To make him never leave with Pia. To never have freed her from the gaming zone. If I hadn't freed her, he'd be here with me right now. But I can't change the past. I can only decide what I do from here.

Words flash on the heads-up display, overlaying the vision.

» Transfer Inventory to another contestant

The only inventory I have is the Reset. But I don't really know what it would do even if I did transfer it to him. As much as I want to free him, that's not the way to do it. I need to find him.

But the memory of him leaving me plays over again in my head. *We weren't meant to be together, Edie.*

Pia, with her bright green eyes and her dark pixie haircut, ruining everything. Smiling at me. Knowing exactly what to do to get under my skin. For all I know this is just another trick. It could be a trick the two of them are playing on me together.

"Where are you, Cole?" I ask, trying to keep my voice even. I can't open my heart to him. It will only make me risk getting hurt.

"You can't come here, Edie," Cole says. "It's too dangerous."

I don't want to find him, and yet I also do want to find him more than anything.

"What's dangerous?" I ask, holding the emotion out of my voice. "And where's Pia? Is she there with you?"

The words flash again over my vision.

This is all a test to see how I react. What I do.

"Where are you, Cole?" I say. "I'll come help you."

"No!" Cole shakes his head. "Edie, you need to be careful. You need to stay away. This place is—"

But before he can say another word, electricity streaks out of the ceiling above him and pours directly into his chest. Cole rears back, coming off the ground, and begins to scream. It makes my toes curl, even in the vision. I try to block it out. To pretend it's not real. To be mad at him. But I can't take it.

I rush forward, trying to get to him, but the vision immediately disappears.

"I'll transfer inventory," I shout.

Words flash on the heads-up display.

"Bullshit," I say, and I try to select it again. And again. Each time the option doesn't work. The only way to help Cole, if it really isn't a trap, is to get out of here. To move forward.

I select ENTER ZONE ALPHA AND BEGIN SIMULATION.

The menu options vanish, and the silver liquid begins to morph around me, pulling away from me. It runs down my skin and to my feet until it slithers away behind me. I turn back in time to see the moving wall of silver flowing upward behind me.

I can't go back. That will result in stasis and eventual termination.

I face forward to see what I'm up against. Instantly I'm sorry. Lightning streaks down, out of the sky and strikes directly in front of my feet. I jump to the side, but another streaks down nearby. Then another.

I run, dashing between the lightning bolts. They sizzle so close that my skin tingles. The hairs on my arm stand on end. If this is only the first challenge, my fate may already be sealed.

xviii

THE GROUND IS A SHEET OF BLUE GLASS.
It darkens at each spot where the lightning strikes. The sky above
is identical to the blue ground below, like a mirror image of it. It's
alive with electricity, shooting streaks of lightning down so rapidly that it's hard to distinguish one from the next. I dare to take
my eyes off the lightning, looking off in the distance. Far ahead
are small dots of blue light, flickering like beacons that call me
toward them.

"Edie, here!" someone shouts.

I turn in the direction of the voice. There stand Zachary and
Taylor. They've made it into the simulation also, though this
might mean death for all of us if we don't get out of here.

They wave at me frantically. They're standing under a slanted
white covering that's keeping the lighting away, one of a handful
that stretch off in the distance. I run as fast as I can toward them,
jumping to the side to keep from being killed. The closer I get,
the more the lightning attacks, as if it's alive. Then I'm under the
covering, safe . . . at least for the time being.

"You guys made it through," I say, trying to shake the feel of the lightning outside of our protection. I jump with every snap. It strikes the barrier above us, sending electrical current into the ground. But it stays away.

Zachary's eyes light up and he smiles. "We got through. It worked."

"We didn't know what happened to you, Edie," Taylor says. "The thing sucked you in. Then, next thing I know, it was wrapping around me."

Lightning hits the barrier again. This time the hairs on my arms stand on end. We can't stay here forever. We need to keep moving.

From off to the left, I hear shouting. Four people are running from one of the barriers out into the sea of lightning. They're too far away to tell who they are, but from the way they move, I'm pretty sure it's not Hudson, Owen, or Abigail. They're dressed like we are, cargo pants and tank tops. I make out a couple words amid their shouts. They run toward another barrier, out in the field of blue glass, but they're still far away.

"Come on!" it sounds like one of them shouts. They dash between bolts of lightning, but it strikes so close, like it's sentient, attempting to kill them.

"They're not going to make it," Taylor says. Her eyes are wide, and I don't know if she sees more with the Oculus than Zachary and I can see.

"Do you see that?" Zachary asks. "Or is that a gue—"

His words are cut short by a scream that pierces the air. One of them stands unmoving, electricity encasing their body. The person's arms are out. Their mouth held wide open in the scream that seems to last forever. Then whoever it is disintegrates as the lightning consumes them.

"Oh shit," Taylor says.

The other three people can't stop to mourn. They keep running toward the barrier. And almost like the lightning is giving them a small reprieve in payment for its victim, it stays at bay, and they make it to the barrier. When they get there, they collapse to the ground.

"We can't get through that," Zachary says. He stands toward the back of the barrier, as far from the lightning as he can.

"Can we make it?" I ask Taylor.

She's still staring out at the other group, but slowly she nods. "One in eight chance," she says.

One in eight. The odds aren't good, but it is a chance.

"Let's go," I shout, and I grab Zachary's arm, dragging him from the safety of the barrier.

Not far ahead is another barrier, our next check point. Once we get there, we can figure out where the next one is. And the next, until we're across the field of blue glass.

"Are you nuts?" Zachary says, yanking back on me. "We can't go out there."

Every second we wait isn't doing us any favors. We have to go. I glance back to the other group. They're on the move again, heading for what I'm guessing is another barrier, but it's too far away for me to see.

"We have to, Zachary," I say. I'm trying to keep my voice even, but I know I'm yelling. "We stay here and we die. There is no going back. Only forward."

His face is tight, and he looks like he's about to keep arguing with me, and in that moment it strikes me. He's scared to death, and rightly so.

"Look, god boy," Taylor says. "This is no worse than the shit you put us up against. And if you don't start moving right this second, Edie and I are going to leave you here. Is that what you want?"

He looks to me, maybe gauging my reaction, to see if I really would leave him here. And though it would kill me to do it, I would. I have to keep moving. Everything depends on it. Still, I don't want that to be an option.

"You can do this, Zachary," I say. "You can totally do this."

He grumbles something under his breath, but with the lighting, I can't hear what it is. Then he says, "Let's go."

We take off, running, and immediately the lightning attacks, aware of us. Maybe drawn to us, like we're metal rods pulling on it. We dash left, right, moving forward, toward the barrier. It's so close. I don't think I breathe the entire time. But my feet pound the blue glass as I run. The image of the other person, electrified and disintegrated, quickens my pace. I've never run so fast in my life. Then we're under the first barrier and safe.

I bend forward, placing my hands on my knees as I attempt to catch my breath.

"One down," Taylor says. "And they made it, too." She points to the other group. They're to the second barrier and moving. The lightning seems to have lessened where we are as they run, almost like it can only focus on one group at a time.

I blow out a huge breath. "We need to go now."

"We need to rest," Zachary says. His dark hair is going in every direction, like he's just been through a hurricane. But if I'm right, while the storm is focusing on the other group, we have to go.

"No time for rest," I say, and I drag him out from under the shelter.

We run, dashing again so fast I think my legs might give out. If I trip, I am dead. But my theory seems valid. The storm of lightning is nowhere near as bad as it was . . . at least until the other group reaches their shelter. Then the lightning turns on us again in full force. We barely make it to the shelter. But barely is better than not at all.

"When they run, we run," I manage to say between breaths, and this works again and again until we are under the final barrier. There is still one more stretch to go. The other group is out of the field of lightning, on to whatever is beyond. This is great for them but leaves us with no distraction. It also means that whoever they are, they're ahead of us.

"Ready?" Taylor says.

"No." Zachary's answer is blunt but true. Still, we can't wait until we're ready. We never will be. But just before I step out from under the shelter, shouts erupt from far behind us.

I turn and in the distance see three different people running through the field of lightning. It immediately focuses on them. I don't allow any time to feel sorry for them.

"Now!" I shout, and we take off, covering the final distance from the last barrier to the edge of the field of lightning. Forms begin to take shape beyond. Columns and buildings that look like something from ancient Greek and Roman days. I focus on the nearest one, making it my goal.

When my feet finally leave the blue glass, stepping onto ground that looks like white marble, I keep running, not stopping until I reach a white building with columns that stretch up to hold a massive ceiling of stone. There is no sign of the other group that made it here before us. I turn back to the storm, watching it crackle and chase whoever else happens to be on it. We're only about twenty feet away, but the storm stays contained. And for the moment we are safe.

Zachary sinks to the stone steps outside the building and runs his hands through his messy hair. "We seriously could have died out there. Seriously."

I cock my head at him as I try to understand what he's going through. It's obvious that he's scared as hell. But when it comes right down to it, he's as responsible for this entire mess as Chaos is. He's been behind the game of the gods as much as Iva or Raven or any of the other minor gods. And the fact that he would be upset that now he's the one inside . . . it's too much.

"We can still die," I say, hearing my voice rise. My heart pounds as I try to get the adrenaline back under control. "Don't you get it? This is what we've been going through from the second you shoved us into the simulation?"

Taylor looks like she's ready to punch him, but instead she slams her fist into one of the white marble columns. A crack forms, running upward and downward away from her fist. "I hate this!" she shouts. "I hate everything about this. Now where's that key?"

I blow out a long breath and look away from Zachary, because I'm pretty sure I'm going to punch him otherwise. I'm ready to drop. I sink to the ground. Sweat pours off me. My gray tank top is soaked through. Unlike the field of lightning, white light shines above, coming from a sun hidden behind the glare of brightness. It makes the marble ground glow, so smooth and even it's like a rolling pin was used to level it. I press my hands against it, but then stop as my right hand rubs against something.

"Look." I scoot to the side so Taylor and Zachary can see. Carved into the white marble is a letter: H.

"Hudson," Taylor says without hesitation. "He's leaving us a trail."

God, I hope she's right. It would great to know that something is going our way. If Hudson's been here, then maybe that means he's not that far ahead. If only he'd killed Owen by now that would be the best.

The thought is there before I can stop it. And yes, Owen has done so much to deserve to die. But for me to just think it, so casually . . . it's not like me.

Unless this is the new me.

My heads-up display comes to life. The silhouette of Chaos appears. "You have entered Zone Alpha. Proceed ahead for your challenge. Only those who complete the challenge will be allowed to locate the key and pass into the next zone."

It's a reminder I don't need.

"Thanks a lot," Taylor says. "You'd think since my heads-up display got jacked, I wouldn't have to listen to his nonsense."

"So it works again?" I ask.

She points to her right eye. "Only on this side."

If Chaos has fixed her heads-up display for the simulation, then that may mean he knows she has the Oculus. And with its abilities, I am almost certain it's something he would want to get his hands on.

Zachary finally stands up, but he's keeping his distance. I know I should feel bad for yelling at him, but everything is too much of a mess.

"Look, Edie," he finally says, taking a step closer to me and Taylor. "I never really thought about it."

Taylor whips around to face him. "Never thought about what? People dying because of the shit you made up? You know my brother died, right? You know that?"

He nods and swallows. "I know. I'm sorry." He glances around, looking out at where we need to go. "But I think—"

Taylor gets right in his face. "You think what, god boy? And be really careful what you say here, okay?"

To Zachary's credit, he doesn't back down from Taylor and her wrath. "I think that . . . Okay, the storage banks . . . I think that if we can get to Main Control Room Alpha, we'll be able to access them."

"And what?" Taylor says. "Will that bring Adam back? Because as far as I remember, he died in the simulation."

Zachary licks his lips before speaking. "He may have died, but if I'm right, he's still stored there. You all probably are."

I'm not sure either of them blink.

Then Taylor says, "What are you saying, god boy?"

Another swallow. "I'm saying, that if we can actually get access to the storage, and if his memory bank wasn't one of the ones that was destroyed, then we can bring him back."

Bring him back. The words hang there in the air like real things. If there is really a chance that Adam could be brought back . . .

I try not to move. This is not the time to draw attention to myself. The muscles in Taylor's face contort as she tries to come to terms with what Zachary is saying. I get it. She doesn't want to believe him, not if it means she'll lose Adam all over again if what Zachary is saying is a lie.

"Why are you telling me this now?" Taylor says. "How come you didn't mention this before, back when we were inside the storage area?"

He points to his eyes. "The heads-up display. I guess I got one, too. And during that whole intro to the simulation thing, I tried to poke around a bit behind the scenes of the simulation."

Of course he did. Zachary may be a god, but he's also a programmer.

"What did you find?" I ask. Unlike Taylor, I am willing to step out on the bridge of hope.

"I saw the control room," Zachary says. "There are all sorts of data signatures pouring off the place. Code scrolling around. Data storage statistics. Outer world simulations. It's all in there. And—"

"We get in there, we get control to everything," I say. "Not just control of our world, but of everything."

Zachary nods. "Everything. It's the only thing that makes sense. Chaos is too weak to control most of it, allowing things like the Creators to destroy chunks of the simulations. Only power of the gods can stop them. Can access the storage banks. Power like you two have. You get there. You get control. Anything is possible."

Taylor finally blinks, maybe the first time she has since Zachary mentioned it. Then she says, "Truce."

The word hangs there. The meaning of it is strong, filled with hope. Full of success if the truce holds.

"Truce," Zachary says. "We get to the end of this simulation. We get into Main Control Room Alpha. And we bring your brother back."

Hope fills my chest. Hope is what we need. It's the only thing that will hold us together and get us to the end.

I put my hand forward, palm down. Zachary places his hand on top of mine. Taylor only hesitates a second before placing her hand there, too.

"Truce," I say. "It can't be broken."

"It won't be," Taylor says. This is everything to her. This is what she needs. I only hope that it works out like Zachary thinks it will, because I don't want to see Taylor lose everything all over again.

Shouts come from behind us, stirring us from the moment. The group of three that was behind us are getting close. Without knowing who they are or if we can trust them, it's better to leave before they get here. We exit the temple and set out across the white marble. The landscape starts with a sparse building here or there, but it begins to fill in with each step we take. Soon a road appears, constructed of black glass inset into the white. Buildings line the sides, built from steel and stone, but constructed to again look like something out of ancient Greece. At first there are no other people around, but soon, they, too, begin to fill in. They sit on balconies and watch as we walk by. They sip drinks and eat from platters of food. They cheer for us. Throw flowers at our feet. They're NPCs, no doubt, created for the simulation, but the whole thing gives me a really bad feeling. The only good thing is that the road leads in one direction. We aren't at risk of picking the wrong way. There's still no sign of anyone in front of us. And if the group behind us made it off the field of lightning, they're not visible either.

Overhead the sun doesn't move in the sky. It's permanently noon. More people and buildings begin to fill in. Statues and obelisks line the streets also, and soon, human heads hanging from poles.

We stop walking at the sign of the first head.

"That's gross," Zachary says. "I never put anything like that into my simulations."

"Wait, didn't you create the doll simulation?" Taylor says.

Zachary twists his lips up in thought. "Maybe. Why? Did you like it?"

She puts her face in his. "Hell no, I didn't like it. Those dolls were psychopathic murderers. Do you have any idea what they did to people?" She motions up at the head. It swings gently, as if there's a breeze.

"Kind of," Zachary says. "But I had to. It was my job. What? Did you think they should just escort you through? You think that would help figure out who should win?"

"No," Taylor says. "I think your entire simulation is stupid. Everything about this place is stupid. I think the gods are stupid."

The zone around us seems to freeze. The people on the balconies stop chatting and cheering. The breeze stops blowing. The nearest head stops swaying. Then it falls to the ground, landing at Taylor's feet, splattering everywhere.

Her eyes are wide as she gazes at it. Zachary looks like he wants to pee his pants.

"Look, Taylor," I whisper. "Chaos is here. He's listening." He has to be. There's no other explanation for what just happened.

"So what?" Taylor says. "Let him listen."

Fear twists in my belly, but I try to ignore it. We've snuck into this simulation. The last thing we need to do is draw attention to ourselves.

"So maybe you should—"

"Don't tell me what to do, Edie," Taylor says. "If Chaos is watching, and I hope he is, then he better prepare. Because when I get to him, he will be sorry for every single thing he's ever done." She looks upward, face to the sun. "Get ready, Chaos."

And without another word, she kicks the remains of the head aside and continues down the road.

"Is she always like this?" Zachary whispers.

I nod but don't say a word. Taylor has been against the gods from the start. But this is worse than before. Her anger is getting to her. Pushing her. And if we don't find a way through this simulation quickly, it may be her end. The only good thing is that she and Zachary are now on the same side.

The chatter picks up once more, and the people return to their drinks and cheering. As we round the corner, people begin to line the sides of the black glass road. They throw flowers at our feet. I crunch one under the sole of my heavy boot. It cuts through the sole.

"Ow!" My knee almost buckles as whatever it's made of cuts into the bottom of my foot.

Zachary bends down and picks one up. It's bright green and red and looks like a flower, but it's made of sharp metal. "Don't step on any more," he says, holding it out to me.

My foot throbs, but I don't see any blood. I don't think it cut through the skin. The petals of the flower are sharp enough to slice off a finger. I'd keep one if I didn't think it would cut through my clothes.

The road angles upward, and we begin the long hike. All I can see over the top of the hill is the incessant sun. But when we finally crest it, something else comes into view. The road leads directly to a giant colosseum.

xix

TAYLOR, WHO'S CURRENTLY LEADING us, stops and stares. "I've seen something like this before."

"Rome," I say. "They have one like it in Rome." I've never been to Rome, but I've seen plenty of pictures. Aside from the color, the colosseum in front of us is nearly identical.

It's a giant arena with archways circling around it at four different levels. In Rome, the Colosseum is fashioned of white stone, maybe limestone. I'm not an expert. This one here, in the simulation, is blue, like the glass ground we crossed to reach this place. It shines in the brilliant sun making me wonder if it's also made of glass.

"People used to fight to the death in the Colosseum," I say. A heavy ball forms in the pit of my stomach. Whatever is ahead of us can't be good.

"It's like before," Zachary says.

"What's like before?" Taylor demands.

He points to the massive blue structure. "During the last war of the gods, the new gods created some of the games. This was one."

It fits together in my mind. "And Chaos was one of the new gods back then."

He nods. "But he's still creating the simulation however he wants. And if that means a fight to the death in a giant arena, then that's what we have to look forward to."

Taylor eyes Zachary, sizing him up. "How are your fighting skills?"

He brushes his hands off on his pants like he's removing invisible dirt. "Not the best. Which is why I'm thinking . . ."

"What?" I ask.

"Maybe we can find a way around it," he says.

As nice as the thought is, I highly doubt it will be an option. Around us, the people still cheer. I'm certain I hear my name. *Edie. Edie.* Whether they cheer for me or against me, I don't know.

"I'm not a coward," Taylor says. "And as far as I'm concerned, we might as well get this over with. All we're doing now is wasting time."

"But what if—" Zachary starts.

"No what it," I say, taking a step forward. "This is how every simulation has been. Every zone. We have to face it. We can't avoid it. It's like in your stupid doll simulation. We had to face those psychotic dolls. We had to fight them. Or that spider girl. She killed people. She nearly killed me. This is how the game works. We face whatever is down there waiting. We deal with it. Then we find the key and move on."

Zachary doesn't say a word. I glance around. The people watch us. They wait for us to continue on with the simulation. It's what they're programmed for.

"I got your back," Taylor says, and she starts forward, down the hill.

"Come on," I say to Zachary, and I grab his arm and link mine through it, half to steady myself and half to encourage him.

Once we begin moving again, the people begin to fall in behind us. They pop up umbrellas decorated with fringe and glitter to keep the sun off their heads. They wear gowns that brush against the black road as they walk. And they keep their distance, as if they don't want to be caught up with us.

The colosseum seems to grow in size the closer we get. Slowly it blocks out the sun, and we fall in its shadow. I clench my hands into fists. The black road ends at a large archway. Most of the people filter through the other openings, off to the sides. But we're different. Special. We walk through the archway and immediately come to a set of stairs leading down. Over the stairs hangs a sign.

ONLY THE STRONG WILL SURVIVE.

"We got this," Taylor says, and she starts down the stairs. I don't know if she sees our victory with the Oculus or if she's just being optimistic. Both, I hope. I'll take anything that will give us an advantage.

I don't think Zachary has said a word since we've started walking again. I finally turn to him.

"Look, it's not like I want to do this either," I say. "But we have to."

He shakes his head. "I know. It's just that being here, inside the simulation . . . it's different."

"Yeah," I say with a small laugh. "Because we're the ones who might die."

He nods but doesn't respond.

"Can you fight?" I whisper so Taylor doesn't overhear.

He shrugs. "I hope we don't have to find out."

I hope the exact same thing. But I'm used to my hopes being shattered. I grab Zachary's hand and lead him down the stairs.

The stairs fill in behind us as we walk, sealing away the sun.

We're being pushed forward, given no other choice. They lead downward, at least thirty of them, and dump us into a dark gray room, the same color as our tank tops. When I turn back, there is no sign of where we came from.

"So what do we—"Taylor starts, but something slams into the ceiling, shaking the entire room.

"What was that?" Zachary asks.

Whatever it was, the force it creates makes my teeth knock together. The faint taste of blood slips through my mouth, as if I've bitten my tongue.

"Greetings, contestants!" Chaos's voice echoes through the small room. "Worry not. Relax. In just a short amount of time it will be your turn for glory."

Our turn. This must mean that whatever is going on in the arena, the group before us is up there, facing it.

"Relax,"Taylor says with a laugh void of humor. "And how are we supposed to do that?"

The room is empty except for the three of us. No food. No seats. I sink to the ground because whatever is up there, I'm going to need my strength for it. Zachary sinks down next to me, but Taylor stays standing.

"Can you see anything?" I ask her. The ceiling above us thuds again, something slamming into it.

Taylor glances upward, then in all directions. "One of them is going to die," she says.

If this is true, then their group will be down two overall since they already lost someone in the lightning.

"Can you tell who they are?" I ask.

"I can tell you who they are," Zachary says. "They're from the other simulations. Players who are still alive. When Iva opened the simulation, they were able to get in, just like us."

Taylor's head snaps back the way we came and her eyes go

wide. "Oh, that makes sense then."

"What does?" Zachary says.

She narrows her left eye, the one with the Oculus. "I keep seeing people coming into the simulation. If it's open, then that's how they're doing it."

"How many?" I ask. On the one hand, more people keeps the attention off of us. On the other hand, more people means more trying to get the key and get to the control room first.

Before Taylor can answer, the ceiling above us slides aside, revealing the shining sun directly above. The floor, a giant platform, begins to rise, higher and higher until it comes to a stop level with the ground above. Whatever waits for us, it's our turn.

We stand in the center of the colosseum. Around us, the bright blue stands are filled with the people we'd seen outside. They're dressed in bright clothes that stand out against the blue background. The umbrellas still cover their heads, and they sip drinks. But worst of all, I see them passing money back and forth, as if they are placing bets on our survival.

"Welcome to the Zone Alpha Fighting Arena!" Chaos's voice booms around the colosseum. "Contestants, we thank you for your participation!"

"It's not like we had much choice," Taylor mutters.

Aside from the three of us, no one else is on the floor of the arena. I scan the whole thing slowly, in a circle. There are columns and barricades and a couple of trees scattered around, but no one to fight as far as I can tell.

"Please introduce yourselves," Chaos says. I can't imagine he's really here. I think it must be like the heads-up display—a simulation of his voice—because if he is here, then that would mean that the final zone where the control room is would be unprotected. But I am guessing that whatever happens here, details are being fed back to him.

Taylor steps forward first. She lifts her face to the crowd and fixes on them a look that tells them she wants them all dead.

"Taylor," she says. "Sister of Adam, soon to be risen from the dead. Bearer of the Oculus."

At this last part, a collective gasp rushes through the crowd.

"The Oculus," Chaos says. "When you lose, it shall be mine."

Maybe it truly is him after all and not just an NPC.

Taylor spins in a circle, trying to pinpoint the source of Chaos's voice. "When you lose, I'll cut the eyes from your head and devour them," she says.

It's gruesome but also the perfect thing she could say. Never show weakness. Assume victory. It reminds me that we will get through this.

Zachary goes next. "Zachary Gomez," he says. His voice, like mine, is broadcast loud enough for everyone to hear.

"A petty god among us," Chaos says. "Coming for your execution early, I assume."

Execution early . . . as if the stakes for Zachary are as great as they are for us.

Zachary bites his lip and glances around, like he's looking for the nearest exit. But to his credit he says, "You assume wrong."

I let out the breath I've been holding since Chaos first spoke. If Zachary can pretend to be brave even when he's not, then our odds of success increase exponentially.

"I'm never wrong," Chaos says.

Zachary looks at me and smiles, like he has a secret. I smile back.

I step forward, ready to get this behind me. But all the people watching me makes me second guess myself.

They're not real people, I tell myself. They're NPCs. The only reason they're here is to fuel the zone.

I think about lying right then. Using another name. If I use my real name right now, it announces to Chaos that I've gotten into the simulation. But if I don't use my real name, if I pretend to be someone else, then I'm allowing fear to control me. There is only one thing I can do.

"Eden Monk," I say, using my real name, not even going with the nickname. "God killer. Bearer of the Power." I only use my normal voice, but my words echo around the entire arena.

The crowd falls silent. Whispers run throughout the stands. Clouds swirl across the brilliant sky above. This Chaos had not been expecting. I shouldn't have been able to get in, and yet here I am.

"You killed my brother," Chaos says. His voice is even but filled with cold malice. "And the power that runs through you is not rightfully yours. Once it is reunited with its other half, I will pull it from your bodies bit by bit as you wither away until you are nothing but dust. Then I will consume it. And when that happens, nothing will be able to stand in my way."

I don't blink. I don't move. His words are filled with my fate. Except . . . then I remember the prophecy.

"When we meet, I'm the one who will kill you," I say. "At least that's what the prophecies say."

"The prophecies are wrong!" His voice loses its calm control, instead roaring like thunder across the colosseum. The sky darkens. The clouds swirl faster. The sun is blotted out.

I don't even realize I'm shaking until I clench my fingers into fists to keep them still. I can't back down. I can't show fear. Not now.

"The prophecies are never wrong," I say. "Now can we get on with it?"

A full minute goes by during our standoff. The whispers continue. The sky remains dark. But after the minute, the clouds part and the sun returns. Once again the crowd places bets, cheers, and celebrates. Their lives are not on the line. Ours are. And Chaos's is. But until we meet in Zone Digamma, we have to play the game. We have to reach the end.

A new platform is lowered down to the ground of the arena. From it steps a familiar figure, dressed in a bright yellow dress that contrasts against her dark skin. Next to her stands something half lion, half eagle. It bares its teeth at if to protect her from anything that would come near. It's possibly her companion. Her bodyguard. Or perhaps it's a kid like us trapped in her simulation and unable to break free from her spell.

"Raven?" I say.

Her face remains passive as her eyes meet mine. She carries a tray as she walks toward us, the lion creature at her side, supporting her. She's limping, and I remember that Taylor had severed her leg off back during the struggle for the Oculus. The yellow dress is too long to see her leg . . . or what remains of it.

"I've selected weapons for each of you," Raven says. "To make things fair."

As if anything has ever been fair.

"What are you doing here?" Zachary asks. His face, unlike hers, is a combination of anger and confusion.

Her mouth doesn't move, but words form in my head. *He's forcing me to be here. To do this. I'm sorry.*

I open my mouth, ready to respond. But that would only let Chaos know that she's spoken.

Fight him, I think back to her.

He's too strong. Raven's thoughts reach my mind. *He'll kill me if I don't help him.*

So many responses run through my mind, but I'm not sure any of them will make a difference. Raven had wanted the Oculus so badly. But had she wanted it for herself or was it for Chaos all along?

You're strong also, I think, remembering how she's captured all of us except Hudson. *Don't let him win.*

Raven only presses a finger to my head in response. It's such an odd gesture, like she's trying to tell me to think about something. But when she pulls her finger away, nothing has changed.

"Your weapon, Eden Monk," Raven says aloud. Her voice carries across the arena. An ax appears on the tray she holds. It's not just any ax either. It's the ax that won me the labyrinth simulation. The one I originally found in my parents' supplies. I can't take my eyes off it. This has to be a sign that someone is helping me. And I would place my own bets on the fact that Chaos does not know about it.

I try to act like seeing the ax is no big deal as I reach for it. I don't dare meet Zachary's eyes. "It's okay, I guess," I say.

Okay minimizes it. Feeling it in my hand is perfect. It lets me know that we will succeed. We have help beyond what is known to Chaos.

Raven limps to Taylor next. "For you, Taylor, sister of Adam."

On the tray appears the giant bow she'd used in the labyrinth. Next to it is a quiver full of arrows. I'm not going to touch one to find out, but my guess is that the tips are laced with poison, just like they'd been before.

Taylor lifts the bow and quiver and lowers them over her shoulder. She doesn't thank Raven. She doesn't say anything for the crowd to hear.

Raven waits for a response, but Taylor only crosses her arms and glares.

Finally Raven moves to Zachary. Silence fills the void, and I'm guessing inaudible words pass between the two of them. Words that are being kept from Taylor and me. But they're being silent too long. Chaos is going to get suspicious.

"Could we hurry up?" I ask, acting like I'm ready to begin the challenge.

Raven smiles finally, maybe for the first time since we've seen her. Then on the tray appears a metal ball about the size of a grapefruit.

Zachary picks it up and stares at it. "What am I supposed to do with this?"

If he were Hudson, I'd say he could throw it like shot put. Nobody could beat Hudson. But Zachary Gomez is not Hudson. Whatever it is, I'm hoping it gives him some sort of advantage also.

"You're supposed to attempt to win," Raven says. Then she limps back to the platform with the lion at her side and is slowly lifted from the floor of the arena.

"Well, my citizens of Zone Alpha," Chaos says like an announcer. "I believe we've waited long enough, but the wait is over. Let the games begin!"

The crowd erupts in applause and the name calling begins. Some cheer for us, standing and waving their hands. Others spit out venomous ways they hope we will die. If we do die, I can almost imagine our heads back beside the roadway, hanging from poles.

"Stick close together," I say, edging next to Taylor and Zachary. We press our backs together and wait.

A hole opens in the ground, and a platform is raised. Standing on top of it is a man decked out in full gladiator attire. Black leather covers him, and his face is mostly shielded by a helmet. He raises a sword and runs directly for us.

In less than a second, Taylor nocks and arrow and fires at him, hitting him directly in the chest. The man falls to the ground dead. He's lowered into the ground, but as soon as he's out of sight, a new platform is raised. This time a new creature appears, half-man, half-bull, like the creature at the center of the labyrinth. He snorts and growls and springs for us.

Another arrow flies, but it bounces off him. She fires another, but it's the same result. He gets closer with every second.

"Do something," Zachary shouts.

Taylor lets another arrow go, but the creature's skin it too thick. I dash forward, cutting under his bulky arm, and I swing the ax, catching him in the stomach. The blow is solid, and he falls to the ground, lowered like the gladiator.

"Are we having fun yet?" Chaos says.

We are definitely not having fun, but my adrenaline is pumping. I'm twenty yards away from Taylor and Zachary, and before I can get back to them, another platform raises between us, cutting off my path.

This time three monsters appear. One turns to me, locking its eyes on me. It spits venom directly at me. I barely jump out of the way. Then I run, as fast as I can, for one of the barriers. Something to hide behind. I reach it as another stream of venom shoots out.

I have to get close to it to kill it, but if I get too close, the venom will hit me.

I peek out from behind the barrier in time to see Zachary and Taylor running in opposite directions from each other. Zachary dashes to one of the columns and attempts to hide behind it. Taylor positions herself behind a barrier, like me.

Each of the monsters is different. The one chasing me is small and quick, and slithers around like a lizard. It's bright orange and covered in scales. Scales I'm not sure my ax will go through. The one facing off against Taylor is tall and slim and iridescent. It seems to be able to snap in and out of visibility, making all her arrows fall short of hitting it. And the one that has Zachary cornered against the column has pinchers like a crab. It grabs out, trying to catch Zachary. He darts one way and then the next, evading it. But it's taking chunks out of the stone column that's protecting him. Pretty soon the entire column collapses. Zachary takes off running, retreating away from the thing.

This is bad. This is really bad. The creature in front of me shoots more venom, this time aiming over the top of the barrier. I jump back just in time. The venom hits the sandy ground in front of me. I can't stay here. The only way to stay safe is to get away from it.

I run from one barrier to another, but the creature follows. I pull on the power. There's no need to keep it secret now. But it won't come. I don't even feel a spark of it. It's like it's been taken from me. Or muted in this arena so I won't have an advantage.

I scan my inventory quickly on my heads-up display. The apple is still there, but it's grayed out, mocking me. However I win, it won't be with the power.

Taylor shrieks from across the arena, but I can't afford to look her way. I run from the current barrier and climb one of the trees. Branches extend far to the sides. The creature sees me and shoots venom upward. I scramble out of the way.

Some of the venom falls back, landing on the orange scales. They bubble at the contact, and the creature hisses in pain.

While it's down, I take my chance. I drop down from where I am and land on the creature's back. Before I can overthink it, I chop my ax downward, over and over, until I break through the thick scales and reach the creature's brain.

When the creature finally falls silent and collapses to the ground, I roll off it, trying to catch my breath.

"Oh, it's a victory for Eden Monk!" Chaos calls. "But it looks as if Zachary Gomez, our godly contestant, is in a bit of trouble."

I roll over and jump to my feet. Taylor stands next to the body of the creature that hunted her. She yanks an arrow from its chest. But Zachary is in serious trouble. Every object without thirty yards of him has been destroyed, leaving only piles of rubble. He runs back and forth, trying to evade the crab-like creature, but it's almost like the creature is toying with him.

I look to Taylor who nods. Then we both run in the creature's direction.

It spins when we get close, and in half a second it snaps out with a claw, nearly catching me. I throw my ax, still dripping with blood from the other creature. It sinks into the hard shell of the crab creature, sticking there. This only seems to make the creature more angry.

Taylor lets loose a volley of arrows, one after another. They hit and bounce off. One finally catches between the joints. But poisoned or not, it doesn't slow the creature.

"Wait! I finally got it!" Zachary says, and he rushes up to the crab creature with a bravery I never would have dreamed possible. He presses something on the metal ball he's been given. Two blades shoot out from the side. Zachary throws it into the air, above the creature. The blades spin, round and round, as it guides itself and lands on the creature's back,

"Get back!" Zachary shouts.

It's not a second too soon. The metal ball snaps and locks into position. It beeps once, twice . . . five times. Then it explodes in a ball of sparks and electricity.

I flatten myself to the ground, barely missing the explosion. Bits of my hair are singed, but I'm alive. We're all alive. And the three creatures are dead.

XX

THE PEOPLE IN THE STANDS BEGIN TO descend, coming for us. If this is the next phase of the game, then we are in serious trouble. I'm sucking air and about to collapse. But before they reach the arena floor, a circular wall made of blue bricks begins to pull together in the center of the arena around one of the massive white columns.

"Come on," I shout, and we run for the center. We're barely inside when the bricks seal closed, forming a protective barrier around us. At the same time, the first people reach the arena floor. But instead of coming for us, they shuffle toward the dead carcasses of the creatures. As we watch from inside the short brick wall, they devour the dead creatures. The blood and body fluids leak out and cover people's face. Their stench fills the place.

"That is seriously nasty," Taylor says.

I don't look, but the slurping sounds are hard to ignore. Zachary's normally brown skin is green, and he looks like he's going to throw up at any second.

"You okay?" I ask. My own stomach rolls. I try to keep it steady.

"No," Zachary says. "How do we get out of here?"

It's a game. We won. We need to claim the reward before we can move on.

"We need to get the key," I say.

"Which is where?" Taylor asks. She still clutches the giant bow, but she only has one arrow left in her quiver.

I'm still gripping the ax also. I think about hooking it to my belt, but if something else attacks, I need to be ready. Zachary's weapon is gone, exploded into nothing. Then the platform we stand on begins to lift and spiral around the white column, slowly moving upward, to the top. This seems to get the attention of the crowd of people because from below there's a shout. I look down to see them pointing at us then rushing toward the base of the column. But we're at least twenty feet in the air by now. They can't reach us.

Unfortunately this doesn't stop them from climbing. Two then four then eight people begin to climb like monkeys, crawling up the column and toward us. And unless I'm imagining it, they are ascending faster than we are.

"Is there any way to speed this thing up?" I ask Zachary.

His eyes glaze over, and I realize that he must be accessing it through his heads-up display.

"Not that I see," he says.

I focus my display on it, too, and a menu appears. But the only valid option is Stop Ascent which is not valid at all. I don't know if the people are trying to stop us. Or maybe kill us? I don't want to find out. But they are getting closer.

Taylor nocks her final arrow and leans out over the blue bricks, way farther than she should be able to. Then she lets it loose.

One person falls, but there are so many others. If I throw my ax, I won't have it anymore. It's not worth the trade. The platform continues to slowly spin upward. But just when I'm sure the people will reach us and climb onto the platform, it stops moving.

"There!" Zachary shouts and he points at the sides of the white column. They glow with silver symbols and letters etched into them.

"What is that?" Taylor says. She's clutching the bow, ready to hit anyone who comes too close.

But as soon as I see the combinations of the symbols, it falls into place. "It's the segment of the key," I say. "We each need to collect it."

I focus my heads-up display on it, and sure enough, a menu option appears.

>   INTERACT
>   COLLECT
>   DISCARD
>   HELP

I select COLLECT immediately, and the piece of the key—code of some sort—is transferred to my inventory.

Zachary and Taylor do the same, and it's not a second too soon. Fingers grab at the sides of the blue bricks, but the people begin to fall away, down to the ground of the arena. When they hit, they vanish, as if they had never been there.

The platform glides back to the ground, spiraling once again around the column. When it touches down, the bricks pull apart, creating an exit for us. But no sooner do I take out step out of it, something slams into the column, sending fiery shattered remains everywhere. It's a fireball, like we'd seen before. The hunter is back.

xxi

"YOU'RE NOT SUPPOSED TO BE HERE,
Edie," a voice says, booming across the now-empty arena. It's a
female voice but sounds robotic, like it's actually a computer or
someone trying to mask their voice.

This is the cost of revealing myself. And even though I'm ter-
rified, I can't let whoever is out there know that.

"But I am here," I shout back. My voice also carries.

Another fireball hits, again smacking into the column. This
time it cracks in half. The upper piece begins to fall toward us.

"Run now," Taylor shouts.

The three of us take off. The marble column smashes into the
arena floor, making the ground shake like an earthquake. Another
fireball hits the ground to the side of us. We dash around it and
keep running.

"Where's the exit?" Zachary says. He covers his head which I
think is silly until a shard of flying rock hits me in the forehead.
We need to get out of here.

At the word "exit" a pathway appears on the opposite side of

the arena from where we entered. It's the inverse of the other, a white road against a black backdrop.

"There!" I shout, and we run toward it.

It's impossible to know where the hunter is because the next fireball hits behind us, as if fired from the way we're going. Then another hits, off to the side. There is no sense in the source. Though we're running as fast as we can, with nothing else around, we're easy targets. I step on debris. I trip on broken rocks. I evade five more fireballs. And then the white road is there, beckoning us. A fireball hits just at the edge of the road, but no sooner than our feet touch the road, the robotic female voice says, "Watch your back, Edie."

I hold my breath as we race up the road, looking for the exit. But no more fireballs come. Black buildings line the roadway, but the farther away from the arena we get, the more the space between the buildings grows until there are no more buildings at all. Then the white road ends at a silver waterfall that reaches up as far as I can see. It's our passage to the next zone.

"Stay together this time," I say, stepping close to Taylor and Zachary. Then, all at once, we press our palms to the flowing silver.

Exactly like before it flows out, surrounding me, pulling me in. One second Taylor and Zachary are there. The next they are gone. That's okay. I'll find them in the Zone Beta.

Like before, I'm encased completely in the silver. I focus on my heads-up display, expecting it to come to life. But instead a vision fills my mind.

Raven and I stand back on the field in the arena. She leans close and presses a finger to my head. This is what had happened. I remember it.

Except . . .

As the vision fills my mind, it takes on new life and expands. We're standing at the top of her temple. Animals flank her: a dragon, a tiger, a zebra.

"Edie, I can help you find him," she says.

"Who?"

"Cole. He needs help. I can get you to him."

Cole.

I bite my lip as I try to harden myself against him.

"He left me," I say.

Raven shakes her head, her long black hair with red tips shaking gently at the motion. "He didn't. I told him he had to. I told him it was the only way."

"What was the only way?" I ask.

"The vision," Raven says. "You each got one."

"I saw Thomas," I say.

Raven nods. "And Cole say Pia killing you unless . . ."

"Unless what?" My heart pounds, and almost like the animals can sense my discontent, the tiger paces toward me and rubs up against my leg.

"He had to get Pia away from you," Raven says. "Otherwise she was going to kill you."

Oh, how much I want to believe this. It would explain everything. It would reaffirm Cole's feelings for me. I couldn't have been so wrong. Not Cole. He wouldn't betray me. I know that.

"He left with her," I say slowly.

"To protect you."

Not to leave me. To protect me. This is the answer I want and need.

"Where is he now?"

Her face darkens and her eyes cloud over. "She found out. She read his mind."

"He's in trouble," I say. The image of him in electrical bonds screaming in pain returns to me. It can't be real, except if what Raven is saying is true, then there is a very good chance that it is.

"You have to free him," Raven says. "I can help you find him."

"Where?"

Raven purses her lips and a small smile forms there. "I'll get Chaos to trust me. I'll find out how to find him."

I shake my head. "We need to find him now. If Chaos has him, his life is in danger."

"No," Raven says. "Not Cole. Chaos can't kill him. If he could, he would have by now."

"Why?" I ask. But the second the words leave my mouth, I know the answer. "Oh. The gods can't kill humans," I say.

Raven nods. "And even if he wanted to break that law, he can't. The prophecy won't let him."

If the world were normal, I would be relieved. But the simulation can definitely kill us as can the person who is hunting me. That person has definitely been sent by Chaos, first to keep me out of the simulation, and now that I'm here, to kill me.

"How long will it take you to find out where he is?" I ask.

Raven holds up a finger. "Not long. Look for a sign from me. I'll use it to guide you."

Before I can ask what kind of sign she's talking about, she presses the finger to my head once again, and the vision ends.

I'm back in the cocoon of flowing silver. Back in the simulation. But I have another ally, or at least I hope I do. I have to trust Raven because I have to find Cole. A sign from Raven. I don't know what that will be, but I hope that when I see it, I'll know.

My heads-up display comes to life as if no time has passed, and the silhouette of Chaos appears.

"Congratulations," he says. "You completed Zone Alpha."

He's silent for a moment like he expects a response. I don't say a word. I wait for this to be over. Unlike back in the colosseum, I don't think this is truly Chaos interacting with me, but more of an interface with programmed responses.

"Items granted in one zone may not be carried to another. You will have to leave your newly acquired weapon here."

The ax. That's what he's talking about.

I place my hand on it. "I keep it."

"You don't," he says. Then the ax vanishes.

Rage fills me. How dare that be a rule? Aside from not being fair, I rightfully should have that ax. My parents had left it for me. But I keep my anger inside, just under the surface.

"I'm ready for the next zone," I say, willing the silver barrier to vanish in front of me.

Chaos laughs. "Are you really?"

I glare at him through the heads-up display. "I'm ready."

"Then please don't let me stop you." Chaos's silhouette disappears and the concentric circles appear once more. The outermost circle, Zone Alpha, has turned green. The second circle, Zone Beta, is lit up blue. The remaining ones inside that are grayed out. We've gotten through one. We have five more to go.

I select the circle, and the others fade away. Then the barrier of silver around me peels backward, letting me through to whatever is next. When I turn back, the silver barrier is there, blocking any chance of returning the way I came. Not that I would consider doing that. Whatever is ahead, I have to face it.

I step out onto a dull gray surface. Ahead of me is only the gray plane and a gray sky.

"Hello?" I say, hoping Taylor or Zachary are within earshot.

There's no answer.

"Hello?" I say again. My voice is sucked into the nothingness around me. There is no one here but me.

I step out farther from the silver barrier, toward whatever is ahead. Maybe they're here already and are in front of me. I'll find them and we can face this zone together. Or maybe they haven't gotten here yet. If I leave, I might not find them.

I stand in the same spot for well over ten minutes. There is no sound. No objects. Only me and the emptiness. I call out for them every minute or so. I wait. But the longer I wait, the more sure I am that they have come and gone. They could have waited for me, and with time all twisted up, maybe they gave up on me.

I wait five more minutes. That's all I can take. I have to see if they're ahead or if there is any sign of them.

I count my steps as I start out across the ground. Ten. Twenty. The silver barrier gets farther away. I look back, scanning for Taylor and Zachary. I go over Raven's words. Cole hadn't betrayed me. I look for a sign. But there is nothing.

Nothing.

Give up, a voice in my head seems to say.

I push the voice away and keep walking. I would never give up. Giving up would only result in death.

You're going to die if you stay here, it says. *This place will kill you.*

I am not going to die. I am going to survive and get the pieces of the key and get into Main Control Room Alpha. I am going to defeat Chaos.

You never will, it says. *Your friends will die. You will be responsible. If you don't die, you will live forever in stasis knowing that you couldn't save them.*

My friends won't die. And I will find Cole.

Instantly the image of Cole appears. His hands and feet are bound and he still screams, as if he's facing torture that never ends. I squeeze my eyes shut to try to make the image go away, but it's like the more I think about it, the harder it is to get out of my mind. I have to save him.

He doesn't want you.

That's not true. Raven said it wasn't true. She said he was trying to save me by leaving with Pia.

Raven is a liar.

I bite my lip. Raven has been deceptive, and she was behind the entirety of Simulation Avine. What if she did lie about Cole?

She did.

But what if she didn't lie? Either way, I have to find Cole. Even if everything she said was false, I can't know he's suffering and do nothing.

Give up now, the voice says.

"Stop talking to me," I say aloud. I've had enough of this voice of uncertainty. It has no place here.

Yet the more I push it away, the more persistent it becomes. I hardly notice as the edge of the dismal gray ground comes into view. My own words have become a mantra in my head, trying to push away the negativity of the voice, yet knowing that many of the things it says are true.

You will never survive, the voice says, and then it falls silent.

I stop walking, searching in my mind for it, because it was there for so long that it almost became a part of me. Then I look down. The ground under my feet is no longer dull gray. It's brilliant yellow, like a sunflower, even though the sky above is dark.

I whip around, looking at the place where I just was. There are others out there, wandering aimlessly. Other players. I should help them. But I can't force myself back onto the gray surface.

I can't die. I have to survive. Not only survive. I have to win.

I call for Taylor and Zachary again, and this time, I hear something off to my right. Not crying. But a low moan, like someone whose world has ended.

"Zachary!" I shout, and I run toward him.

He's sitting on the ground, knees to his chest, shaking. I reach down and place my hand on his shoulder. Only then does he look my way.

"Are we going to die?" he asks.

There is no way I can believe he's a god right now. He's too much like us in this moment. Too vulnerable.

"We're not dying," Taylor says, hurrying up to join us. She no longer has the bow, the same way I don't have the ax.

"But the voice . . . ," he says.

"Is bullshit," Taylor says. "Now get up. We're only at the start."

That's it. Each zone has an entry boundary that we need to cross. The lightning on the field of blue glass in Zone Alpha. The gray field of doubt here in Zone Beta. It doesn't thrill me to realize this, but it helps cement the rules of this place in my mind. It would be great to know what to expect, but if that's not an option, then at least we know to expect something.

Zachary slowly gets to his feet. His face is ashen, and there are still a couple scratches from the fight with the creatures. But otherwise, he's ready to go.

"Let's go," I say, and I set out, forward. There are long lines that run in a grid pattern ahead, and we use these to guide our way. Soon, the lines extend out to the sides also, like a giant grid. And pretty soon, they are over us and under us, too, visible through the ground which is now transparent.

I step on one, about to comment on how much it reminds me of a holographic grid when the square I step on lifts upward, separating me from Taylor and Zachary. The squares they stand on do the same. Taylor moves downward and off far to the right. Zachary heads forward at least twenty blocks. And in case I thought there was any chance I could run back over to join them, at least half of the other squares fall away, leaving huge gaps and no clear path.

I wobble, almost losing my balance, but I shoot my arms out to the side until I'm steady.

"What is this, Edie?" Taylor calls. Unlike me, she's completely stable on her platform.

Each square is about two feet by two feet and nearly transparent. I look down, through my square, but if there is something down there, I can't see it. Ahead of me are four more squares, each the same size. A path.

I step forward to the next square. The second my foot touches it, the square behind me shoots backward a good ten feet. But a different square comes over from the right, attaching to the new square I stand on.

"What did you do?" Zachary shouts. His square is far above, at least five levels, and only attached to one other square.

I moved to a different square, watching Taylor and Zachary as I do. Taylor moves up two levels and to the left. Zachary stays in place.

"It's a game," I say. "Each time we step on a new square, it makes other squares move."

Taylor isn't content to believe me. She steps forward, and the square I'm on pops downward one level. I wobble because I'm not expecting it. Zachary nearly falls off the side.

"Don't move!" he shouts. "Let me get stable."

Taylor scowls at him but stays in place until he's standing once again. Then he turns to look at me. "I've seen stuff like this before," he says. "It's a game. We need to find the end."

"What?" Taylor says. "Like a board game? This isn't *Candyland* you know."

Memories of playing *Candyland* with Thomas return to me. Granted, with all the game playing we did at home, he'd outgrown the bright-colored game quickly, but not before we'd played at least one hundred times. He always wanted to be the red gingerbread man.

"Not *Candyland*," I say. "But similar."

Taylor puts her hands on her hips. "I suck at games."

I can't help the smile that creeps onto my face. "Well, then it's a good thing I'm fantastic at them. The first thing we need to do is test out our movements. Don't move unless I tell you to."

"What about me?" Zachary says. "You act like I'm an idiot. If you haven't noticed, I'm pretty good with games, too."

"Yeah, well, I could beat you at *Catan* any day of the week," I say.

"Challenge accepted," he says.

"Anyway, it makes sense for one of us to be the main control point," I say. "Otherwise, we won't know what controls what."

"So let me be it," Zachary says.

Though he's a bit away from me, I study his face. Does he think I'm not up to the challenge? I more than am. I was always the smartest kid in computer science, hands down.

"I got it," I say and look away before he can argue with me. "So only move if I tell you to."

Taylor looks bothered by the entire thing. But it's not like she's trying to take control. That's one thing I love about her. She knows what she's good at, and she knows where she needs help.

Unlike you, the voice of doubt says in my head.

I look back, to the river of doubt we crossed, but it's out of sight. Yet the doubts remain. I hate the doubts. I push the thought aside and step to the right.

Both Taylor and Zachary's squares move. I make a chart in my head, tracking the movement, watching not only how the squares we stand on move but how all the squares move. Far ahead are three glowing beacons. They have to be our destination. And the first step is getting close to them.

Slowly, each of us moving one square at a time, we approach them. Everything is going exactly like planned. Then Taylor moves, exactly like I tell her to, to the right. My next move is going to be me moving ahead. But on the square ahead, a spike shoots up, making the move impossible. It's not the only square with spikes, either. At least twenty cubes are now impossible to reach.

"Step back," I call over to her.

When she steps back, the spikes disappear. I hurry forward, covering the six squares where the spikes had been, then I tell her to move again. Another square bumps into the one I'm on, and I'm not prepared. Neither is Zachary, because the same thing has happened to him. He wobbles and falls over the side of the square. His shout throws off my balance even more, and I topple. I try to grab the edge, but the pull of gravity is too much, and my fingers slip. I fall into the abyss.

XXII

THE WORLD OF FLOATING SQUARES ZIPS by as I fall. My arms scramble to grab hold of something, but there is nothing safe. Nothing reachable. I am going to die. And so is Zachary, all because my stupid pride was too much to let him help.

My heads-up display flashes. Death Imminent. As if I needed some kind of reminder. I start to grasp the power, to build something to stop my fall. But then there's Zachary also. We're falling too fast.

Wait. The power isn't all I have. My inventory also has another item.

I parse through the menu of the heads-up display and select Reset.

Confirm use of Item Reset, my heads-up display says.

"Confirm!" I shout at the same time I select it. Every second counts. I brace myself, ready to hit whatever is at the bottom of the zone.

Use of Item Reset confirmed, the heads-up display says.

Immediately my surroundings change. I'm standing on a cube at the beginning of the playing field. Zachary and Taylor are right next to me. I'm breathing hard, still thinking I'm about to die. So is Zachary for that matter. It takes a few seconds for my mind to figure out and accept that I am no longer falling.

"What happened?" Taylor says. "You guys fell off the side of the world. I thought you were dead."

I was dead. Or nearly was. Would have been if I hadn't used my item.

"Reset," I manage to say as I catch my breath. "It's what I picked as my item at the start of the simulation. I used it."

I pull myself to my feet. We're back exactly where we started, the grid of squares ahead.

"Are you kidding me?" Taylor says. "We have to do all that again?"

I nod, not caring. I'm happy to be alive.

"You want to take the lead this time?" I ask Zachary. It kind of pains me to do so, but I also don't want to die. I've played lots of games, similar ones to this, but not this complex. And with not only my life but my friends' lives on the line also, I can't make another wrong move.

"You can," Zachary says.

I shake my head. "You got this. I should have let you from the start."

"You're really smart, Edie," he says. "You're like the smartest girl I know."

My face feels warm, but I try to brush off the compliment. "Not that smart," I say. If I was, I wouldn't have almost died.

"Yeah, that smart," he says. "And I'm really glad you're alive."

"Enough, you guys. Let's get this shit over with." Taylor steps forward.

We all do. We retrace our steps back to where the first blocks move. But instead of telling us what to do, Zachary asks me. "What would you do?"

And we talk about each move, just like that. Sometimes we're so far apart that I have to shout. Another time, Taylor almost gets sliced open by one of the spikes. She's ready to kill us, I think. But within a couple hours, the destination squares are finally visible.

Each is a different color, and each moves in and out of being reachable as we get closer. Four different times one of us is transported to a different square, but we retrace our steps. We get back.

Taylor steps on her destination square first. Then Zachary. Finally me. The rest of the game board falls away, into the abyss. And above us fireworks begin to shoot into the sky.

"We did it!" Zachary shouts. And he grabs me in what may be the most awkward hug in the entire universe. It makes me wonder if he's ever hugged anyone in his life. And given that I have no idea what his life is really like or how long he's been alive, that could have been a very long time.

I hug him back because I'm so shocked.

"See, I told you that you were smart," Zachary says, finally stepping back from the hug once I've let go.

"Wait, what about me?" Taylor says. "Don't I get a hug?"

Before Taylor can react, I grab her in a hug and squeeze her tight.

"I am so glad you're my friend," I say, and I mean every word of it. Taylor has been here through everything.

I'm not sure what surprises me more: the fact that Taylor hugs me back or when she says, "Yeah, I'm really glad you're my friend, too, Edie."

After I let go, Zachary steps in like he's going to hug her.

Taylor steps back. "Nope. I still don't like you, god boy." The look on her face makes me thing Zachary will end up with two black eyes if he actually tries to hug her.

At this, Zachary laughs. "But I just saved your life."

She shakes her head. "That's not how I see it. Now where's the key?"

Almost like her words are dictating it, from the center of where we stand on the three colored cubes, a giant white column appears. It grows in signals and currents like electrical circuits being woven together. And when it has grown so high that I can no longer see the top, the three cubes we stand on begin to ascend.

Zachary wobbles, but Taylor grabs hold of his arm. "Do not fall," she says.

His eyes go wide. Fear of Taylor holds him in place. The cubes ascend until the yellow playing field is far below and we're high up in the dark sky. Then the cubes stop, and glowing silver letters and symbols appear on the side of the white column.

"Collect it," I say, and I access my heads-up display. The menu appears and I select COLLECT. Like before in Zone Alpha, the piece of the key is transferred to my inventory, listed along with the first piece. That's two down. Three more to go.

Once we've all three collected the piece of the key, the zone below us falls away, and a yellow path forms in the air from the column where we stand off into the distance. At the end of it, I can barely make out something shimmering. We hurry down it, and as we get closer, the silver barrier appears like a flowing sheet of liquid mercury in the air.

"See you in Zone Gamma," I say, and I press my palm to the moving silver. It immediately morphs around me and pulls me in until I'm entirely encased in it. Zachary and Taylor vanish from my sight, concealed in their own entries to the next zone. The barrier of silver flows in front of me and behind.

I've done it. I've completed two zones. I have three more before the final zone where the control room is.

Also where Chaos is.

I take a moment to catch my breath. Taylor, Zachary, and I have all gotten through. How many others are there, though? And does it matter?

If it does matter, I can worry about it later. For now, I need to get on with the simulation.

I open my eyes and blow out a long breath. Then my heads-up display comes to life. I expect to see the image of Chaos, but instead the screen is bright yellow with only a single icon on it.

A black raven.

Look for a sign from me, Raven had said. This has to be it

I don't hesitate as I select the black raven. It immediately begins to glow white and slowly pulse. I select it one more time, as a confirmation, and my surroundings blink away.

I'm in a long white corridor. No doors, no windows. Only one way to go which is ahead. I start walking, ignoring the worry that Taylor and Zachary are going to wonder where I am. I can worry about that later. For now, I need to . . .

A scream tears through my thoughts, ripping into my heart. I know that scream. I've heard it before, not long after I first met Cole. He'd had a nightmare, screamed out in the dark. And I know with absolute certainly that it's the same scream. This is Cole.

"Cole!" I shout.

Another scream. I take off running, not caring if I'm moving straight into a trap. Raven could have set this entire thing up, luring me into some sort of stasis to keep me from reaching the end. But that's a risk I have to take.

He screams again, closer now. Then his scream is cut short by something that sounds like the sizzle of electricity. After that there are no more screams. I may be too late.

xxiii

I RUN SO FAST THE WHITE CORRIDOR
is nothing but a blur. I listen for another scream, not sure if I
want to hear one. If Cole screams, it means he's still alive. If he
doesn't . . . I can't think about that. I almost call out to him again,
but the silence is now deafening and keeps my mouth shut. I don't
know how long I run. Time stands still.

Without even realizing it, the white corridor spreads far apart
until I'm now in a vast white warehouse with white shelves
stacked high with jars. Florescent lights shine from far above,
casting shadows everywhere, making the world feel monochrome.

I stop running, sure I'm being watched. Slowly I move until
I'm next to one of the shelves, hidden in the shadows.

"Cole," I whisper, barely audible even to my own ears.

Something falls to the ground, shattering, like broken glass.
Maybe one of the jars. I turn to look at the shelf next to me. Each
jar has a screwed-on lid and is filled with gray liquid. I dare to
reach out and pick one of the jars up. As I tilt it sideways, something bobs to the surface. Something that looks like a black glossy

egg, growing like it's in a test tube. Like the black eggs I've seen in my visions of the future. The future that will come if we don't stop Chaos.

I nearly drop the jar I'm holding as something scrapes along the surface of the floor. Glass rattles from a few rows over. I quickly set the jar down and crouch down until I can peek through the shelves.

A shadow moves across the shelves.

I hold my breath. Something is out there. Something that is not Cole. The shadow moves slowly, but as it turns a corner, I get a glimpse of what I am up against.

It's tall and thin and has an elongated head that curves upward and back as it grows. Its arms claw at the shelves as it lifts itself up and begins to climb, growing with each moment that passes. Its movement rattles other jars. Another one falls to the ground.

There's hissing and thick gray dust. Then a second shadow joins the first.

This is not good. This is so not good. I have to find Cole, but I also don't have a single weapon on me to fight these creatures.

Wait. That's not true. I do have a weapon.

I try not to breathe as I pull on the power. My worries over whether it will come at my command vanish as it manifests. Relief flows through me. I blow out a breath . . . too loud.

Both shadows stop moving and their elongated heads turn my way. I don't move. I don't breathe. I grab the power and I begin to reshape bits and pieces of the world around me. Pieces of the shelves. The floor. The lights. I craft a long black sword with an edge so sharp, one wrong move and I'll cut my own hand off. Then I dare to take a step forward.

The creatures seem to sense my movement because they too move forward, in the exact same direction I did. This could be a coincidence. I take another step. So do they. It is no coincidence.

I turn and run the other way, down the long corridor of shelves. I almost bump into one as I round the corner. The last thing I need are more jars shattering and more of these creatures hunting me. The shelves go on forever in the warehouse. I keep running. I turn a corner, and then I see them.

They swing from the shelves, crawling up and sideways and over the tops. They get closer with every second. I don't want to face them.

I look everywhere for Cole, and though it pains me to hear it, when another scream fills the air, relief rushes through me. I shift direction, toward the scream, and I run like my life is depending on it. Like the fate of the world depends on it. I don't worry about keeping quiet. My heavy boots pound on the ground. I bump into a shelf, and glass jars rattle.

Cole screams again.

"I'm coming!" I shout. "Hold on!"

I don't dare turn back. I can almost feel the heat of the creatures behind me. They hiss and spit. I finally round a corner, and there is Cole, held up against a wall by bonds of glowing white electricity around his wrists and ankle. Pulses of current run across his skin, and his face is pulled tight in pain.

"Cole!" I shout.

His eyes go wide at his name and he spots me. But his eyes are filled with terror.

That's when I hear the hissing right behind me.

I turn and swipe the blade of the black sword out, tearing clean through one of the creatures. It splits in two pieces which fall to the ground, but thick black gel begins to ooze out of it. I dash back, barely evading a long claw on the second creature. I jump to the side and swipe out but miss the creature. It launches forward again and again, and though I try hard to hit it with the sword, I miss every time. The black ooze continues to spread across the ground. Smoke rises where it seems to burn through the hard floor. I don't want to know what it's made of, but I'm willing to bet that if it can disintegrate the ground it will have no issue with my boots.

The creature moves toward me, and too late I realize that it is pushing me against the wall. The same wall where Cole is held in bondage. I can't let it trap me. If I try to save Cole only to get myself captured, too, then there will be no hope.

"Run, Edie!" Cole shouts.

He's crazy if he thinks I will leave him here. The creature continues maneuvering me, and I try to play along like I don't realize what it's doing. Closer and closer it gets. My retreat is blocked. If I don't do something immediately, I will die.

I pretend to fall, and I scream out as I land hard on my knee. The sword clatters to the ground. Still I keep my hand on the hilt. And as the creature moves in to attack, I swipe upward, cutting through it all the way from its groin up through its head.

I jump to the side just as the black goo begins to pool from it. The wrong side. Cole is on the other side. I don't wait. I jump over the growing ooze and land hard. The sword does fall from my grasp this time, but I grab it before the black goo gets to it and attach it to my belt. Then I rush to Cole.

He mutters something that sounds like, "You shouldn't be here."

I don't say a word. Instead I grab the power and pull on the bonds that holds his arms and leg. There's some sort of encryption around them, and as I mess with them, fresh waves of electricity emanate from them, pulses across his body. He winces and tenses, and where the currents run, his skin is raw and red. But I don't give up. I pull at the encryption, trying every technique I can think of until finally I break it.

His right ankle pulls off the wall. I immediately move to his right arm. Then his left arm. As I release this final bond, Cole sags forward, losing his balance. I catch him, because if he falls to the ground, he's going to land right in the pool of black gel.

"We have to go," I say, trying to get his focus back in place. His head lolls to the side, and he lets out a low moan. He has no crutch. No prosthetic. Nothing to support him but me. And I can't lift him across the black pool of death.

There has to be some way to get across it. I can figure it out. Without the threat of the creatures, I can stop to think for a moment. But no matter what I work through in my mind, with Cole unable to move, he's doomed.

"Come on, Cole," I say. "Pull on the power."

He lifts his head the smallest amount and looks at me, almost like he's forgotten I'm here.

"Edie?" he says.

I nod. "I'm here. But you have to help me. I can't get you out of here all by myself."

From down the rows of shelves, the glass jars rattle against each other. Something is out there. Another creature? Chaos? All I know is we can't stick around to find out.

"Use your power, Cole," I say.

He barely shakes his head. "It's gone, Edie. She took it."

She has to be Pia. But I don't mention her name now. She is not the concern. Getting out of here is. But there is no way Pia could have taken Cole's power.

"She didn't," I say.

"She did. I've tried. It's not there." Defeat fills his eyes. But I am not willing to fall prey to that defeat. I also find it impossible that Pia would take Cole's power. She's only a kid, like us. Not even the gods we've encountered have been able to take our power.

I squeeze my eyes closed and the image of the giant compass

rose returns to me. Back when we'd been on the compass rose, when we'd kissed, there'd been a spark. A sign of the power, stronger when we were together. That's all I need now. One single spark. It has to be there, buried inside him.

I lean forward and place my lips gently against his. His lips are swollen and raw from where he's bitten them from the pain, but I don't focus on that. Instead I focus on the power that is inside both of us, ready to be used.

I hold my lips there, wishing, hoping, and then there it is. The spark ignites.

I jump back, afraid to let it linger too long. But it's enough. Cole's eyes light up. He's felt it, too.

Again the jars rattle. Then the horrible sound of one of them smashing on the ground fills the air.

"Cole," I say. "We have to go."

His eyes move to where the sound came from, and the defeat slides from his face, replaced by determination. He's back. And so is his power.

The air around us seems to move as Cole manipulates it and pulls pieces of it together. Then a crutch manifests in his hand. It's not a second too soon. From down one of the rows of jars, a shadow moves.

"Come on," I say.

Cole shoves the crutch under his arm, and together we jump the pool of black acidic ooze. Then we run.

The creature must hear us, because more jars shatter as it changes direction.

"Don't stop!" I shout. I don't look. All I do is run and make sure Cole stays next to me. I'm sure the creatures are at our heels. But we run until we break free from the endless shelves. It's only then that I dare to look back.

Three creatures face us. They stand in a row and hiss, as if they are tasting our death.

I pull on the power, and I begin to build. Cole must figure out what I'm doing, because together we construct an invisible barrier out of pieces of the code that make up this room. And when the creatures launch forward and smash into it, I finally let out a breath I think I've been holding forever.

They hit the barrier over and over, smearing black blood everywhere. I step back, unable to take my eyes off it.

"What are they?" I ask. Now that the situation is not so immediate, I can process what I've seen.

Cole turns my face toward him. "Don't look, Edie."

Even after everything he's been through, he's still worried about me. I grab him and pull him close, hugging him so tightly he may never be able to get me to let go. His skin is full of electricity still, warm to the touch. It pulls on the power that runs inside me. It flickers to the surface of my skin and almost seems to combine with his.

How it should be. How it was always meant to be.

"Edie, I'm so sorry," Cole says, pulling back from the embrace. "I . . ."

He stumbles on his words. And I know I should make it easy for him. I should tell him what Raven said. But I still have to hear it for myself.

"You left," I say. I bite my lip and wait. Please let what Raven said be true.

Cole puts a hand on either of my shoulders and looks me directly in the eyes. "I was trying to protect you. To protect all of you."

"You left," I say.

He nods. "It was Pia. Small things. Things I wanted to ignore. I didn't want to believe that she could have changed. I wanted her to be the same. But then I had the vision."

"What vision?" I ask.

He looks back at the barrier we've created. One of the creatures lies broken on the ground, seeping blood that pools up against the barrier but does not burn through. The other creatures are slowing, though they continue their assault.

"From Raven," Cole says. "She gave me a vision, before we came to the Nether Zone. It was Pia, killing you. And she told me the only way for it to not come true was if I got Pia away from you. But Pia . . . well, you know this. She was reading our minds. And even though I tried to block my mind from her, I guess she was able to get through. She knew that I didn't trust her. As soon as we crossed the lava river. We'd barely touched the shore when she brought me here."

It's everything I want to hear. Everything and more. And it confirms my beliefs, too. Cole would not betray me, and Pia could never be trusted.

I look around at the white warehouse there at the edge of the storage shelves. "Where is here?" I ask. A second creature has fallen, but this has only seemed to increase the energy of the third and final creature. It slams into the barrier, trying to weaken it.

Cole gives a small shakes of his head. "I don't know. But we need to go."

We do need to go. But first, I lean forward and press my lips against his ear. "I believe you," I whisper.

Cole turns his head, and his lips meet mine. Gone is every single doubt I've ever had about what has happened. The kiss mends the wounds and makes them vanish. I put every bit of the worry and hurt and stress to the side, only thinking about what I have here, now. Cole is everything, and without him, nothing was right.

Off to our side, the creature slams into the barrier, stirring us from the moment. I pull back with a start. Later we can finish what we started, but for now, we need to get out of here.

I press the palm of my hand to Cole's scar on the side of his face. A small spark of electricity runs from it to me, through my body, and down my spine.

"You ready?" I say.

He glances back to where he'd been held and tortured. And by someone he'd thought he could trust. Then he looks away.

"Let's get the hell out of here," Cole says.

We take off, away from the creature and the shelves of jars with more creatures just like it. Once we get to the end of the simulation, we will have to find this place and destroy it. Cole uses the crutch as well as he had back when I first met him, before the simulated prosthetic. Maybe even better. He not only keeps pace with me, he's ahead as we come to the long white corridor. The sounds of the creature behind us hitting against the barrier lessen and lessen until we can no longer hear it. The white stretches on forever, but it's not until we reach the end and there is nowhere else to go that I realize we don't have a way to get back into the simulation.

"We need to get back in," I say.

"To where?" Cole asks.

That's right. If he was taken here the second he reached the Nether Zone, then somehow he's skipped the entire Simulation Omega. I explain quickly, going only with the major details. Then I access my heads-up display. I blow out a breath of relief when the icon of the raven appears.

"Does your heads-up display work?" I ask.

Cole blinks a few times as he tries to access it, and his face darkens. Then he shakes his head. "It's all static."

From down the corridor where we've just come, a hiss shatters the silence. The creature has broken free. It will be here any second.

Okay, I can think this through. *IF-THEN-ELSE*. If Cole

never entered the simulation, then his heads-up display never got programmed for it. If I can program it, then he'll be able to get into the simulation, else . . . we're both going to die.

"Trust me," I say and I place two fingers on either side of his head.

"Always," Cole says.

I grab some of the interface code from my heads-up display, and I start the tiniest of connections through my fingers, using the power that bonds both of us as a conduit. I start small, just to test it, but as soon as I see that it's going to work, I increase the output.

The creature hisses again, and lets out a shriek that chills my blood. I don't want to find out what happens when it reaches us. I keep transferring.

"Can you see anything?" I ask.

"Little bits," Cole says. "Blue circles."

It's working. I transfer as much of the program as I can.

"Tell me when you see the raven," I say. I only hope that Raven's presence in my program means that she's overlaid code in my heads-up display. If she has, it will transfer to Cole along with everything else.

The creature is getting close. The stench of its black ooze fills my nostrils. The hissing gets louder. I keep going.

"Grab my sword," I say. I can't take my fingers away or the connection will be broken.

I feel Cole take the sword from my belt. I don't dare look. I send every bit of code across, copying it.

"Wait," Cole says. "I think I see something."

Oh please let this work. "A raven?" I ask.

"Almost," Cole says.

Then the creature is on us.

Cole swipes around with the sword, sending the creature flying backward. But the sword has taken all it can of the creatures' blood. Where contact was made it melts, dividing into two pieces. Cole drops the part he holds before the remaining acid reaches his hand. Then he says, "I see it."

"Select it!" I shout.

I pull my fingers away and grab his hand, and with my eyes, I select the raven on my own display. It lights up and then I'm being sucked in. But just before the world vanishes, something hits my arm, like a spray of water. Except it burns like acid.

Then the world shifts and I'm back inside the silver zone transport. I'm also alone. Cole is nowhere to be found.

xxiv

THE SILVER MORPHS AND FLOWS around me, but I fall to my knees. My arm throbs. I force myself to look at it, knowing what I'm going to see. Sure enough, there is a splatter of bright red spots on my right forearm where the acid from the creature hit. It sizzles as it burns through my skin. It hurts like someone is driving a needle-pointed knife in each spot with surgical precision.

I press it against my leg, trying to get the pain to lessen, and then I take in my situation. There is no sign of Cole. Also, on my heads-up display, there is no sign of the black raven. Instead the six concentric circles appear. This third one, Zone Gamma, is lit up bright blue. The first two zones, Alpha and Beta, are green. Complete. The final three are still gray, like tasks left undone.

I force away a fresh wave of pain and try to collect my thoughts. Hopefully Cole is in his own silver zone transport, ready to enter this new zone. Since I copied my program to his heads-up display, my progress should have been transported along with it.

Chaos appears on the screen, his simulated face with its mock

congratulations.

"Look at you," he says. "You've made it through two zones so far. I'm happy to report that of the over fifty contestants that have started the simulation, only thirty-four have made it this far."

His avatar face beams like this is great news. And sure, this means some have been eliminated from the competition, but it also means that those kids have died. Been erased. But then I remember Zachary's promise. He could bring back Adam. That's what he'd said. If he's telling the truth, then he could bring back others also. And even though none of the other contestants have been on my side during the games, if there is also a chance to bring them back, then I'm going to try.

"Wonderful news," I say, trying to act along with the simulation. I need to get on to the next zone. I've spent enough time already. Taylor and Zachary must have been there for hours.

"It looks like you are injured," Chaos says. "Statistics have shown that those entering a new zone with an injury are five times more likely to perish during the simulation."

I grit my teeth at the pain that emanates from my arm. I can't even pretend to be upbeat about this statistic. As far as I'm concerned, Chaos can take his numbers game and shove it where the sun will never shine.

"I'm ready to move into the next simulation," I say, keeping my breathing even.

Chaos smiles. "You won't survive long."

He vanishes and the concentric circles appear once more. I select the third one, Zone Gamma, and they, too, disappear from my heads-up display. Then the moving silver shifts around me, slithering behind me as it pulls away, leaving me at the beginning of the new zone. I look around for Cole. For Taylor. For Zachary. No one is there. As far as I can see I am all alone.

XXV

AHEAD OF ME IS A BROWN EXPANSE OF
dirt. Wind blows, causing dust to fly everywhere. I can't see Taylor, Zachary, or Cole, but they could be right near me. With visibility so low, I can't see more than five feet in front of me.

"Edie!" someone shouts. I'm sure it's Cole, but with the wind whipping, the voice is stretched thin.

I put my hands out and move in the direction of his voice. "Cole? Where are you?"

"Edie, stay where you are," he says. "I'm coming."

I hate standing still, but I also don't want to get lost. Sure enough, in under a minute, a silhouette walking with a crutch under one shoulder takes shape in the dust and then manifests into him.

I grab Cole in a hug, because now that I know he's here, I don't want to lose him. "You made it in," I say.

Wind hits against us, sending my curly brown hair everywhere. What I need is a way to tie it back more securely, but until then, I pull it together and knot it at the base of my skull.

"This is the simulation?" Cole says.

"Zone Gamma," I say. "I think my progress got transferred to you also. You got to skip the first two zones."

"What? Skip the fun?" Cole says. "I may have to complain to the management."

I let out a laugh. The idea of someone willingly going backward in the simulation is ludicrous.

"Don't worry," I say. "We still have four zones to look forward to."

Cole gives me a cute little grin that almost has no place in Simulation Omega. Except our bond is the only thing that has let us get this far.

"Where's Taylor?" Cole asks.

I shake my head, trying to look through the mess of a dust storm. "I don't know."

We call for Taylor. I also call out for Zachary. The second I do, Cole's eyes go wide.

"Zachary as in Gomez?" Cole says. "As in one of the gods?"

I immediately know what he's thinking. "He's here helping us."

Cole scowls. "Helping you what? If I recall correctly, he was behind the labyrinth."

It's definitely an exaggeration. "He was one of the programmers, not behind the whole thing. But he saved me and Taylor. We'd be dead right now if it weren't for him."

He blows out a breath. "We can't trust the gods."

I put up a hand to stop him before he goes down a path we don't have time for. "We can trust them a little bit," I say, which I know is lame, but it's the best way I can think to phrase it. "Raven is the one who showed me where to find you. Zachary saved us. And Iva got me and Taylor into the simulation after you left us at the side of the lava."

This last part comes out like a slap.

"I told you—" Cole starts.

"I know," I say. I wish I could take back the words, but also, this is not the time for the conversation. "I'm sorry. And we can talk about this later. But for now, let's find Taylor and Zachary."

"Just be careful," Cole says.

I know he's trying to watch out for me, but when it comes right down to it, I'm the one who saved him. But I don't respond because I am so done with this conversation.

I shout Taylor and Zachary's names again, and for a second, I'm sure I hear something ahead, in the distance. The wind whips by, blowing my hair free once again. It seems to come in waves. I wait for it to clear, then I grab Cole's arm and drag him forward with me, toward where I think the voices originated. We pause when the wind picks up, plow forward when it wanes. We keep calling out. And the farther we go, the more sure I am that we're going to find them.

The next time we call, I am sure it's them. And they're close.

"This way," I say, and I start forward. But the dirt is everywhere, and I'm breathing it in. I pull my tank top up over my mouth and nose. I can't do anything about my eyes. Not if I want to see. The world is brown. Up, down, ahead, and behind. That's all there is. But from within the brown dust, two shapes begin to form.

"There!" I say, and I rush forward.

The second they're in view. Zachary grabs me in a hug. Not like a romantic hug but more like he's overjoyed to see me.

"Where have you been, Edie?" he asks. "Do you have any idea how worried we've been about you?"

"Yeah," Taylor says. "You were gone for hours."

I'm about to explain when Cole appears out of the dust storm, coming up to stand next to me.

From the way Zachary jumps back, it's like he's been electrocuted.

"Well look who decided to show up?" Taylor says. She narrows her good eye at Cole. The Oculus stays just skewed enough to remind the world that it is not truly a part of her. She steps forward and gets in Cole's face. "Give me one reason why I shouldn't kill you right now."

"It's cool," I say quickly before Taylor can just kill him anyway.

"Edie said you left her," Zachary says. He manages to stand his ground, even though Cole is at least six inches taller than him.

Cole nods slowly. "Edie and I have already talked about it."

That may be the case, but it's not good enough for Taylor. She stares him down until he gets out the explanation of the vision and how Pia was going to kill me.

"So Raven helped you," Zachary says, pursing up his lips. "I wonder why."

Cole shrugs. "Why not?"

Zachary acts like it's a ridiculous question. "Because Raven only helps herself."

I cock my head, thinking this through. "She gave me the ax. And Taylor the bow. And she showed me where Cole was."

"Which was where?" Taylor says.

I shudder at the memory of the creatures, and I fill Taylor and Zachary in on what I saw and what happened.

Zachary runs a hand through his hair. "They sound like destroyers."

"Destroyers?" Cole asks.

"What are destroyers?" Taylor says.

The wind still whips around us, but with our faces toward each other, we do somewhat of a good job keeping it out.

"Destroyers are something the ancient gods came up with. Creatures formed from primordial essence. They're bred for nothing but destruction, like their name implies. They grow, and when their eggs are planted in the ground, they destroy everything.

Eventually they burn out and die, but not until they've completed their job. Never before they've completed their job."

I think of the sword, bubbling away in the acid of their blood after slicing through them. A weapon might work to kill one of them, but I'm not sure how to fight an army of them. And what I'd seen was an army, waiting for its moment to attack.

"What do we do about them?" Cole asks.

Zachary presses his lips together as he thinks. "Well, for starters, we do not let any more of them out of the storage jars. If they never hatch, they shouldn't be a problem."

"That's great advice," I say. "But I wasn't the one who released the first one. It was alive in there. It shook the jar. Made it fall to the floor. What about that?"

"Yeah, that's a problem," Zachary says.

"Solved how?" Taylor says. Her eyes are scanning, her mind working through visions of the future. "Because if I can believe what I'm seeing here, eighty percent of the time I see those things crawling all over the earth, leaving death in their trail."

"Those aren't very good odds," Cole says.

"Those odds suck," Taylor says. "Ninety-five percent of Earth is wiped out by destroyers."

Earth is already is bad shape. If the destroyers get loose, even if we can bring everyone back from storage, there won't be anything left to bring them back to. And they won't be able to fight the destroyers.

Zachary turns to Cole. "What do you remember about the warehouse?"

Cole's face pulls tight. "Not much. I woke up there. I was already tied up at that point. And then . . . well, it's not like I had much of a chance to look around."

The memories of Cole's screams run through my mind. He'd been tortured in an effort to get the power out of him. I try not to think about it, or about how well I would have done under the same circumstances.

"So you don't know how to get there?" Zachary says.

Cole shakes his head.

"That's okay. We'll figure it out," I say.

"We'll have to," Zachary says. "Because if we don't, none of us will care who gets to Main Control Room Alpha first. All we'll care about is—"

A giant explosions stops his words. In the distance, through the dust, a giant fireball fills the air. It sends smoke and dust everywhere. The impact knocks me over.

"We need to get out of here," I say, trying to keep all three of my friends in sight.

Nobody disagrees. We link hands and make our way across the dusty land. The wind and heat push against us, almost like they want to hold us there in the middle of the desert we're crossing. But we can't stay there. Whatever this zone holds is ahead.

Another explosion rocks the world behind us.

We run, stumbling but trying to keep a straight line. Bits of shrapnel fall from above, remnants of the explosion. We have to get out of here.

"Someone is hunting us," I manage to stay to Cole. With one hand I'm holding onto him, with the other, Zachary. Taylor leads the way, keeping what I hope is a good hold on Zachary's other hand.

"Who?" Cole shouts amid the whipping wind.

"I don't know," I say. "But they've been here since the start. They're trying to kill us."

Cole actually smiles. "So everything is like normal then?"

A small grin slips onto my face. "I guess so."

Another explosion, closer this time. But the only consolation is that the air is clearing, filling with mist instead of dust. The ground gets softer, too. I look down to see moist soil instead of the hard-packed dirt. One foot slips, and I slow to a walk. Cole's having a harder time of it with the crutch. With each step, it sinks a good three inches into the soft soil.

"Do you guys hear that?" Zachary asks.

Far in the distance, the wind still whips around, but it's all behind us. Ahead of us is a different sound. A fresh, welcome sound.

"Water," Taylor says. She spits on the ground. Her saliva is filled with dust from the area we've just crossed.

I edge forward, carefully placing each step. Fog is thick in the air, but it's also rising, exposing a pond ahead of us. It's fed by a small creek that bubbles over rocks. Immediately my sensors go on high alert. It reminds me too much of the babbling brook in the garden we'd crossed so long ago.

"Don't go near it," I say to the others.

Zachary is the closest to it. He turns to look at me like I've lost my mind.

"Are you kidding? My mouth is filled with dust," he says.

I hold up a finger. "Just wait. It could be poisoned."

But Zachary only shakes his head. "It's not poisoned. Look." He points to fish that swim around in the water. They're bright orange, koi, unless I'm mistaken.

There must be at least ten fish, and they swim and float like they don't have a care in the world. They're mesmerizing, and I can't pull my eyes away from them. Taylor bends down and dips a hand in the water. The fish slowly move away. She scoops out the water and lifts it to her mouth. I open my mouth to tell her I'm not sure if that's a good idea, but then my vision swims.

It's okay, Edie, Raven says in my mind. She's there, filling the space on my heads-up display. *You can drink the water.*

"But . . . ," I start. There must be a good reason to not drink the water.

Raven shakes her head, her long dark hair slowly moving side to side. *It's fine. The water won't hurt you.*

I blink, trying to get her out of my heads-up display, but she stays there.

Edie, would I lie to you? Raven says.

This comment is enough to stir me from the vision. Raven would definitely lie to me. She admitted that Chaos is forcing her to help him.

"You would," I say aloud.

Raven softly smiles. *True. But you have to drink the water. It's the only way to get through this zone.*

That right there may be the only truth that's come out of her mouth. I nod slowly.

Taylor drank it and she's still standing. Maybe Raven talked to her, too.

I step forward and squat down. Cole is next to me.

"Don't leave me, okay?" I say.

He brushes some hair off my cheek, pushing it behind my ear. "Don't leave me. Ever."

From off to my left, Zachary clears his throat. "I think we have to drink it," he says.

I nod. Then instead of dipping my hand into the water, I press my face down to it and drink deeply.

I let the water wash the dirt and grime from my face. I hold back my hair even though I'd love nothing so much as to take a shower and get clean. I'm sure I have dust deep in my ear canals.

The water is vibrant blue, and the bubbles from where the creek feeds into it drift across the surface. Each time they pop, a musical note fills the air, like someone tapping on a xylophone. There's a hint of sweetness in the water. It reminds me of sucking on a honeysuckle. Just a drop and yet the perfect amount.

From off to the side, a noise brings me back to the present.

Someone is walking away. I can't tell who it is because I can't see their face. I stand and wipe the water from where it drips off my chin.

"Hey, who's there?" I call. I'm the only one still standing in the clearing. Not five minutes ago, there were more of us. I try to remember who, but the names escape me. But I'm sure I should be with them.

I look back to the water. One more small sip won't hurt. I dip my hand in and hold it to my mouth, letting the water trickle into my mouth. Having the dirt and dust off me is a little slice of heaven. Why was I so dirty anyway?

On the other side of the pond is a row of bushes. They have bright pink flowers, and bees buzz around them, collecting the nectar. A path leads through the bushes but it's pretty well overgrown. Still, I'd seen someone going that way. If I follow the path, I can find them.

I push through the bushes. "Hello?" I say. The row of bushes is thick, and soon I'm immersed in them. I look back, but I can't see the way I came from yet. Then something stings me on the right forearm.

I swat at the bee, watching it fall to the ground. My arm immediately swells up red, and I scratch it in case there's a stinger inside. Then I push forward. The row of bushes finally ends. I hold them apart and step through, letting them fall closed behind me. Ahead of me are dozens of people wandering around, cloaked in gray, like all color has been removed from the world.

I turn to look behind me, but the colorful bushes are gray also. No sign of pink flowers. No sign of bees. Just shades of gray.

I step forward and walk to the closest person I see.

"Hey," I say, tapping on his arm. It's a guy, maybe my age. He's got cropped blond hair and a thin build, like a runner.

His eyes meet mine and light up in slight recognition. "Hey, it's you," he says. "I have something for you."

"For me?" I don't know him. I can't imagine why he would know me.

"Well, yeah," he says. "The girl with the curly brown hair and the gray eyes. That sure sounds like you."

I can't see myself to know if he's right.

"I know it sounds crazy, but this giant snake told me I'm supposed to give something to you," he says.

"What is it?"

"I don't know. Something I stole earlier. Not sure what it's for. But I guess I stole it for you."

He doesn't reach out and hand me anything. Instead words flash across the front of my eyes, briefly. They're gone before I can read them.

"Thanks," I say, unsure what just happened. Whatever it was, it's done now.

"Yeah, no problem."

I leave him there and continue forward. But each step I take, I can't remember what I'm doing here. There is some reason—there must be—but I can't place it.

XXVI

I WATCH PEOPLE WALK AROUND. NO-
body seems to care where they're going. They wander along, stopping and staring, as if they're trying to think of something but can't quite remember what. I don't know why they care. I'm not sure why it matters.

Someone bumps into me from behind. It stirs me from my thoughts.

"Sorry," they say.

I turn to see a guy looking at me. He's tall, well over six feet, and he has spikey blond hair. He's pretty well built, and when I finally turn around, he smiles.

"I wasn't watching," he says. "I didn't mean to run into you."

I shake my head. "It's okay."

"No, really, I'm sorry."

It's not a big deal, but I guess he wants to talk or something.

"Okay, this is a really weird question," he says. "But do you know your name?"

I laugh out loud. It's the silliest question I've ever heard. "Sure.

It's . . ." But the second I try to actually pull my name into my mind, it slips away. Weird symbols seem to float over my vision, but I ignore them.

"You can't remember, right?"

I place my hands on my hips and draw for my name again. "It's . . ." But it seems like the harder I try to remember it, the more it slips away.

He smiles again. A really great smile that instantly makes me like him. "Me either. I can't remember it. It's so weird, right?"

"Really weird," I say. I blink a few times, still trying to grab my name, because what kind of person forgets their own name?

"Glad I'm not the only one," the guy says.

It is a small amount of consolation. And a voice seems to whisper across the colorless expanse of people. *Don't worry about it. It doesn't matter. Nothing matters.*

The voice must be right. It's better off this way.

"Do I know you?" the guy says.

I tilt my head and study him. A memory nags at the back of my mind. It pushes against his smile, like it wants to be heard. There is something about him. Something familiar. Something . . .

"I think so," I say.

He blows out a long breath of relief. "Good, I feel the same way. But I can't remember. But you know, if we both don't remember then maybe that's a good thing."

"Yeah, maybe," I say. "Where were you before this?"

I ask not so much because I'm curious, but because I'm hoping it will answer my own questions. I'm here now. But before now . . . I don't know.

Something moves off to the left. Something huge that is hidden by the crowd. I turn, but whatever it was, it's gone. Kids like me walk about, looking as confused by all this as I am.

"Before now?" he says. His eyes light up, and his mouth opens the smallest amount. He remembers, and he's going to tell me.

"Yeah. Before you got here," I say.

But then he shakes his head. "I was . . . somewhere. But you know what? I don't think it matters. I think maybe this place is all that matters."

I nod, processing his words. I don't know who I am or why I'm here, but little bits of logic ping at my mind. I must be here for some reason. And there must also be some reason why neither of us can remember.

A girl walks by. I tap her on the shoulder to stop her. She has dark skin and short bleached braids. She's also got a couple scars on either of her cheeks, in a row, almost like they were put there intentionally. She scowls at me the second she sees me.

"What do you want?"

I open my mouth, ready to ask her name. What she's doing here. But she glares at me like she hates me, so instead I shake my head and say, "Never mind."

"Yeah, okay," she says, and walks off.

"You want to look around?" the guy says.

It's so impersonal, and something nags at me. Connections. I need connections to figure out what's going on.

"What can I call you?" I ask. I don't want to think of him as 'the blond guy.'

He shrugs. "John? Andy? Thomas? I don't care."

Thomas. Something about the name sends a flash of worry directly to my brain. I know someone named Thomas. Someone in trouble? Maybe? Maybe that's why I'm here. I could need to find this Thomas person.

"How about Andy?" I say.

"Good enough," the guy I'm now referring to as Andy says. "How about you? You look like an Emily."

Emily. Again the name causes worry to form in my mind.

I shake my head. "Call me Samantha." It's the first name that comes to mind. It's good enough.

"Samantha it is," Andy says. "Let's look around."

He takes the lead, making me feel like he's trying to prove he's in control. It's a little off-putting, even if he has a nice smile. But maybe he knows more than he's letting on to. We push through the people. It's not hard since most of them aren't talking and don't seem to have much of a purpose.

Purpose. I need a purpose. *IF-THEN-ELSE.* The three words form in my mind. If I'm here in this place and I don't remember why, then there must be some reason. I need to find out that reason, else I could be . . . lost here forever.

Lost here forever. The last words seem to form on their own. That's what is at stake.

"We need to find a way out of this place," I say, pulling on his arm to stop him.

"How do you know?"

"Why else are we here?" I say. "No one here is doing anything. There's no reason to be here. Right?"

He considers my words then nods. "Yeah, true. So we look for this way out."

I relax the tiniest amount. It's good to be on the same page.

The world around us is shades of gray and brown. Sepia except nothing is standing out. But maybe if we find something different—something that doesn't belong—that could be a clue as to how to get out.

"But where's the way out?" He twists up his mouth, like he's trying to figure it out.

"Logic," I say. "This place has to be logical. Like we came in from somewhere. So there must be a way to leave."

"Where did we come from?"

Small memories slip into my mind. Drinking from a pond.

Moving through some bushes. The color disappearing.

"Wherever the color is," I say.

I turn slowly in a circle, trying to take it all in. There are the kids, like me, like Andy. The dark-skinned girl with the bleached braids. The guy with the spikey blond hair I talked to earlier. Again I see something move through the crowd, slithering and staying out of sight. Then it's gone. There's another guy, off to my left, standing on one leg with a crutch under his arm because he's missing the other leg from the knee down. He has dark hair that hangs almost to his shoulders, but he's not looking our way. Almost like he knows I'm watching him, he turns and my eyes meet his.

Half his face is covered with a giant scar that runs from his eye down to his chin. But instead of detracting from the way he looks, seeing it instantly fills me with relief. I know this guy. I'm certain of it.

"Let's ask him," I say, pointing to the guy.

The guy I'm calling Andy twists up his face in disgust. "Really? Why?"

Without even realizing I'm doing it, I take a step away from him because how rude is that?

"I think I know him," I say. Then without waiting to see whether Andy follows me or not, I start over to the guy. He has something important. Some kind of information. I'm supposed to talk to him.

"Hi," I say, unsure what kind of reaction I'm going to get.

"I know you," the guy says.

I nod slowly. That feels right. I don't know how or from where, but I'm sure he's right. "Yeah, I think I know you, too."

By this point, Andy decides to follow and comes up on my right side. He flashes his smile, but it's nowhere near as nice or warm as I originally thought.

The guy with the scar has one thing that we don't. He remembers his name.

"I'm Cole," he says.

The second the words are out of his mouth, my eyes widen. I know his name is Cole. And I also know that whoever he is, I like him way more than just as a friend. But I don't know if he knows this. I don't know how to act through this.

"We need to find the way out," I say.

"Yeah, I was thinking about that," Cole says. He's got a really cute accent, way different than mine or Andy's. Like someone from the south. But not Georgia. More like Louisiana. He points with his crutch over to a dead tree. "Did you guys see that?"

I hadn't even noticed it before, but now that Cole mentions it, my vision seems to focus in on it, almost like everything else fades away.

"Have you gotten a closer look?" Andy says. He acts like he's trying to be friendly again, but it's almost like there is invisible animosity between the two guys.

"I tried," Cole says. "But . . ."

"But what?" Andy says.

"You have to see." Without another word, Cole sets off, using his crutch so well it's hardly noticeable that half his leg is missing.

We walk closer to the dead tree, but as we walk, two things happen. The tree grows larger with every step, and leaves sprout from its branches. It is transforming in front of us until by the time we stop about twenty feet away, it towers so high above us that I can't see the top. And the leaves rather than being gray and brown like everything else around, are bright vivid colors, green and orange and yellow, like it can't contain all the life inside it.

"That's why," Cole says, point at the base of the tree.

Wrapped around the tree is a snake so thick, its body width is nearly as wide as I am tall. It curls around four times until its tail reaches up and drapes over a high branch, then extends back down, ending just above the ground. Its eyes are closed, but as soon as I spot it, the snake's eyes fly open. They're black and thin like slits, but they have the tiniest amount of green lined through them.

You've made it this far, the snake says. But it's talking directly into my mind, not aloud. I glance to Andy, but he doesn't act like he's hearing anything.

I know you, I think to the snake.

It flicks its tongue out, tasting the empty air. *You do. Do you remember?*

I shake my head. This snake has somehow been in my past. But the details won't fill in. *You helped me once.*

Did I?

I glance at Cole and Andy, but they're standing motionless, almost like time is frozen around them. Nobody else is moving either. Only me and the snake and the leaves in the tree, blowing softly in the wind.

You need to remember, the snake says.

At his words, symbols flash across my eyes. I squeeze my eyes closed and they vanish. I try to remember.

What have you done with the power? the snake says.

Power. There is something about the power. About where I got it.

An image of a throne room, with a golden throne at the top of a small flight of steps fills my mind. An old man sits in the throne. Dies in the throne.

He was your enemy, too, I think.

The snake blinks its eyes. *He was always my enemy. From the beginning of time.*

Little bits and pieces come back to me. An old god. I'd killed him.

Are you a god? I ask the snake.

I am, the snake says. *One of the ancient gods, from ages long ago. We ruled the earth before the old gods. When the old gods came—well, we thought of them as the new gods back then—they tried to take control. They determined that our time was done. They claimed we were destroying humanity. They asked us to leave.*

Our council convened, and it was recognized that most of our numbers should be cast aside. Perhaps these new gods were correct. As happens with many gods over time, their care for the earth had waned. But among us, there were a select few that secretly vowed to maintain control. From these new gods we sensed the chaos that would come. We knew we would be needed.

These new gods fought us in a war that nearly destroyed the earth. They killed many of us. But a few of us, like me, survived. We let them believe we were dead. We stayed hidden. We built up our power. We waited. The time would come. We always knew that. But these new gods didn't. They never expected to hear from us again. They never put in any precautions to protect against us.

Over time, the new gods became the old gods, and the destruction they sprinkled over the earth became too much. The time had come for change. The time had come for a new generation of gods to take over.

As the giant snake communicates with me, images play through my mind. Of the ancient gods. The war. New gods taking over. And slowly, as had happened before, a shift in power became necessary. It is now the time of change.

What do you need me to do? I ask. I clench my fists, wanting to spring into action but not understanding anything.

I need you to remember, Eden. I need you to remember who you are. Why you were born. And what you are meant to do. It's why you're here. Why I've brought you here. Why I've brought you all here.

Eden. That's me. That's my name. And all of us. He's talking about the people that stand around me. Cole. The guy I'm calling

Andy. The other guy who'd given something to me earlier. The girl with the bleached braids. A couple others that look vaguely familiar.

Then the snake's tongue flicks out, lashing over my forehead, trailing down my arm. Sparks run through me, like invisible power under my skin. Symbols flash across my eyes. This time I recognize them as a word: MEMORY.

Remember, the snake says. Then he begins to uncurl himself from the tree, slithering forward until his tail winds down and he is finally free. He slithers off, away from us, into the bleak land ahead.

I watch the snake's departing form until it is completely out of sight. The sparks still run through me. I focus on them, feeling them move like they are a part of me. The word is still there, floating in front of my eyes. I focus on it. MEMORY. Then I blink.

Memories flood my mind. The labyrinth. A giant wooden horse destroying a city. My friends. Cole. Taylor. Hudson. Zachary.

Owen.

I spin around, and there is Andy—Owen. I almost shrink back, but I stop myself. I'm not scared of Owen.

The snake had been clear. We're all here. We're all needed.

Owen doesn't remember. I do. The word had been there, in my heads-up display, transferred to me by Hudson. And Hudson, in turn, had stolen it from someone else, possibly the very person he'd been following: Owen. The MEMORY item should have been his, but the snake had told Hudson to steal it from Owen and transfer it to me.

"The snake is gone," Owen says, pointing to the tree. It's still full of life. Full of hope in this desolate place. But one by one, the leaves begin to fall from the tree.

I hold my face steady, but the power flows through me in waves. I know what I need to do with it. I need to not only make myself remember. I need to help the others remember, too.

I glance to Cole, wondering if he feels the power, too. Sure enough, he's studying Owen. Anger flows across his face.

"You remember?" I ask Cole.

He nods.

"Did the snake talk to you, too?" I ask. "Did you hear?"

"All of it," Cole says.

I let out a long breath, thankful I am not alone in this knowledge.

"We have to use the power to bring back their memories," I say.

"What are you two talking about?" Owen asks. I'm guessing that Cole and I are the only ones who heard the snake. The only two with the ability, since we have the power.

"Nothing," I say. "But we need to go."

I start walking away from Owen, not looking back, but he grabs my arm and stops me. His fingers dig into my muscle, almost hard enough to hurt.

"Go where?" Owen asks.

I look him right in the eye. "Let me go."

"But where are you going?" he says, still not letting go.

If I had my sword or my ax, I would . . . What? Would I kill him? Could I? I bite my lips but hold his gaze.

"None of your business," I say, and I yank my arm out of his grasp.

Cole gets right in his face. "Don't follow us."

Owen puts up his hands and steps back, acting like he's Mister Innocent. And maybe here, without his memories, he kind of is. But underneath, he's still Owen. Still the same asshole he always was.

"No problem," Owen says. "I was leaving anyway."

Cole and I walk away, leaving Owen there by the tree. I turn back only once, just in time to see the last leaf fall from the branches, leaving it barren. And when we are far enough away and out of sight, we stop.

From our vantage point, and with my refreshed memory, names and faces coalesce. Abigail with her cross necklace clutched in her hand. Taylor, somehow connected with Hudson, except she's scowling at him like she doesn't know him. Rex from Simulation Avine. His sister Amanda. I even see Queen Simone and Damien. They're all here, in the simulation. They've all lost their memories. And we have to free them. But first, we have to separate our friends, find the exit point so we'll have the advantage. So we'll get the key and get out first.

"Let's start with Hudson," I say to Cole, and we hurry over to where he and Taylor argue. He's jogging in place, full of unlimited energy, but with no memories, it's like he doesn't know what to do with it.

"Hudson, you have to come with us," I say.

Hudson's eyes go wide. "You know my name."

I nod, and that seems good enough for him.

Taylor is an entirely different story. She fights and argues with everything we say until Cole finally manages to convince her that he's telling the truth by whispering her brother's name: Adam.

It's like when I'd heard Thomas's name. A small sliver of the past that is powerful enough to seep through the mask blocking the world.

There's no sign of Zachary Gomez anywhere, and I worry that we're going to have to leave him. But we push through the crowd, to where a small pond seems to suck in every bit of color, like a black hole pulling in light. We find Zachary there, looking into the pond.

He doesn't even look our way as we approach.

"It's full of colors," he says, pointing through the still surface. Underneath the otherwise gray surface, an iridescent carnival is going one, with colors swirling and mixing into every shade possible.

"It's beautiful," Taylor says.

Hearing her say this is so uncharacteristic, like she's taking a moment to look at the beauty of the world. Or maybe this part of her is always there but she keeps it hidden under her hard shell. Either way, we have to bring back the old Taylor.

"You ready?" I ask Cole.

"Ready," he says.

We link hands, and I let the power slip out of me, combine with his, and release into the zone around us. It flows out almost like waves of light that travel through the air. I know it's working because Taylor's good eye lights up. The Oculus remains the same, unmoving, all-seeing. Hudson is next. Then Zachary. I have to assume that every other kid trapped in this zone will begin to remember, too.

Immediately something begins to grow from the center of the pond. It's a giant white column that stretches up far into the air. The pond begins to lift.

"Get on!" I shout, and I step onto it. It's moving slowly enough for us all to get stable before it's too high.

"Wait!" someone shouts.

It's Owen, running for us, for the column.

"Faster," Taylor says, stomping her foot on the platform, like that will help.

Owen jumps, but his fingers miss the edge of the platform. We're free from him . . . for the time being.

"Edie, come back!" Owen shouts. "Come on."

He's completely delusional if he thinks I would try to help him now. But he had tried to convince me to work with him before. Even if he was the last person left, I still wouldn't help him.

The platform continues to rise and the column grows. And

when it stops, we collect the segment of the key that appears in glowing symbols there at the top.

From far below there's shouting. Not just Owen, but others. The pond morphs and flows like a path, and we run down it, away from the column. But around us, lightning begins to fill the air.

Abigail. Shit. She still has her lightning power. And with us now ahead, she's going to want to stop us.

I dare to glance back. She's got her fingers outstretched. Her eyes closed. Owen stands next to her, screaming at us to come back.

I look away and see the silver waterfall. We're almost there. But before I can reach it, something hits me from behind. There's a shock of electricity, and then everything goes black.

XXVII

"EDIE," A VOICE SAYS IN MY MIND.
"Edie. Wake up."

The voice is familiar. Really familiar. My eyes don't want to open. It's too much effort. They're dry and with them closed, everything is peaceful. The world is black.

"Edie. Come on."

It's the voice again. The world begins to fill in. I need to see the person behind the voice. It feels like I'm drawing sandpaper across my eyeballs, but I force my lids open. Light pours into my vision, blinding me only for a moment. Then shapes begin to fill in.

"She's coming around," another voice says.

Taylor. That's who the voice belongs to. And the other voice is Cole. Cole who'd betrayed me. Except he hadn't. He'd protected me . . . and it almost cost him his life.

"What happened?" I manage to say. My voice is hoarse, like I haven't talked in days. What I really need is water.

"Abigail and Owen," Hudson says, popping into my vision.

"They attacked. Caught us by surprise." His hand is on the center of my chest, only a couple inches below my neck, but he quickly pulls it back like I've caught him doing something he shouldn't.

"Abigail still has her lightning power," Taylor says.

Of course she does. Cole and I still have our power, taken from a god. And her power . . . the lightning . . . she took it from the old king on top of the mountain back in Simulation Avine. And now, thinking about it, I'm willing to bet he was one of the old gods also, hidden in the simulation.

Raven's simulation.

Raven, of all the minor gods, is the one I'm sure we can trust the least.

I sit up as the world slowly fills in. Taylor. Hudson. I turn my head, looking for Cole. He's there, on his crutch, standing next to Zachary. But there's an invisible boundary between them. Cole's eyes meet mine, and I can't help the smile that grows on my face.

Hudson reaches down, offering me a hand to help me stand. "You know you almost died just there," he says. "And heck if I know how you didn't. But not gonna lie. It would have sucked to finally find you again just to have you die on me."

"You healed her," Taylor says, completely matter-of-fact.

Hudson crosses his arms over his chest. "I didn't."

She rolls her one good eye. The Oculus stays in place. "Whatever."

"What makes you think I can—" Hudson starts, but he stops talking.

I don't have to ask why. Symbols begin to scroll across my heads-up display, like a stream of data full of various colors and types of symbols. There are words I recognize, ancient symbols. There are even things that remind me of emoticons, though I can't believe the gods use those.

"System resetting," Chaos's voice says through the heads-up

display. It's his simulated voice, like this is what happens when there's a . . .

"Power failure," I say aloud, blowing out a breath. A system reset will give us a little wiggle room.

Taylor nods. "The system must've gotten fried from the lightning."

"Where did Abigail get power like that?" Zachary asks. He stands back, not quite part of the group. But he's as much a part of it as any of us right now.

I step to the side, giving him room to move forward and join our tenuous circle.

"There was this old god," Hudson says. "At the top of Mount Olympus, in the last simulation. He was programmed to be like Zeus or something. And the quest was to get the lightning. We tried. He totally kicked our asses. Then Abigail stole all his lightning. She channeled it through that necklace of hers."

Zachary's eyes go wide and he quickly glances to me.

I nod.

"What did he look like?"

Hudson shrugs. "An old guy. Sat in a throne. Acted like he owned the place. But when he started fighting, he was fast and could teleport from one place to the next. Totally not fair. I mean, we would have figured out a way to get the lightning from him, even if Abigail hadn't shown up. That's how it was programmed."

But Zachary shakes his head. "I don't think he was programmed," he says. "I think he was—"

"One of the old gods," I say.

"Yep," Zachary says, confirming my suspicion. "Planted in the simulation, either by Raven or without Raven knowing. And you guys killed him?" He kind of bites his tongue on this last part, like he's not sure what the answer should be.

"Abigail did," Hudson says. "She took his lightning and he

withered away. Turned to dust.”

“Oh.” Zachary’s response is not what I expect. But then I remember my conversation with Elise. The old god that I’d killed had been her and Iva’s father. And maybe there’s something similar going on here.

“You were related to him?” I ask.

“Unfortunately,” Zachary says. He doesn’t expand and I don’t press. And the problem remains. Abigail has the power of one of the gods.

“He must’ve been the god who was helping her,” I say, and I quickly relay the story Abigail shared with me, leaving out the more personal details, about how she prayed for her father to die. And how she claimed god responded to her. Agreed to help her . . . if she protected Owen. The only good part of this is that if he is dead, he’s no longer helping her . . . aside from her having his power.

“You weren’t the only one with help, Edie,” Zachary says. “Remember?”

I know Zachary’s talking about himself and Elise helping me. But my mind immediately goes to the giant snake. Without his help, I’d still be trapped back in the other simulation. And he’d been the one who’d given me the power to kill the old god. I could be dead in the labyrinth right now if not for him.

“Wait, you helped Edie?” Hudson says. “Aren’t you just one of us?”

By us, he means the kids in the simulation. I let out a laugh. Cole shifts his weight to his crutch but doesn’t smile. And Taylor says, “Oh, you haven’t met god boy.”

“Didn’t we agree to not call me god boy?” Zachary says.

“I never agreed to that,” Taylor says.

“Wait. You’re a god?” Hudson says.

Zachary stands tall, and this time, instead of acting shy about it, he crosses his arms. "Yep. I am." He offers no more explanation.

"He's a minor god," Taylor says in a loud whisper intended for everyone to hear.

"The key word being god," Zachary says.

"Don't get touchy," Taylor says, but there's a hint of softness in her voice. If I didn't know better, I would swear she's actually coming to accept Zachary.

"Are there more old gods left?" I ask Zachary, part to change the subject, but also to know what we're up against. Chaos is behind this simulation, but that doesn't mean there aren't any other gods hidden inside.

"Chaos is the only one," he says. "As far as I know. But I'm obviously not told everything."

"So you didn't know about the warehouse?" Cole says. "You didn't know I was being held there?"

It's almost a challenge.

Disbelief crosses Zachary's face. "No way. If I'd known, I would have . . ."

"What? Freed me?"

"Yeah, I would have freed you." His voice is solid and without question.

Cole gives a small nod, and some sort of unspoken truce seems to pass between them. One more truce that can only help us succeed.

The symbols on my heads-up display stop scrolling and vanish. Replacing them is a single command.

RESUME SIMULATION?
» YES
» NO

I can tell that everyone else has seen the same thing as me.

"Does this mean that we're not in the simulation right now?" I say, trying to work through the pieces of logic. With the gray barriers around us, there is nowhere else to go.

"We must've gotten kicked out," Zachary says. "Like really out."

"So we can leave?" Taylor says.

I glare at her.

"Just kidding," she says, putting her hands up. "I am ready to kick some serious Chaos ass."

"Ditto," Hudson says.

"And me," Cole says.

Relief flows through me. Our group. Our truce. Back together and solid.

"Not me," Zachary says.

"But—" I start.

He shakes his head. "This is my chance. I need to figure out what's going on with that warehouse. With the destroyers. Because if they get loose . . . well, we don't want that to happen."

I know he's right, but I also don't want him to leave.

"Will we see you again?" I say. I hold my voice even, trying to keep my emotions in check. But the fact of the matter is that I've gotten kind of used to him being around.

Then he steps toward me, and I think for a second he's going to kiss me. Instead his eyes meet mine, not blinking.

"You're meeting us at the end, right?" Taylor says, stopping whatever else he was planning on doing. "We have a deal."

Zachary smiles. "I'm good for my word," he says. Then he vanishes, his god powers working here outside of the simulation.

"I don't trust him," Cole says.

Taylor actually reaches over and musses Cole's brown hair. "Oh, don't get all worried. Just 'cause he likes your girlfriend doesn't mean he's a bad guy."

Cole actually blushes. "It's not that."

It's totally that. Even an idiot could tell. And I can't help but be a little bit flattered.

"And what deal do you have with him?" Cole asks.

She looks away. "None of your business."

She must know I'll tell Cole later. There's no reason not to.

"You do realize that every second we wait, Owen and Abigail are getting ahead of us, right?" Hudson says.

I kind of love how everything is back to normal. Pia is gone. Hudson is in a hurry. Taylor's determined. It's comforting in its own special way.

"Yeah, Hudson's right," I say. "You guys ready?"

Cole, Taylor, and Hudson all nod. Then I select Yes from the choices on the heads-up display. Instantly the world shifts away from the gray void. The wall of moving silver appears.

"See you guys on the other side," I say, and I press my hand on the flowing silver.

xxviii

THE SILVER SLIDES AROUND ME, MAK-
ing everything else vanish. Are Cole, Taylor, and Hudson right there near me? In a physical world, they would be, but this is a simulation. They are nothing but a programmed representation of themselves as am I.

My heads-up display comes to life, and the silhouette of Chaos appears.

"Congratulations," he says. "You completed Zone Gamma. Interesting how you managed to recover your memory without Memory as your selected item."

"Yeah, interesting," I say, holding my voice steady. Hudson had stolen MEMORY from Owen and given it to me, at the request of the ancient snake god. Simulation or not, Chaos cannot know about this.

"Of course, by doing so, you have allowed all those trapped in Simulation Gamma to also proceed."

I knew this was the cost. There was nothing that could be done about it. My and Cole's power helped everyone. Now everyone

I saw in there is moving on to the next zone. And it's not that I don't want to help them—well, except for Owen and Abigail. I would happily have them plucked from the simulation.

They're necessary. Iva's voice echoes in my mind. It's not real. It's a figment of my imagination. And also wrong. Owen and Abigail can't be necessary.

"I'm ready for the next zone," I say, blocking out thoughts of Owen. My best option is to keep moving forward.

"Zone Delta," Chaos says. "The hardest yet. Thus far none have survived." His final words of discouragement, not that I would expect anything less.

The silhouette of Chaos disappears and the image of the concentric circles appears. Three of them are colored in green. Three remain, including the center. We're halfway there. We can do this.

I select the fourth circle. The silver fluid around me pulls away from me, dumping me out into the world, leaving me behind. It forms a wall behind me. No turning back. No leaving.

Cole is already there, leaning on his crutch. I hurry over to him and grab him in a hug.

"I really missed you," I say. With no one else around and no threat imminent, it's what I've been waiting to tell him. "I couldn't stand it when I thought—"

He puts a finger to my lips. "I can't think about it, Edie," he says. "I had to do it, but it almost killed me leaving you like that. But she left me no choice."

She has no place in this conversation.

I answer by leaning in and pressing my lips to his. All it takes is one kiss and then every barrier is broken. I run my fingers through his hair. I explore his face. His back. Cole holds my face and he's so warm. So perfect. My heart had broken when I'd thought he'd gone off with her. And sure, maybe I'm risking it breaking again, but it's a risk I'm willing to take.

"Can you guys stop that?" Taylor says, walking up to join us.

I let the kiss linger for another moment then pull back. When this is all over . . . Well, there are lots of things that are going to happen. But until then, I need to focus on getting to the end.

"Sorry," Cole says.

"Yeah, no one likes PDAs." Then she hollers, "Hey Hudson, over here."

Sure enough, Hudson is only about twenty yards away. He turns at the sound of her voice and sprints over to join us.

"What did I miss?" he says.

"Nothing you wanted to see," Taylor says. "Now how are we going to get through this shit?"

By shit, she's talking about what lies ahead of us. We're under a roof that extends about thirty feet out, but after that, it's raining. Water droplets seem to hang in the air, thick and slow moving, and so close together.

"That's a lot of rain," Cole says.

"That's more than rain," Hudson says, and I notice that he's soaking as if he's already been out in it. He shakes his head, water slinging off his blond hair. "It's like being underwater. There's no air."

Instead of a river of lightning or dust or fog, we're in a literal river of water, in this case thick rain.

"How long can you hold your breath?" Hudson asks.

"Long enough," Taylor says. "But don't go running off ahead of us."

He puts a hand to his chest. "I would never. Now are you guys ready?"

I grab his arm. "Wait. You took the Memory from Owen. You stole it from him."

He shrugs. No big deal. "The snake told me to do it. Right after we got into the first zone. Owen and Abigail knew I was following them, so I joined up with them even though they didn't want me to. They didn't have much choice. We all wanted to survive. Then I had this vision. Talked to the snake. He told me what to do. When Owen opened up his heads-up display to interact with the first part of the key after that stupid colosseum, I activated the option to transfer the item. He never even knew."

But the snake had known that if I remembered, I'd be able to use the power to open up everyone else's memories also.

"Thanks," I say. "You saved us all."

Hudson cocks his head and smiles. "Only partly. You're the one who remembered."

"Yeah, and good thing," Taylor says. "I didn't know what the hell was going on looking at the world through the Oculus back there. It was like a million visions and no idea what they were supposed to mean."

Seeing futures and not understanding why had to be confusing.

"And now?" I say. "What are our odds of success?"

I hold my breath, hoping the number will be in our favor.

Taylor smirks. "Thirteen outcomes I see from this point," she says. "And of those four succeed."

Four in thirteen. It's not good, but it's better.

"If we don't get going, we'll never find Owen," Cole says.

"Cole's right," Hudson says. "I spotted him and Abigail earlier."

Shit. We need to go. We need to face whatever is ahead.

I glance out at the river of water drops ahead of us. Off in the distance, purple lightning crackles. An added complication. Lightning will make the water electric, increasing our chances of death.

"I'm ready." I take a deep breath, drawing in as much air as I can, and we run into the river ahead of us.

What I'm not expecting is the temperature. Each drop of water is like ice, and without thinking, I blow out the breath in a gasp. When I suck in, I get a mouthful of freezing water.

I gag on it and cough. Cole looks to me, and I convey that I'm okay . . . for now. Then he motions with his head the direction we need to keep going. I nod, and we continue forward.

The lightning gets stronger the farther we go. It's steady, flickering in a rhythmic pattern. The water gets thicker and colder the closer in we get. I can barely see Taylor and Hudson off to our right, just ahead of us. But then we step forward and there's a break in the water that extends far ahead.

The water is like a sheet behind us. But it's not what I'm worried about. We stand at the edge of a giant circular chasm. Lightning flickers over the center of the chasm, crackling purple and blue and red in a pattern that goes round and round like the water that fills the chasm.

I blow out the breath I've tried to hold, and I suck in fresh air but almost gag. It's fetid, like rot fills everything.

"It's a whirlpool," Cole says. Except for the swirling motion, the water is almost calm, going round and round in a perfect pattern. The lightning is silent, as if the world has been muted.

We join Taylor and Hudson there at the edge of the chasm, but we're not the only ones here. Abigail and Owen stand not fifty feet away, staring out at the swirling water and electric sky. They aren't alone. Other kids stand along the edge, too, all around. Kids I've never seen before but who have apparently made it this far in the simulation. Other competitors. Others who might get to the end before us. There must be at least twenty others, standing alone or in groups of two or three, scattered about. Even as I watch, five more hurry up from the sheet of rain that lies behind them as if the entire zone is a circle with this as its end point.

Then the swirling picks up and the water begins to suck down more rapidly. The lightning flashes and changes from purple and blue to orange and yellow. Sound fills the air like wood being thrown against a rock wall. The water climbs higher as the center of the water dips deeper.

"Do you see that?" Hudson says.

I do see it. See it but don't want to believe it, because inside the whirlpool something is forming. Something with teeth large enough to swallow an entire ship. Then the teeth open into a gaping mouth, and the head of a monster lifts from the whirlpool and darts out, grabbing one of the kids who stands on the edge of the chasm.

There isn't even enough time for the kid to scream. He's pulled under. The mouth again disappears below the surface of the whirlpool, and it calms down. The lightning changes back to purple and blue. There's a monster inside the chasm. Somehow we need to get past it.

XXIX

ABIGAIL SHRIEKS AND BREAKS INTO
sobs that easily carry across the silence to us. I can't even pretend
to muster up the effort to feel sorry for her. She has sided with a
monster from the very start of this entire thing. From even before
she met Owen, she knew the only reason she was in the simulation was to help him. Not to mention she's tried to kill us on
multiple occasions. I have better uses for my energy than to feel
sorry for her.

"There's nowhere else to go," Hudson asks. "Look at this point.
It's a giant circle."

I am not one to give up before trying, but Hudson is only
voicing what every single one of us thinks. If we skirt around
the edge, we'll only be back where we started. Entry points from
all sides but no exit. It's us against a giant chasm with a monster
inside. No bridge. No trees or buildings or boats. Even if we had
a boat, the whirlpool would suck us down. And the sky is nothing
but a crackling mass of lightning emanating from a black starless
night.

I glance back to Abigail and Owen. It looks like they're arguing, no doubt about the same thing we are. Then Owen presses a finger to either of his eyebrows.

"That's how he talks to his dad," Hudson says. "He's done it the entire simulation. It's how he defeated the monsters back at the colosseum."

"Then maybe he knows how to get across," Cole says, watching Owen.

IF-THEN. The logic immediately moves through my mind and calms me. If Owen is cheating, then we can use it to our advantage.

We watch, and Owen and Abigail don't move. They stay on the side of the chasm like everyone else. Then the lightning picks up and changes color and the whirlpool begins to swirl faster.

"Back up!" I shout.

We back up, against the river of water we came through, but it won't allow us to reenter. Then the teeth form in the center of the whirlpool and the head appears and lashes out of the water. It snaps its mouth for a kid on the edge of the chasm, but somehow the kid manages to get out of the way, scrambling and falling backward.

The monster is not satisfied. It snaps its jaw again. Owen says something to Abigail, something she must not like because her eyes go wide and she shakes her head and backs up. Owen scowls and pushes her away. Then he runs for the monster, getting directly in the path of the gaping mouth. Its teeth close over Owen, swallowing him whole. I don't breathe. He's there and then he's gone, disappearing in the monster's mouth and under the whirlpool.

Abigail screams and runs directly for us. She's wearing the same flowing white dress like she had on in Simulation Avine. Its billowing skirt flows out behind her like an apparition.

"Please help me!" she shouts. She's ugly crying and screaming and I can hardly understand a word of what she's saying. It sounds like a hysterical mix of begging and cursing and praying to a god who just stole her only reason for living away from her in the most gruesome way possible.

I can't take my eyes off her or the spot where Owen was. In the chasm, the water calms, returning to the smooth swirling. The lightning resettles to blue and purple.

"Shit," Taylor says. She reaches toward her belt, for a weapon that isn't there. Abigail is almost to us. Her face is streaked with makeup, dark lines that trail from her eyes down to her chin. Her dress now clings to her legs in spots from the moisture in the air.

"Don't hurt her," Hudson says, stepping forward, in front of Taylor.

"Why not?" Taylor says. "She's been helping Owen." She clenches her empty hands into fists. Even without a weapon, I think she could destroy any one of us barehanded if she wanted to.

"She's deluded," Hudson says. "She doesn't know what she's doing."

I'm not sure that's entirely true. Abigail has been hurt, maybe more than any of us, but that doesn't excuse her seeing Owen trying to kill us and siding with him. But flashes of Taylor killing Dominic return to me. Stabbing him over and over again until he lay motionless back in the labyrinth. As much as I despise Abigail, I can't have that happen.

Abigail falls to the ground. She throws her head into her hands and sobs. "Help me, please!" She claws at my heavy boots with her hands. Her fingernails are painted cherry red, perfectly manicured.

I can't stand this girl. Can't stand anything that she represents. But I also can't turn my back on her.

"How do we get past this monster?" Cole demands.

Abigail keeps sobbing and begging us to help her.

"How?" He reaches down like he wants to get her to look at us, but aside from grabbing her by the back of the head, she's not moving. And Cole is not the kind of guy who's going to do that.

Taylor has no such worries. She grabs a huge handful of Abigail's blond hair and yanks on it, pulling her head upward.

"Tell us how to get through this zone now," Taylor says.

"I don't know!" Abigail wails.

"Last chance," Taylor says.

Abigail shakes her head and continues crying. Snot mixes with the makeup turning her face into an official disaster zone. Then the lightning begins to change color again and the swirling of the water picks up.

Taylor lets go of Abigail's hair, causing her head to fall back down. "Feed her to the monster."

"No! I'll help you!" Abigail shouts.

The lightning is bright orange and yellow and increasing in intensity with every second that goes by. Any second now the monster is going to strike. I press back, pulling Cole with me, toward the unbreakable wall of water behind us. We can't be eaten by this monster.

"How do we get past the monster?" Taylor asks Abigail. "Last chance or I throw you in."

The teeth are forming. Down the shore of the chasm, kids shout and try to run. They press up against the wall of water. There are more of them now. More food for the monster.

"You don't," Abigail shouts, pointing at the swirling water which nearly reaches the top of the chasm.

"What do you mean, we don't?" I demand.

"You can't get past the monster," Abigail says. "There is no way past it. That's what Owen said."

There has to be a way past it. If there's not, then we're trapped in the zone forever.

But then Raven's words return to me. *You have to drink from the pond whether you want to or not. It's the only way through the zone.* This has to be the same. Owen had gotten in the path of the monster, almost like he was giving himself up as a sacrifice. Except Owen would never do something like that. He'd never sacrifice himself to save anyone. He'd only do it if it was the thing to do. If someone gave him that information.

If there is no way to get past the monster, then the only thing to do is . . .

The teeth jut up from the water, ready to feast.

"Jump!" I shout.

Cole looks at me like I'm crazy. Maybe I am crazy. But I also know that I can't let Owen get ahead, and if I'm right, then he already is ahead. I need to stop him. Understanding dawns on Cole's face. I leap into the air the same time he does. I glance back in time to see Taylor and Hudson running for us. They dive for the chasm, leaving Abigail behind. Then the jaws of the monster close over us.

XXX

AIR WHOOSHES AFTER ME, THRUSTING
me far into the gaping mouth of the monster. There's a sucking
sound like water being pulled down a drain. Darkness settles in. I
think to grab for Cole's hand, but I'm moving too fast. I scramble
around, trying to find something to hold onto. The surroundings
are moist and slimy, and my hands slip over them as I fall, down,
down. I twist around, slamming into one wall and falling farther.
The monster is like a giant snake with no end. Finally I land,
bouncing on a trampoline-like surface covered in slime. The wind
is shoved out of me on my landing, and I make a noise sure to
alert anyone nearby of my presence.

I can't see a thing. Even my heads-up display shows nothing
beyond a few symbols slowly scrolling across the screen.

"Hello?" I barely whisper.

There's only a groaning sound in reply. Then something lands
hard next to me, causing me to bounce back upward into the air.

"Who is it?" I ask once I land and my head resettles. My body
aches from the fall.

"Edie?"

"Cole?" I reach forward and find him, pulling him close to me. I wrap my arms around him, needing to know we're both okay.

"Into the monster?" Cole says. His mouth is close to my ear, warming me. "You thought jumping into the monster's mouth was a good idea?"

I can't help but laugh. "It was my only idea."

He pulls his head back then puts a hand on either side of my face. I still can't see a thing, but it doesn't take a genius to know he's looking right at me. "Nothing like thinking things through," he says. Then he kisses me, and without the light, it's even more delicious, like a kiss stolen.

It ends as someone falls on top of us.

"Ugh, that hurt!" Hudson shouts.

"You landed on my shoulder," I say. "How do you think I feel?"

He doesn't get the chance to answer before a final person lands on the ground.

"Taylor?" I say.

"You're crazy, Edie," Taylor says. "You know that?"

Crazy maybe. Okay, probably.

"At least we're all together," I say. I try to stand, but the ground is so soft that my knees buckle. It's like a bouncy house with all the lights out.

"Together in the belly of a monster," Hudson says. "And now we . . . ?"

"We get out of here," Cole says. Light erupts from the spot where he is, illuminating our surroundings. A ball of fire rests on his outstretched palm. His power, back to full force.

"Glad you're back," Taylor says. "Edie's other boyfriend couldn't make fire."

I almost snap out a retort, but then I catch the look on her face. She's trying to egg me on.

"Whatever," I say, acting like it doesn't bother me.

Taylor actually smiles. "Good, Edie. You're getting smarter."

"I was always smart," I say.

"School smart," Taylor says. "But that's not the only thing that matters."

How right she is.

"There's a path over here," Hudson says. He grabs Cole's forearm and angles the light to where he's looking. Slime drips down from above, falling on his short blond hair.

"This place is gross," Taylor says. She swipes the slime out of the way, but it gets all over her arm. She tries to wipe it on her pants, but the entire effort seems a bit futile.

"We're in the belly of the monster," Cole says. He holds the fire close to the slimy wall and rests his other hand on my arm. His crutch has not made the trip with him.

Instantly the ground begins to rumble. I fall to my knees, knocking into him and making him fall over, too. The light bounces around, creating shadows everywhere.

"This has to be the way out," Hudson says.

"Hudson's right," Cole says, standing again, using my arm for support. "And I don't think we should wait around to confirm it."

I meet his eyes, then I glance down at his missing leg. Without a crutch or a prosthetic, it's not feasible for him to go anywhere.

"Just a crutch," he says.

I shake my head. "You need your hands free. And we need the light."

Cole scowls, darkened by the shadows and his scar.

"Now's not the time to be stubborn," I say.

Taylor laughs. "It's always the time to be stubborn when you're Cole."

"Whatever. Fine," Cole says. "But it's temporary."

"Understood." Then I pull on the power and draw what I can

from our surroundings. There isn't much visible except for the slimy flesh of the monster. But a small bit of delving beneath it, and I find bone. Teeth and bone. I deconstruct the bone and create a prosthetic for Cole, attaching it where his leg ends beneath the knee. The monster is not happy with my pulling it apart. It begins to rumble again, but this time it doesn't stop.

"Now, you guys!" Hudson shouts. He can't run ahead because Cole has the only light, so Cole pushes forward and leads the way. The shaking around us continues. Maybe the monster is eating again. Maybe it's angry. Whatever the reason, we need to get out of here.

The corridor is narrow and leads ever downward, and all I can imagine is that it is some intestine, curling around. It has to come out. The basics of monster digestion are not what I want to think about. We plow forward, through the dark. The tunnel only gets narrower. Soon, we have to crouch down and walk single file. Still we press forward. And maybe it's my imagination, but the ground becomes more solid, the walls less slimy. The grumbling of the monster diminishes.

Then Hudson says, "Is that a light up ahead?"

Cole lessens the glow coming from his fireball, and sure enough, far ahead, down the corridor, there is definitely something bright. There is also dirt beneath our feet. Stones and rocks around us. Wherever we are, we've left the monster behind.

"Put it out," Taylor says, motioning at Cole's light.

Cole pulls his fingers together into a fist, and the fire goes out. We creep forward. If Owen is up there, it would be great to catch him by surprise. But when the corridor widens until it's wide enough for all four of us to stand next to each other, there is no sign of Owen. There is only a mountain with no sign of the top ahead.

"That's our way out," Cole says, pointing upward.

It has to be true. We traveled down the belly of the monster, far down. Now we need to travel back up. Owen is nowhere to be seen, but there are footprints that lead up the dirt-covered ground. He's gone ahead of us. We have to keep moving.

We find a stream and at the risk of it wiping our memories, we drink. There's no other choice. Without water, we could die. And I am not going to die. Not now. Not when we are so close. Then we set out, up the mountain.

Halfway up, we find a staircase carved into the rock. Instead of making our trek easier, each time I lift my leg to raise it to the next step, cramps form in my muscles. I don't know how long this can go on. How much more I can take. But I push through.

A mantra plays over and over in my mind. *Just one more step. Just one more step.* I can't stop now.

"How much longer?" Hudson says. Sweat covers us, and we haven't said a word for the last couple hours. Speaking has become too much of an effort.

"Soon," I say, trying to be encouraging but failing miserably.

"And you know that how?" Taylor says.

"I just know." It's a flat-out lie.

Keep going, the voice in my head says. *You're almost there. Your enemy is ahead.*

Owen is ahead. That is my enemy. One of my enemies. The list continues to grow. But it's enough to power me on. Whatever internal motivation the others use, I don't know. But when the peak of the mountain finally comes into view, I sink to the ground.

"Don't stop now," Cole says, pulling me to my feet.

I nod and wipe a few tears that have leaked out the corners of my eyes. I won't stop. Can't stop. And then we reach the top and look at what is on the other side.

XXXI

THERE IS NO VALLEY. NO OTHER SIDE of the mountain. No downward trek. Instead, the giant compass rose stretches before us. The world is black, and the edges and outlines of the compass rose glow in moving neon lights, like race tracks in a video game. I walk forward, toward the center. Eight different directions. The world shifts, and as we stand in the center, I can't tell which way we came from.

Then the center of the compass rose begins to rise, high into the air, as a column grows upward. We've reached the end of the zone. We link hands as the platform rises, and when it stops, we each collect the glowing symbols etched on the side of the column. Four segments collected. Four zones completed. The column vanishes and we're back in the middle of the compass rose. With eight paths, there is no way to tell which way is out.

"How do we get to the next zone?" Hudson asks, slowly spinning in a circle.

I bend down and look for the symbols that had been there before. Except this time, there are no symbols. Each direction

looks the same. Then near the end of one of the compass points, I see Owen.

"There he is!" I shout, pointing at Owen. With his dad helping him, he must be going the right way.

Hudson takes off first, but I'm right on his heels, knowing Taylor and Cole will follow. Blood pumps through my veins. The compass rose seems to grow as we run down the point, making the end seem farther and farther away, but eventually we reach it. Then the ground underneath me shifts and changes. The compass rose and neon lights vanish, leaving a sleek ground of pure black. In front of me is a flowing wall of silver.

"We made it," I say.

Nobody answers. I turn, but there is no sign of Cole, Taylor, or Hudson. There's also no sign of Owen.

"It's okay," I say to myself. "Move forward."

I lift my hand and press it into the waterfall of silver. The flowing metal morphs around me, pulling me in, closing me inside. I let out a deep breath. Four zones complete. Two more to go.

My heads-up display flickers and the silhouette of Chaos appears. He's more filled in each time, as if our getting closer provides him with strength to show himself. This time I can nearly see his face. His brown hair shadows it. His shirt is blue.

"Congratulations," he says. "You completed Zone Delta."

I say, "I'm ready for the next zone."

"You're not ready," Chaos says. "No one is ready."

I don't respond. It's only one more mind game. Another test I will not fail. I wait. Finally his silhouette disappears and words appear on the readout.

Choose one letter to assist in Zone Epsilon.

Listed thereafter is every letter of the Greek alphabet, even the ones that are no longer common, like Digamma and Sampi. I scroll through the list, trying to find a pattern when I notice there are a few of them missing. Delta. Iota. Nu, Epsilon. Another one, Pi, is there and then disappears, like they're being eliminated one by one.

There is no way of knowing what they mean. Another vanishes as I watch. Maybe it's not so important which one I get as long as I collect one.

I think about the generic code Zachary Gomez used to get us into this simulation. `Om1cr0n5`. I have no other reason to pick any of the letters. I think of it as a good luck charm. Then I select the Greek letter Omicron.

The remaining letters disappear, and the Omicron is transferred to my inventory. It's there along with the four pieces of the key. I'm almost through. The simulation is almost complete. But almost still means I could die. I can't let my guard down now.

The image of the concentric circles appears with four of them now shaded in green. I select the fifth circle, and the others dissolve. Then the silver waterfall in front of me pulls to the sides, forming my opening. I step through, ready for whatever is ahead. Except this is a lie. I am not ready for it. Maybe my luck really has run out.

Owen stands there, alone, looking out at an endless field of green grass. He turns as I pass through the silver barrier. I freeze the second I see him. But there is no turning back now. I ball my hands into fists, willing Cole, Taylor, and Hudson to appear.

"You're alone," Owen says. Then he actually has the nerve to smile at me. After everything, he's smiling.

"My friends are coming," I say.

Owen crosses his arms, making his muscles pop. "When?"

I glance back. The silver barrier is gone. There is only an endless sea of green behind us also. Please come, I think.

But the barrier doesn't appear and neither do my friends.

I bite my lip. "Soon." And I cross my own arms and try to look as confident as I can.

Five minutes go by. Neither Owen nor I say a word. But with every second I lose confidence. What if they don't come? What do I do then?

Finally Owen shakes his head and takes a step toward me. "It's just you and me, Edie," he says. "That's how it was meant to be. Don't you see that?"

I try not to let anything register on my face. I have to play this smart. Owen could easily try to kill me right here, right now.

"See what?" I say.

"This." He motions to me and then him. "We're supposed to get to the end together. The two strongest ones. The two with the most to offer. That's how it was always supposed to be."

He's not right. But I also know I need to pick my words carefully. My options are limited. I could try to kill Owen, but I could easily fail. My other option is to pretend to work along with him. It's far from ideal.

"I don't trust you," I say.

Owen actually laughs. "Good. I'd worry about you if you did."

He's so carefree, like he really believes this is all part of some great plan.

I glance out at the expanse of green grass. It looks calm and inviting. That, too, must be a lie. It has to conceal more. I have to move forward into the zone, but I don't see any way to get rid of Owen. There is not really anywhere else for him to go.

I nod out at the openness ahead. "I'm going that way. How about you give me a ten minute head start. That way we don't have to be together."

Owen's mouth drops open slightly. An act of surprise. "Why wouldn't we want to work together? We have so much of a better chance of surviving that way."

I hate that his words make sense. I don't want him anywhere near me.

"We can't work together."

"Why?"

His question hangs there in the air. I fumble for the right response.

"You're cheating, that's why," I finally say.

"Cheating? By getting help? And you're not?"

I hold my face still, trying not to show anything. "Why do you think I'm cheating?"

Owen laughs. "You're friends with one of the gods," he says. "That Zachary guy. He's been helping you this entire time. There's no way you would have been able to get out of the labyrinth if not for him."

I bite my lip. I don't want Owen's words to be the truth, but they are. There is no denying them.

"So what?" I say.

"So we work together. Out there."

I will Cole to appear, but nobody does. It's still just me and Owen. The minutes tick by. And what if Owen is right? What if this is one more trick of the simulation, separating me from my friends, making me work with my enemy?

"I'm coming along," Owen says. "Whether you want me to or not. So why don't we just be civil?"

Civil. Owen has tried to kill me. Tried to force himself on me. He is not a civil person. But I'd rather have him with me than behind me, waiting for me to let my guard down. Whether I want it to be or not, this is the best way. But the first chance I get, I'll find a way to stop him.

"Fine," I say, crossing my arms. "We work together."

A huge grin breaks out on Owen's face. A grin I used to think was so perfect. A grin I know now is filled with deceit. "Great, Edie. You won't be sorry."

I already am sorry.

I step forward into the grass. Immediately something skitters under my foot, making me jump back. I look down but don't see anything except grass waving gently in the wind.

"What?" Owen says.

I point downward. "There's something in there." Something hidden. The grass is here to cloak it.

Owen places one of his boots into the grass, stepping solid. "It's fine. You're imagining things."

Fire burns through me. I am imagining nothing.

I test it again with my foot, but this time nothing moves. Still, I did not make it up.

"Whatever," I say. If Owen doesn't want to be cautious, that's his issue.

"Just stay behind me if you're scared," he says.

Bullshit. I'm not scared and I'm not staying behind him. Even though I don't want to, I place my other foot also into the grass. Both feet are in. I am committed. I blow out a deep breath and take a step. Then another. Five more steps and I start to question if I really felt anything in the first place.

Then Owen says, "Shit! What was that?" He jumps and lifts his right foot into the air, swinging it around wildly, nearly bumping into me.

I freeze. "What was it?"

He looks down, studies the tall grass. "Something grabbed at my foot. I felt it through the boot."

I almost let a petty smile creep onto my face, but I don't need to. He knows that he should have listened to me.

"You told me so, right?" Owen says.

I shrug and blow out another breath. And then I see it.

Something black and red flashes through the blades of grass. I jump back, but my foot doesn't land on solid ground. Instead it squishes something big. It reminds me of stepping on a giant cinnamon bun, except it also makes a sickening crunching noise.

I look to Owen, but my eye catches on his leg. Crawling up it is some sort of black and red crab monster.

"It's on you!" I shout.

Owen freaks and swipes at the thing, but another one is attached onto his bare arm. I'm so distracted I don't notice the one crawling up my right leg until it's well past my knee. Its pinchers sink into my flesh, and I shriek.

I swipe at it, and the second it lands on the ground, I try to stomp on it. But the things are fast, and another one claws up my back. I swat at it, but when another pinches me in pain, I twist around too fast and fall off balance. Then I'm on the ground and covered in them.

I cover my face and try to get to my feet, but there must be twenty of the things on me. It cannot end this way. I try to stand and barely make it to one knee when Owen grabs me and yanks me to my feet. I twist and shake and fling the crab things off me until I'm finally free. My pants are torn where they had been attached, and the skin underneath burns.

Owen swipes at three crabs that claw at his knees and ankles. He's detached the one from his arm, but blood drips down to the grass, creating a frenzy beneath him.

"Run!" I shout.

We take off, running through the vibrant field. The crab monsters swipe out with pinchers dripping with venom. The grass is alive. We run faster, and the world becomes a blur. The grass grows thicker, and burrs stick to my legs, but I keep going. If I stop for even a second, I will die. I don't question this. It is fact. I dare to look forward, for the end to the grass, but everything is green. It's only when I no longer feel anything brushing against my legs that I finally look down.

The grass is gone. The ground underneath our feet is green, the same color as the grass, like it's been put in place as some sort of optical illusion. But it's only hard rock, green to look like grass, but solid and smooth.

I stop running and bend over, placing my hands on my knees to catch my breath. I did it. I got across the boundary to this zone. But then I remember that I didn't do it alone.

I hate it. I hate every second of it. But I'm also not too proud to acknowledge the truth.

I look over to Owen. His face is red, his skin is splotchy, and he's also breathing hard. "Thanks," I say.

"No problem."

Simple. Straightforward. He's not even a jerk about it.

"What do you think is ahead?" he asks.

I straighten up and look forward, across the new zone. Zone Epsilon. The ground where we stand is solid green and hard, like smooth emerald formed here when the zone itself was created. Beyond that are four large stripes each extending away from us: Red, black, green, and yellow. They're each so wide that they encompass the entire horizon ahead.

"I don't know," I say. My brain fights me. I don't want to work with Owen, but I also know that I have to. It's the only way. And maybe the Greek letters we chose before entering have something to do with whatever is ahead.

"What letter did you pick before you got in here?"

"Iota," he says. "You?"

"Omicron."

"Any idea what it means?" he asks.

I shake my head. "Can you ask your dad?"

And like it's no big deal, Owen says, "Maybe." He presses a

finger to either of his eyebrows and his eyes focus on his heads-up display. But the focused look is soon replaced by one of frustration.

"What's up?" I ask.

He pulls his fingers away from his eyebrows. "My dad's not answering."

"Why not?" I ask.

Owen's face is half worry/half annoyance. He tries again. And again. And the normal confidence that fills his eyes is missing.

"He's not responding," Owen says. "He's always answered right away."

Something must have happened to him.

"Maybe he's busy," I say, though the words sound false to me. I think the better guess is that Owen's dad got in above his head. He destroyed the memory banks. He cheated in the simulations. He hacked in when the gods didn't know. He pried into the business of the gods, but maybe he underestimated them.

Maybe we all underestimated them.

"What do you know about Chaos?" I ask.

Owen shakes his head. "Just that he's the last of the old gods. Kind of surprised my dad when he found out. He thought all the old gods were dead."

But they weren't. And possibly Chaos discovered Owen's dad messing around with his simulation and had done something about it. I haven't met Chaos, but I can't imagine any of the old gods happy to have a mortal, like Owen's dad, messing around in their business.

"We need to keep moving," I say.

Owen taps his eyebrows again. "Let me try one more time."

I let him try, though I know he'll fail. Owen's dad must have been eliminated. Owen is alone.

It doesn't work. But Owen, instead of looking defeated, is filled with a new confidence.

"It's okay," Owen says. "He never helped me in the labyrinth. I don't need him here."

I almost point out that Owen would still be in the labyrinth simulation if his dad hadn't pulled him and Abigail from it, but I keep my words to myself. The more I appear to ally myself with Owen, the better my chances of survival.

"We have four choices," I say. "Red, green, black, and yellow." I start toward the colored stripes, walking until I'm only about ten feet away. I stand at the split between the green and the black.

"They're like lanes," Owen says.

Lanes. It reminds me of a racing game. Lots of racing games have the same end point and a few different tracks the player can take to reach the end. Each track is easier and harder in different ways.

"We need to pick one and take it," I say.

Owen seems to consider our choices, looking from one to the next. "You know whenever we had a choice before, Abigail would always pray for the right answer."

"Abigail's not here," I say. As far as I know, she's still on the edge of the chasm, afraid to jump into the gaping mouth of the monster.

"It used to work better before," Owen says, almost like he hasn't heard me. "But then she took the lightning. Since then, the gods don't seem to be answering her."

That's because by taking the lightning she killed the very god who was helping her.

"We don't need to pray to some god for answers," I say. We can figure it out."

The side of Owen's lips curl up. "That's what I always liked about you, Edie. You were always so confident in being able to figure things out. You never once doubted yourself."

I bust out laughing before I can stop myself. If Owen only

knew the truth. I have doubted myself so many times I could never count.

"What?" Owen says.

I shake my head. "Nothing." Then I look back to our choices. Red is on the far left. Next to it is green, then black, then yellow. Each stripe is easily one hundred feet across. Each is plain and simple with nothing to distinguish it. I think through each choice. Yellow: it's normally associated with caution. Red: it's most likely to be danger. Green: Full ahead . . . unless it's a trick. And black: the very absence of all color. The one with no meaning. It could be our best bet.

"Black," I say pointing to the dark stripe before us.

"Why?" Owen asks.

I fix my mouth and stare him in the eye. I don't want to explain my logic to Owen. I try to figure out why. If it's pride, then that's all the more reason to tell him my thought process, because what if I am wrong? There are no second chances. Not anymore. I already used up my reset. So I go through my thoughts, and as I do, he slowly nods.

"Absence of color," he says. "Good thinking. Let's do it."

I don't want to feel relief that he agrees with me, but inwardly I do. I don't let it show on my face.

"Great," I say. "Let's not waste any more time." Then I start for the entrance to the black track ahead.

XXXII

THE SECOND WE STEP FOOT ON THE black track, the rest of the zone vanishes. Huge walls go up on either side of us, blocking out red, green, and yellow. The walls are black, but images of outer space begin to spin by on them, like we're moving forward in space, and they are here to help make the illusion feel more solid. Five steps forward, and the ground behind us begins to rumble.

I turn in time to see the ground disappearing, crumbling away into whatever is below. It forms a gaping hole, and it's coming right for us.

"Run!" I shout.

I take off forward on the black track. There is no choice. No chance to be cautious. My feet pound on the hard ground, but the rumbling only gets louder. I'm not going to make it. Next to me Owen runs as fast as me. It's no use.

The falling ground catches up to us, then my next step comes up empty. I fall into the opening. I scramble with my hands trying to find some hold, but there is nothing to hold onto. But

instead of falling downward, I stop and hang there in the midst of the stars and galaxies. It's like we're so far out in the middle of nowhere that the pull of gravity on us doesn't exist. I watch the rest of the black track collapse, turning into floating space debris around us. Then there is no way to distinguish one way from the next. Everything looks the same.

"Which was do we go, Edie?" Owen asks. His face is unsure, and it almost brings me joy. How nice it must have been for him to just ask Abigail to pray their way out of any situation or to call in for some help from his dad.

I move my arms, and against the laws of physics, I spin around, like there is something out here to move me. There is no sign of the black track anymore. No planets nearby. No star that seems any closer than any other. There is only me and Owen and outer space.

I call up the menu on my heads-up display, looking for some kind of hint as to what we're supposed to do. But the only selection available is HELP, and when I select it, a single message flashes on the screen.

FIND YOUR WAY THROUGH TO THE END OF
ZONE EPSILON.

Not terribly useful given that it's information I already knew.

"You see that, Edie?" Owen says. He's pointing off toward something in the distance. Maybe a planet or an asteroid. There are lots of them around, gently floating like we are.

"Not specifically," I say. It's hard to know exactly what he's pointing at.

He comes closer to me, such that our line of sight is the same. "There. Right where I'm pointing. The little speck. It's kind of blue."

I narrow my eyes and attempt to see what he's pointing at. Sure enough, among the moving objects is one that is not moving. "It's blinking a little. Is that the one you mean?"

He nods. "Okay, I know this is completely dorky, but my dad used to watch this space show. I didn't watch it with him because come on? How nerdy is that? But if you lived in our house you couldn't help but catch an episode here and there."

Nerdy or not, I've watched plenty of space shows in my life, seeing as how I used to want to be an astronaut.

"What about it?" I ask.

He grins. "Well, there was this one episode about something called a wormhole. And I think—"

As soon as he says it, I get it. And I can't believe I didn't think of it. I was too busy looking for some sort of puzzle for how to get to the end of the zone.

"You think it's a wormhole," I say. The heads-up display had said, "Find your way through to the end of Zone Epsilon." Through. That's the word that mattered. We have to go through the wormhole.

"Exactly," Owen says.

We start out, moving through space toward the flickering blue object. In the vast area of space, it's the only one that is staying in the same place, like a beacon drawing us in. Owen and I stay side-by-side because I know it can't be this easy. Something will try to stop us from reaching our destination. But as we continue on and nothing attacks, I get less sure of this.

"Didn't you ever want to be an astronaut?" I ask Owen. He'd mentioned watching the space show like it was something to be embarrassed about. But we both grew up right near Cape Canaveral. Everyone I knew wanted to either be an astronaut or work for NASA.

"Well, sure," Owen says. "When I was in elementary school.

Who wouldn't want to be? But do you realize how much math and science you have to take when you're an astronaut?"

"Duh," I say.

He laughs. "Yeah, well I didn't. But once I found out, that was a no-go for me."

He's smiling, but he almost looks embarrassed about it. It's so different that the expressions I saw him wearing back at school. "Why are you so against math and science?" From what I've seen of Owen, he's actually pretty smart. He just doesn't like to work very hard. His skills seem to be getting other people to do work for him. Like me. Abigail.

He shrugs. "Are you kidding? My dad was always trying to shove it down my throat. Him working at that gaming company. All he wanted was a kid who liked the same nerdy things as him. But the more he forced me to practice math or program or anything like that, the less I wanted to. I think he finally gave up trying when I was a sophomore. He still forced me to take computer science, but he stopped nagging me about giving a shit about it."

It's actually kind of funny how different Owen and I are. I had begged my parents to let me take programming courses at FIT over the summer because the ones at the high school weren't enough.

"Anyway, I don't think either of us are becoming astronauts," Owen says.

Given the state of the world and how much repair needs to be done, he's probably right.

The stars and galaxies pass by, but as we get deeper, a stream of data appears and begins to take shape. I've seen it before.

"You recognize that?" I ask, pointing at it. It swirls from a source, spiraling out like a work of art. I tilt my head and music fills my ears, like a symphony composed to go along with it.

Owen looks to where I point then nods. "The Creators."

"Yep. They're destroying the world to create this stuff," I say.

"They're not destroying the world," Owen says.

"Have you seen the world?" I ask.

"I don't need to."

Which means he hasn't. I try to explain what I saw when Taylor and I had gone back to Florida, from the destruction to the dead crawling from the earth.

"You're being overly dramatic," he says.

Overly dramatic? My blood almost boils inside me. Who is Owen to tell me I'm being overly dramatic?

I stop moving and spin to face him. "You haven't seen it, Owen. I have. And let me tell you. It sucks. Everything is gone. Everything we knew growing up. The beach. The ocean. It's been turned into ruin. And I can't believe you would do that."

"I would do what?"

"Destroy the world. I mean, I know you're kind of an asshole, but I can't honestly believe that you think that's the right thing to do."

Owen looks at me like I'm missing an important part of my brain. "What do you mean? I'm not trying to destroy the world."

Does he really believe himself?

"Yes, you are. You told me you are."

He shakes his head. "I'm not going to destroy the world."

I cross my arms. "You said you were going to. If you got the key."

"No," Owen says. "What I said was that the world needed to change. Needed to be different. And to make any changes, some things have to go."

"That's destroying the world."

"That's reshaping the world," Owen says. "Can you honestly say that everything is perfect and great in the world? Would you seriously not want to change anything?"

"No. I would put it back just how it was," I say. "And I would let it take care of itself. It's not my job to decide how things should be."

Owen laughs. "Not your job? Then whose job is it? The old gods? Chaos? Don't you see? They're the ones who have been messing up everything to this point? You think humans just made all these messes themselves? Even after all this? No. It's the old gods. They played all sorts of games among themselves, and if the world or humans happened to get in the way, oh well, so be it? That's why we're here. The old gods are dead."

"Not all of them," I say.

"Almost all of them," Owen says. "And once the final one is gone, it will be up to us to make the world a better place to live. I'm not going to just settle for how things were. I'm making it better."

"You're going to ruin things," I say, trying to ignore what he's saying. But the thing is that Owen is right, at least about the old gods. If I've learned anything so far it's that the gods love playing games. The world had plenty of problems, and I am willing to bet that the gods were involved in many of those problems. But I don't want to admit to Owen that I might agree with anything that he says.

"Look, Edie," Owen says. "When we get to the end, no matter how this works out, all I'm saying it that it's your responsibility to step back and at least consider all the options. That's part of having power. You can't just believe everything that other people say. You have to listen to everything and make decisions on your own."

I push away his words. Or I file them away in the recesses of my mind. "We need to keep going." And I set off, back in the direction of the wormhole. I don't look at what the Creators are making, because all it signifies to me is the world that is being destroyed.

We're getting closer to the wormhole. We pass through a huge open area but then we stop, and here I realize what our true enemy is in this zone. The easy part is behind us. We're now at the edge of a field of asteroids. They move erratically, bouncing into each other, shattering. Somehow we need to cross them.

XXXIIII

THE ASTEROIDS MOVE FAST, BOUNCING into each other, sending shards of rock everywhere. A small rock hits me on the shoulder, cutting into my skin. Blood wells to the surface. But instead of making me want to run away, it only reaffirms to me that I have to get past this. If it was easy, everyone would be able to do it.

Everyone . . .

How many of us are left? From what I've seen, there are still plenty of us remaining in this simulation.

The thought hangs there in my mind. This whole time I have been sure that I will get the key, get to the end. But in every zone thus far, we've each collected the piece of the key, because the only way to leave a zone is to collect the key at the end of it. In my mind, I'd always figured this meant that each level would eliminate more and more until at the final level, only one was left. It was a truth I hadn't wanted to face. But what if it isn't the truth at all?

"You've collected the pieces of the key so far, haven't you?" I ask.

"Of course," Owen says.

He doesn't ask if I have. He knows the answer. Thus far, I have. So has Taylor, Hudson, Cole. Most likely Abigail.

I'm about to ask him about Abigail when a ball of fire flies through the open space and hits one of the asteroids, careening it off course. It lurches forward and comes directly for us.

"Come on," I say, and I grab Owen's arm and drag him into the field of asteroids.

We balance and land on one of the larger asteroids. Then I realize I'm still holding his arm. Immediately I let go.

I'm sure Owen will make some comment about me grabbing hold of his arm, but instead he looks in the direction the fire ball came from.

"What was that?"

Meaning he doesn't know about the person who's been hunting us this entire time. Unless he's trying to trick me.

"Don't act like you don't know."

"I don't," Owen says, but then a different asteroid hits into ours, sending it flying. We're still pressed against it, but it spins, and if we stay where we are, we're going to be smashed into one of the giant rocks.

I push off the asteroid and aim for a different one deeper into the field, but I overestimate how much force I need and slam into it. My hands scrape along the rock as I try to get hold. When I finally do, I don't have time to relax. Another asteroid is coming.

From one to the next, Owen and I cross the asteroid field. We're almost out when a huge rock hits me in the back, knocking the wind out of me. My face slams forward onto the asteroid I'm pressed against. Stars spin in my head.

"Are you okay?" Owen asks. He pulls my head back and turns it to face him. "Shit, that's a lot of blood."

There is actual concern in his face. True concern. And I hate it.

I don't know if it's real or if he is faking it to trick me into believing him more. I push away the pain. There is plenty of time for pain and recovery later. If I let up now, I will die, and Owen will be the one to get through. Alone.

"I'm fine," I say, and I launch off the rock, heading for the edge of the asteroid field.

We battle through the field of asteroids. Owen nearly gets crushed by three of them closing in together. One of the fireballs comes within four feet of me. I lose sight of Owen twice as the giant space rocks move around, blocking our path, keeping us from the end. There are more and more the deeper into the field we go. Just when I'm sure we can't avoid them anymore, we pass through an invisible barrier of space and leave the asteroids behind.

Owen is there, about twenty yards away, and we meet in the middle. And ahead of us is the glowing blue mouth of the wormhole.

"Edie, your head," he says.

I put my hand to my forehead. It comes back covered in blood. I can worry about it later, once we're through.

"It's fine."

"You sure?"

I glare at him. "Can you stop that?"

Confusions clouds his face. "Stop what?"

"Stop acting like you care."

His face shifts the smallest amount and fills with . . . hurt?

"Why is it so hard to believe I care?" he asks. "Why do you hate me so much?"

Blood rushes through me. This. I knew it was coming, even though I never wanted it to.

I glare at him trying to send my anger directly into him. "You tried to force yourself on me. Don't you remember that?"

He shakes his head. "I . . . I know, Edie. And I'm really sorry. I don't know why I did that."

I know exactly why he did it. He's a sociopathic liar. He can't possibly believe himself.

I harden my gaze. "And then in the labyrinth. You tried to kill me. And in Simulation Avine. You and Abigail. With her lightning."

"That was her," Owen says. "Not me."

"You were with her," I say. "And then you actually have the nerve to act nice? To act like you didn't try to force yourself on me? To act like you don't want to kill me?"

The muscles in his face shift around in an internal struggle. "Edie . . . sometimes it's like someone else is in my brain, telling me how to act. It's like I'm only standing back and watching. Maybe I did those things."

"You did," I say.

He nods. "Yeah. Okay. But I didn't want to. And what I really want is to act like they never happened."

I press my lips together and try to calm myself because rage is seriously threatening to boil outside of me. "You can't act like they never happened," I say.

A few moments pass before he says anything. He tries to process my words. Tries to deny them. But I will not back down from them. I am never going to ignore what's happened.

"Then what can I do?" Owen asks. His voice is soft. Not pleading, but filled with a quiet resignation.

I want to tell him there is nothing he can ever do. That his past defines him. But I've done things that I've regretted before also. Not to the same degree, but still, there are choices I would change, given the chance.

"You can try to do better," I finally say.

Deep down, I know Owen will never do better. It's not who he is. He may think he wants to change, but I don't think he really does.

"I can do better," he says, balling up his hands into fists. "I will do better."

I don't believe him. But a small part of me wishes his words were true.

I look away from Owen, back to the wormhole.

"You ready?" I say, ready to leave this other discussion behind us in the field of asteroids, wishing it could get crushed to nothing.

He blows out a long breath. "Yeah, I'm ready."

And we move forward into the blinking mouth of the wormhole.

XXXIV

THE BLUE SUCKS US IN. ONCE INSIDE,
there is no thought of turning back. The sides fly by in a stream
of endless moving shapes and colors. Other zones. Other simulations. There are hints of all of them. A giant wooden horse. Metal
spikes filled with games that try to draw me back. A river of lava.
It's all there. And then it's gone and we're through the wormhole
and on the other side.

Space is gone. We're back on a ground of black glass, one of
the tracks of the simulation. Off to the sides are the other color
choices we could have taken. Red. Green. Yellow. They angle in
together and come to a point, and where they meet, a giant column rises from the ground.

"The key," I say, and we both take off running. I don't see any
chance that Owen won't get the key also. And maybe that is how
it was always meant to be.

When we reach the column, Owen stops and grins at me. He's
forgotten our conversation already.

I haven't and never will. But I smile back and act like we're

friends. Like we're in this together. Because having him believe that may be more valuable than him knowing that I will never trust him.

We step up to the column and the ground begins to rise. The four colors of the track fill the sky in solid stripes like a reflection of what is below. But when the platform we stand on stops moving and we come to the top of the column, unlike before, there are no glowing symbols to collect. No piece of the key.

"Edie?" Owen says, slowing walking around the perimeter of the column. "Where's the key?"

I do the same, trying to find it. But aside from the carvings on the column, there is nothing. No symbols. Nothing to collect.

Nothing to collect.

"Wait," I say. "That's it."

"What's it?"

I scramble through my inventory and transfer the letter Omicron to the forefront of my heads-up display. Instantly a menu item appears.

      TRANSFER ITEM?
    »   YES
    »   NO

"Omicron," I say. "It's what I picked."

I select YES on the heads-up display, and immediately a string of silver glowing symbols appears on the column. It's the fifth piece of the key. I transfer them quickly to my inventory, and the second I do, they vanish from the side of the column.

"Wait, I didn't get them," Owen says.

I shake my head. "Your Greek letter. Grab it from your inventory and transfer it to the column."

Owen does what I say, and a different set of symbols appears there on the column. I try to mentally capture them, but they're gone before I can.

"I got them," he says.

Logic pushes at my mind. If there were various Greek letters to use to grab the pieces of the key, and if Owen and I chose different letters, then there is a very likely chance that the string of symbols we collected here are different.

And both necessary.

"Share your symbols with me," I say.

Owen laughs, and immediately whatever invisible wall that was weakened goes back up between us. "No way."

"But they're different," I say. "And we need them both."

Owen crosses his arms. "Maybe. But I'm not sharing with you. Why don't you share your symbols with me?"

The thought is laughable. And also makes perfect sense. I don't trust Owen and he doesn't trust me, and yet we both have something the other one needs. Maybe each of the Greek letter options parses out a different part of the key. Maybe we need all of them.

A black path extends out from the column, and at the end of it, I spot the moving wall of silver.

"I'm getting out of here," I say, and I start forward, down the path.

"Come on, Edie," Owen say, catching up to me. "You have to let me see your symbols."

I step directly in front of the silver barrier. "I don't."

"But the key isn't complete," Owen says.

I know this. And I also know that it will be a problem . . . for both of us. But I'll figure that out when the time comes. I got the piece of the key I came into Zone Epsilon for. It's all I was able to get. And maybe it's enough.

"See you on the other side," I say to Owen. Then I press my hand to the silver barrier and it pulls me in.

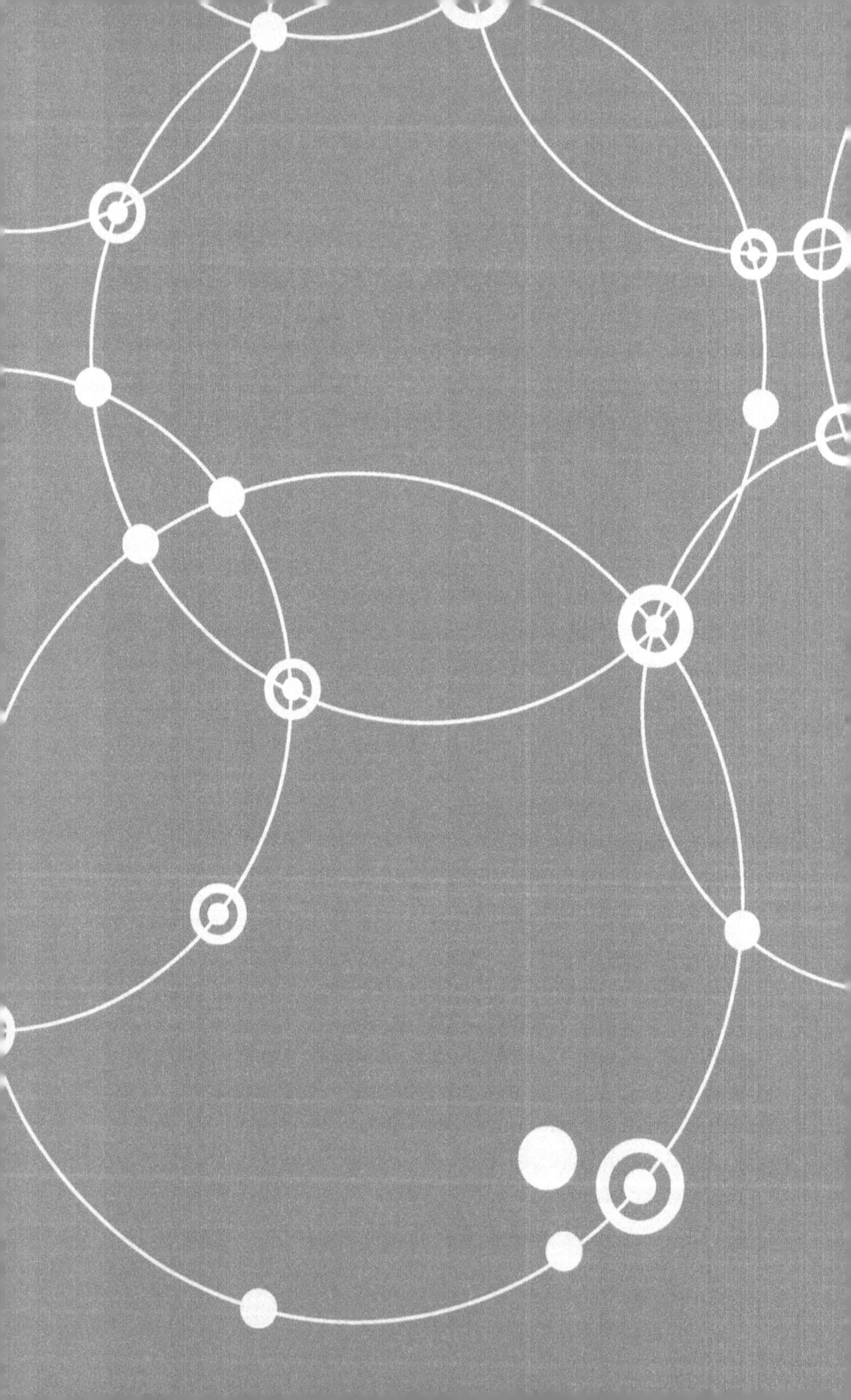

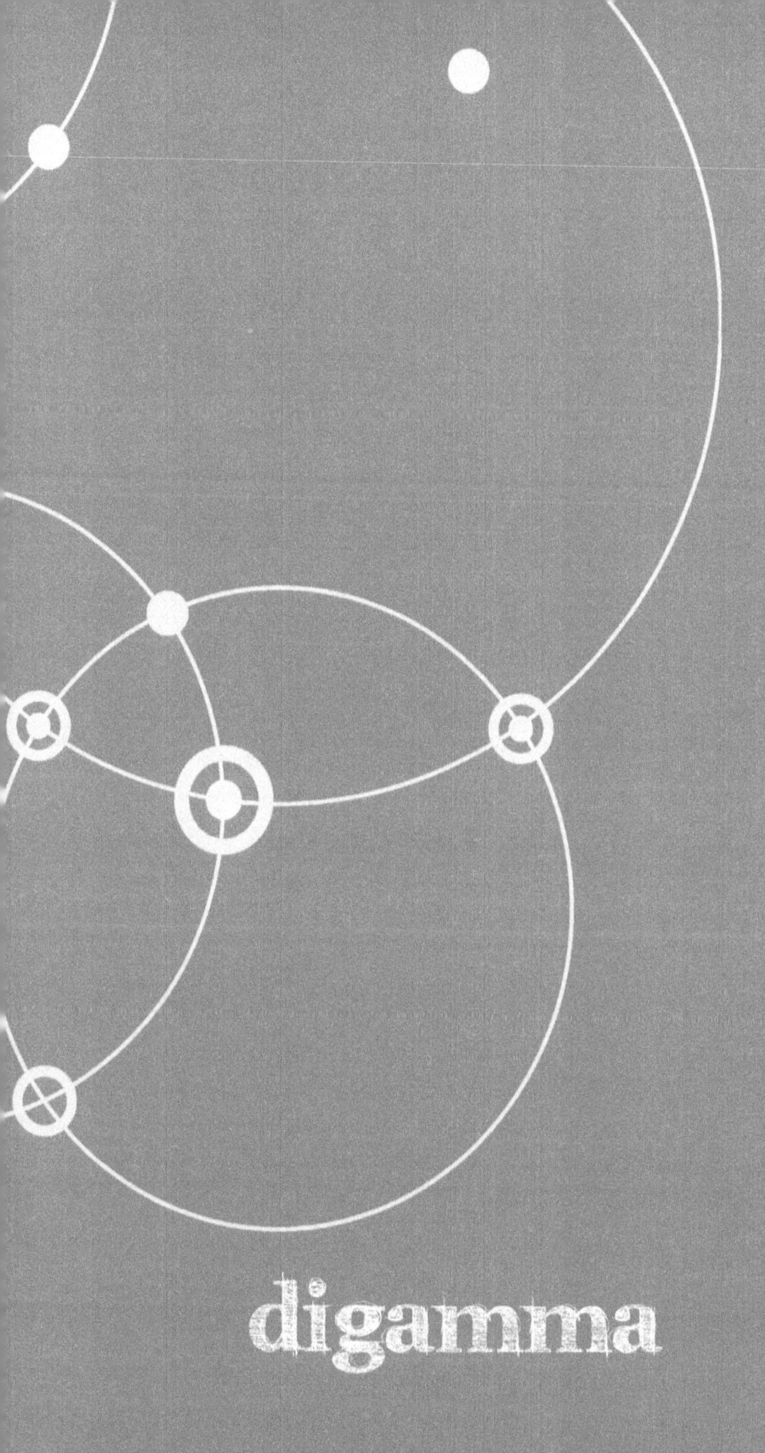
digamma

XXXV

THE SILVER BARRIER ENCOMPASSES
me and spits me out. There is no talking to Chaos between zones. No selection of the zone. No choices. There is only the transition.

This is Zone Digamma. The last zone. The hidden location of Main Control Room Alpha and no doubt of Chaos himself. Before I reach the control room, I'll have to face him. And if the prophecy is correct, I'll have to kill him. I've killed a god before. I have to hope that I'll be able to do it again.

I stand in a world of darkness. Far off in the distance, orange glows in the sky, flickering like fire hidden deep inside the earth. Hills and rough terrain make up the ground, and I stumble as I try to steady myself on uneven footing. From the sky hang black vines. They curl down and tickle my bare shoulders. They tangle in my hair.

I've seen this place before. In Raven's vision, I've been here. Thomas is here. I am more sure of this than I have ever been of anything in my life. I don't know why he's here, but after the vision, I'm certain he is. I have to find him, because if I don't . . .

No, I can't entertain any negative thoughts. But almost like the world knows what I'm thinking, a wave of terror rolls over me. Something is here, in this zone with me. Something that is determined to kill me.

I don't move. The wave passes through me and is gone. Only then do I survey my surroundings. The flickering orange sky illuminates shapes. Mixed in with the vines are black columns that stretch up as far as I can see. There must be a ceiling or some upward barrier, but with the vines climbing down, I can't see it.

I try not to make a sound as I step forward, and I call up my heads-up display to see if any options appear. There is only one.

Use Inventory Item

When I select it, the five pieces of the key are there. Nothing else. The apple and the power it holds is now a complete part of me. No longer part of my inventory. But just to make sure, I pull on it and feel the spark buried deep inside me. It helps calm the fear that washes over me.

I turn around, making sure no one else is here. It's only me. But when I look backward, the terror that rolled over me threatens to come back. I feel it like a sentient being. I can't give in to it. I turn slowly back around and try to figure out where I'm supposed to go.

I need to find Main Control Room Alpha. That's the goal. But if Thomas is here, I need to find him.

You'll never find him, a voice whispers in my mind. It's like a thought that drifts along in the air and implants itself in me.

I will, I think, and I step forward, starting my journey to the end.

I walk toward the nearest column and press my hand against it. Immediately it begins to glow orange. When I pull my hand back, the glow remains but fades little by little until it finally goes away. But it does light up the world around me. The ground, uneven, looks like it is made up of black stones the size of my fist. Each step I take, my ankles wobble and nearly twist. I have to be careful, because if I rush, I could easily sprain my ankle.

I access the heads-up display again, trying to find some way to communicate with Zachary or any of my friends, but there is no visible way to break out of the current subroutine: Use Inventory Item. I'm not ready to use the key.

I continue forward, pressing on the columns as I pass them. Energy seems to transfer between me and them, in both directions, as if somehow I am feeding them, and they in turn are returning that energy to me.

"Edie?"

I whip my head to the right at the voice. It's faint, but I know I heard it. Childlike. Filled with fear.

"Thomas?" I take a step in the direction it came from, but the vines immediately grow downward at my movement. They twist into my hair, holding be back.

I stop moving and listen again for the voice. There is nothing but the faint rustle of wind through the vines, making the leaves on them quake. But I know what I heard, and no one is going to tell me any differently. I yank my hair free from the vines and keep moving toward the voice.

"Thomas?" I say again. If anyone is around, they already know I'm here. My skin crawls at the thought, as if I'm sure I'm being watched. I press my hand to another column, lighting up the path I need to take. But I step wrong, and my knee buckles out from under me. I land hard on it, catching myself with my palms on the hard stones. One cuts into my hand, and pain erupts that radiates up my entire arm.

"Crap," I say to myself. Blood covers my palm. And in the

distance the howl of some kind of wild animal sounds. Then another. And another until an entire chorus of animals howl in the darkness around me.

I wipe my hand on my pants and look directly at my palm. It's nothing but a simulation. This all is. And with the power, I will the skin to heal over. I pull bits from other nearby areas, stretching them, and I watch as it knits together until the only sign left that I was hurt is the smear of blood. At the use of the power, a pulse of energy runs through me, reviving me.

You start to understand, a voice in my mind says. The voice of the ancient god—the giant snake—as if he is here, watching.

I seize hold of the power again and light every column as far as I can see. A path forms in front of me, and the rest of the dark world fades. I pick my way carefully down the path until I come to the end. A door stands there with nothing else around. A door in a frame. It's solid wood, painted black, and has a huge brass knob and knocker on it. I peek around behind the door but see only what I would expect, the continuation of the dark world. The path to nothing.

I have to go through the door. I place my blood-smeared hand on the giant knob and I turn it.

XXXVI

THE KNOB TURNS EASILY, AND I PUSH
the door open. The hinges don't make a sound. I expect to see
the same thing inside the door as what I saw on the other side:
the dark world with the black vines and columns. Instead, a lush
garden appears.

I step forward into the garden, and the door closes behind
me. When I turn, the door is no longer visible. There is only the
garden. My first thought is that it's the same garden where we
first visited, by the volcano. But little by little details let me know
this is not the case. The trees around me are filled with leaves of
all colors, but no fruit. The ground, instead of being soft grass, is
gravel, the color of bone. And the sky above is not blue but orange
and yellow, as if it's on fire.

A path leads forward and I start down it. That's when I hear
the singing. I stop moving and listen.

It's a female voice, but not the sirens. It's more like a church
hymn, with talk of God and grace and other uplifting things I've
never found comfort in. But here, in this garden, the words of

the song seem to dive into my chest and fill me with hope. I start walking again and when I come around the bend, there is Abigail standing at the edge of a pond as clear as crystal. Her dress is so white, it's like fresh milk. Her hair is wavy and cascades around her back and shoulders. She looks out at the still water and she sings, and even though I haven't made a sound, she turns as I walk into the clearing. Like everything else about her, her makeup is perfect, as if she hasn't faced any peril in the simulation at all.

"Edie, I prayed for you," she says.

He face is sweet and full of concern, and whatever is running through her brain for real, I honestly think that she believes she has prayed for me. I almost bite out a sharp response about how she was probably praying for my death. But I keep the thought to myself.

The important thing is that Abigail is here. That means the others could be here also. There's a really good chance of it.

"Have you seen any of the others?" I ask, not mentioning names.

She slowly shakes her head. "No. But I know where your brother is. God showed me."

I freeze at her words. I thought Abigail killed the god who was helping her, stealing his lightning and his power. And anyway, Abigail and her god have only helped Owen to this point. But I can't ignore this. If there is even a small chance she can help me find Thomas, I have to take it.

"Where?" I ask.

Abigail points into the pond. The water is so clear, it reflects back like a mirror. Like the mirrors back in the labyrinth, where Abigail had been trapped. Thomas could be trapped the same way. I have to get to him.

"How do you know?" I ask.

Abigail giggles like it's a silly question. "God showed me. I told you."

I bite my lip and try to believe her. "In the water?"

She smiles sweetly. "It's the starting point."

I glance back, willing Cole to appear. Or Taylor. Hudson. But it's just me and Abigail.

"I'll come with you," Abigail says. "Don't worry." She raises a hand. My first thought is that lightning is going to fly from her fingers and strike me. But instead she grabs hold of the golden cross necklace and smiles.

I don't need Abigail to come with me. I don't want her to come.

Without another word, I dive into the water.

The cold cuts into me like a sharp knife slicing each nerve in my body. I tense up and suck in water then try to cough it up as it hits my lungs. But I'm sinking fast, carried by my forward momentum. I scramble, trying to get back to the surface. Why had I jumped without even taking a breath? It was stupid. Another stupid mistake added to my list.

No, that's not right. Since when have I been negative? It's not me. It's like a voice in my brain that doesn't belong there.

You will fail, the voice says.

I pull at the water with my arms and finally manage to get myself to the surface. Water spews out of my mouth as I try to get air. Finally I manage to suck in a huge breath that restores my energy.

There's a small splash behind me. I turn just in time to see Abigail disappearing beneath the surface. Her white gown billows in the water behind her and then vanishes along with her feet.

"Crap." I take a deep breath and dive after her. I have to get to Thomas first. Her knowing where he is could easily be a trap.

The water is clear enough to see every small plant and fish. I spot Abigail in a second and follow after her, trying to ignore the cold. She swims like she's part mermaid, like the cold doesn't affect her. I want to wrap my arms around myself, but if I do that, I'll never keep up. So instead I pull through the water until I'm right behind her. I hold my breath and keep swimming even though as the seconds go by I don't think I can make it. I'm not even sure where I'm trying to make it to. And then I still have to get back to the surface, I'll run out of air. But as these thoughts are going through my mind, my head breaks through a giant bubble.

The weight of the water disappears, and I fall. I twist my body around and land on my feet, noting that Abigail does the same. Then she puts a finger to her lips and motions ahead.

We're inside an underwater bubble. Overhead the water ripples and fish swim by. The ground is covered in sand and small shells. I take a step and they crunch under my feet.

Edie? It's Thomas's voice again, but it's in my mind.

I nod at Abigail, and we set off toward an alley lined with rocks and trees. The air is warm and arid, and my skin and clothes quickly dry. The alley leads us forward and dumps us out at the edge of a giant circle.

Thomas is at the center, his hands bound, a blindfold covering his eyes. Standing next to him with a hand resting on his shoulder is a person cloaked in a black veil which covers their face. They reach up with a slim hand and pull back the veil. Sharp green eyes meet mine. It's Pia.

xxxvii

"EDIE, I'VE BEEN WAITING FOR YOU,"
Pia says. Her dark pixie hair goes out in every direction. Her green eyes blaze. Her voice easily carries across the giant circle to where Abigail and I stand. She tightens her grip on Thomas's shoulder, and he grimaces and lets out a small cry.

"Let him go," I say.

"No," Pia says. There is no question in her voice.

From somewhere else around the circle there's another voice I recognize. Cole.

"Come on, Pia," Cole says. "Let Edie's brother go."

I look for him and find him standing alone, leaning on a new crutch, the makeshift prosthetic gone. Taylor and Hudson are also there, but they stand elsewhere around the circle, as does Owen. We're all here. We've all made it.

"I won't let him go," Pia says. "Not unless Edie and you both agree to leave the simulation and not come back."

Pia's part in this is full of holes. I don't get why she would care that much. I haven't even seen her in Simulation Omega until

now. And her being here . . . she could have already made a run for the control room.

"What about me?" Taylor says. "Don't I need to leave?"

Pia laughs. "Please. He's not scared of you." But the second the words are out of her mouth, her face freezes.

She's said something she shouldn't have. More than one thing. Chaos must have placed Pia in the simulation in the first place, as a way to trick Cole. To stop him from ever entering Simulation Omega. Meaning Chaos isn't just worried about the prophecy. He truly fears it. Fears Cole and me . . . because of the power.

"You work for Chaos?" Cole says. "You actually work for him?" Betrayal covers his face. But if it's true, the little pieces begin to fall together.

Pia's pixie face twists into a smirk. "Of course. And I can't believe none of you ever caught on. Seriously Cole, I thought you were smarter than that."

The muscles of Cole's face pull together into hatred. "It's not about being smart, Pia. I wanted to believe you. I wanted to trust you. How long were you working for him? How long did you know?"

His unspoken question is if Pia knew what was going on before any of the simulations took place? And if so, had she deceived Cole the entire time, since they first met?

For Cole's sake, I want the answer to be no.

Taylor shifts her stance, ready to pounce. "Yeah, well, Chaos should be scared of me. He should be scared of all of us. Now let Edie's brother go or I will tear your head off." Her fingers flex, eager to fulfill her threat.

Power or not, I'm scared of Taylor. I will never, no matter what, cross her.

A sliver of hope appears in my mind. The fact that Chaos is worried enough about the prophecy and our power to kidnap my little brother is encouraging.

"I'm not letting him go," Pia says. "Not until Edie and Cole leave the simulation."

The thought is completely laughable. Even if she wasn't holding my little brother in her hands, I wouldn't leave. Leaving doesn't just end the simulation for me. It terminates me. Her here, threatening me only fuels my need to stop her. To stop Chaos. I'll find a way to get Thomas without playing by Pia's rules.

"I'm not leaving," I say. "And neither is Cole."

Pia must be expecting my answer. Maybe even hoping for it. She raises a hand. A giant fireball grows there, glowing with light. Then she throws it directly at me.

She's the one who's been hunting us. The final piece falls into place. Chaos brought her here to keep us out of the simulation, and once that was impossible, to kill us.

Abigail and I jump apart barely in time. The fireball smashes into one of the huge rocks that make up the alleyway behind us. Pia fires again. And again. Each time the fireballs get closer. Each time I evade them and look to make sure Thomas is okay. He's still clutched against Pia's side, like an appendage. He twists and tries to get away, but she is not letting him go.

Another fireball comes again. I dart to the side, but Pia shoots of another right where I'm moving to. I'm not going to make it. Then Abigail jumps directly in front of me, blocking the path of the fireball.

It hits her directly in the chest, electrifying her. But instead of killing her, she extends her arms outward and tilts her head back and absorbs it. Pia's mouth drops open in disbelief. Then in immediate retaliation, Abigail points her hand out at Pia.

"Stop!" I shout, but it's too late.

Lightning laced with fire flies out from Abigail's hand. It's going to strike Thomas and I'm going to have to watch him die. But

I'm not giving Abigail enough credit. It's a perfect shot, like it never had a chance of going anywhere else. The lightning strikes Pia directly in the chest.

Pia turns bright yellow, and sparks crackle off her, like a massive ball of electricity. Thomas falls to the ground, out of her perimeter. Abigail sends out more electricity, increasing the size of the barrier of lighting. Pia shouts but with the crackling of the lightning, I can't hear her. Her scream seems to go on for an eternity. Then Abigail pushes her hand out, palm forward, and shoots a ball of fire directly into the center of the mass of lightning.

Pia's eyes go wide just before the fireball hits. Then she collapses to the ground.

"Wait there!" I yell to Thomas and I run toward him. But the second my foot hits the inside of the circle, the entire thing lights up like a pie graph with a bunch of different segments, all different colors. A monster appears on the path directly ahead of me, a giant scorpion. It's keeping me from getting to Thomas.

XXXVIIII

THE SCORPION SPOTS ME AND CURLS its tail, poised to strike. Its pincers reach out, gripping and releasing in preparation to attack.

"Don't move, Edie," Cole says. I glance over quickly and see him facing off to a monster also, a giant ram with horns that curl around in spirals. It glows purple and pink, and smoke comes out of its nostrils.

Across from Taylor is a huge crab. Owen faces a giant of a man with a huge bow pointed directly at him. Hudson faces a lion. Each of us is here. And each faces a monster.

This is the final challenge. The test inside Zone Digamma. I have to get past the scorpion if I want to get to Thomas.

I pull on my power, but I'm shaking and it slips away.

Focus. I have to focus.

"Edie, it's like the zodiac, like Mom used to tell us about," Thomas says, his blindfold now discarded. His voice barely carries toward me as I take a step back away from the scorpion. But he's right. It is like the zodiac. Like each of us is facing off to a

different sign. Six of us so far.

Maybe that's it. I can jump to the next segment of the pie and dash around the scorpion. I run and when I'm close enough, I jump. The second I do, a giant jar appears, and water pours from the mouth of it. I barely have time to jump back into the piece with the scorpion before the water floods over the area where I just stood. It cascades in a never-ending stream. But the scorpion takes this moment to attack, and it comes at me, pushing me back. I dive under its pincers, hoping to get to the other side, but the tail blocks my path. I rush to the side instead.

It turns so quickly it's like a blur. Then it snaps out at me once more. Again, I dive underneath, and I'm back where I started. But I'm breathing hard, and the scorpion acts like we're playing a game. It has infinite energy, and if this keeps up, soon I'll be too exhausted to move.

"Don't you remember his nickname?" Thomas shouts.

Nickname. That's right. Mom gave each of the signs a nickname to help us remember them. To help remember their strengths and weaknesses. And Scorpio, just like every other sign, has a weakness.

What was it? My mind spins as the scorpion attacks again. I evade it . . . barely, then I rush to the edge of the circle and try to think.

Single-minded Scorpio. That was it. The scorpion is intense and focused, almost to a fault. And that fault is my only chance. I have to give it something to focus on. It's the only hope I have to defeat it.

Abigail has jumped to the next spot and now faces a huge goat. Whatever I do, I am on my own. We each are.

Focus.

I pull on my powers again, but with running away from the giant monster, they slip out of my grasp. I try again and get the same result. Taylor screams and runs for the crab. One of its claws grabs out for her, but she jumps, vaulting through the air, and lands on top of it. Cole has hold of one of the horns of the ram, but it's shaking its head and tossing him around.

I can't help them until I help myself.

The scorpion lashes out with a pincer. I jump back, then I edge closer to the water. It scrambles forward, closer to me. I move again. The spray of water hits my back. One more step and the water is going to sweep me away.

The scorpion inches again toward me. I pretend to fall, stumbling slightly, hoping it thinks I'm hurt. Then I take my eyes off it and look down. It's all I can do to not run. Though it feels like an eternity, it can't be more than two seconds that go by before the scorpion pounces.

I fall and roll over backward, changing direction so I'm moving away from the water. The scorpion hasn't thought it through like I have. Its forward momentum carries it directly into the path of the water. Instantly it's sucked away. The water moves so fast that it becomes a blur.

I get to my feet and run toward Thomas, and the second he's within reach, I grab him and pull him close to me.

"What are you doing here?" I ask as I hug him close. He shouldn't be anywhere near here. He should be safe in the data storage banks, back in the volcano. Or at least safe now that we've locked out any more potential intruders who would destroy the place

"Edie, stop holding me so hard." He struggles against my embrace, typical Thomas.

I give him a final hug and let him go, then I get down on one knee so I'm on the same level as him. "What happened?"

Tears well up in his eyes, but he presses his lips together like he's trying to be brave. "That girl was trying to hurt you, Edie.

Why was she doing that?"

There is so much required to answer that question. It's hard to even know.

"She didn't like me," I say.

Thomas sniffs and wipes at his eye where a single tear has managed to escape. "Well I'm glad she's dead."

I hope she's dead. Her charred body lies motionless not ten feet away. I'm not going any closer to it.

"Me, too." I ruffle his hair, wanting to hug him again. "What happened? Did you make it to Colorado?"

His eyes get really big. "I was, Edie. I was with Aunt Kathy. In the kitchen. Uncle Simon was outside. Then he just wasn't there. Then Aunt Kathy wasn't either. They were there and then they vanished. I don't know what happened."

They were put in storage. Uploaded to the memory banks before the world became a battleground.

"What about you?" I ask. I try to keep my voice steady because I don't want to freak him out.

"I don't know, Edie," Thomas says. "I was in the kitchen, and this giant snake came along and he talked to me. Talked to me for real. I know you don't believe me."

"I believe you," I say. "What did the giant snake say?"

Thomas gives me a small grin. "He said he was going to hide me where they couldn't find me. Then everything went dark, kind of like I was sleeping because I kept having dreams. But then I woke up and that mean girl was there and she took me to some kind of giant place with all these weird jars with things that moved inside. And she told me I had to stay there until it was time. I thought she was never going to come back, so I tried to leave. But I knocked over a few of the jars and . . ." His voice trails off.

"And what?" I barely ask. I realize I'm holding my breath, and

I suck in, getting fresh air.

"Edie, I know you think I make up things, but I swear I'm not making it up. But there were these gross slimy monsters and they tried to attack me and I killed them."

Killed them. I want to ask how, but Thomas keeps talking.

"Then the mean girl showed up again and she was really grouchy and she brought me here. And all scorpions aren't that big, are they?"

I can't help but laugh because even after what he's been through, somewhere along the line he's shifted back to being a normal seven-year-old kid.

"Let's hope it's only that one," I say.

Hudson rushes up then. "Did you see that?"

His voice is filled with as much wonder as Thomas's, almost like he's a little kid also.

"See what?" I ask.

"The lion," he says. "I demolished it."

"Good thing," I say. The alternative isn't very promising.

Cole and Taylor run up next, joining us. Owen stays away, on the other side of the inner circle.

"Do you think she ever was truly my friend?" Cole asks, walking over to where Pia's charred body lies unmoving.

The question could be asked about any of us. Who were we before we came into the simulation? Were we on Earth specifically for this purpose all along? Did we ever have a choice in the matter?

I dig deep, looking for the answer. Whether the gods had a part of our conception doesn't matter. I was a normal kid before this all started. I think back on what Cole told me about Pia, about her past. Being bullied. Changing schools. I can't believe that was all a lie. I'm not willing to believe it.

"Yeah, I think she was," I say, standing. I keep hold of Thomas's hand. "I think the simulation changed her." Like it changed all of us.

"Yeah, well I'm ready for this simulation to be over," Taylor says. "So show me Chaos and let's get this moving on."

There is a boom of thunder and a pulse of light that starts at the inner circle where we stand. Abigail comes running, latching onto Owen's arm. The burst of light rushes outward, and when it gets to the edge of the outer circle, everything outside of the zodiac circle vanishes.

A couple other kids begin to appear, spaced out on the circle. Rex, from the refueling zone back in Simulation Avine. Next to him is his twin sister, Amanda. Simone—Queen Simone—appears next, her short blond hair cut into a bob. Next to her is Damien, her guard and fellow-tormenter. They'd taken over the refueling zone and killed anyone who'd come there to get energy. The tall red-headed girl from the labyrinth appears next. I'd assumed she had died in the simulation, but maybe she'd only been trapped there. Now she's here.

A couple others appear, but nobody speaks. I don't know why they're here. I don't want them here.

Then something begins to grow from the center of the circle.

XXXIX

I GRAB THOMAS AND MANAGE TO scramble out of the way before the thing starts jutting upward, breaking the circle, spreading it farther apart.

It's a sharp spike, but soon details begin to fill in. Pink and black glass windows. Sharp angles made of steel. It's not growing. It's more like the ground far beneath us is being pushed up, and the circle we're in is making room for it.

The segments of the zodiac circle break apart, and long steel bridges stretch between them. Thomas and I are on one, but we're the only ones. Cole is in the next segment. He spots us and rushes across the steel bridge. The crutch catches on a gap in the metal, slowing him down, but he yanks it free, nearly snapping it in half, and gets across just in time.

I link my arm through his the second he's in reach, pulling him close.

Thomas stares at Cole like he's from another planet. But in fairness, Thomas has never met Cole. Never met any of my friends from the simulation . . . except for Owen back when we

were dating.

The building is still growing, reaching up so high the spike on top is nearly out of sight. Metal continues to groan.

"I've seen this before," I say. "It's the control room."

Cole nods. "I saw it, too. And we have the pieces of the key. We can get inside."

I doubt anything is going to be that easy.

I point to his crutch which is splitting and isn't going to see it through much more. "You need a new one."

He tosses it aside. The second it hits the ground, it breaks into two pieces. "I made that one in a hurry," Cole says. Then he reaches out for the power. Though he's the one using it, I feel a small pull inside myself, letting me know that they're linked. One power shared between the two of us. I watch as Cole pulls bits and pieces of the simulation around us into a new prosthetic attached at the bottom of his left leg. When he's done, it looks perfect, blended in almost seamlessly beneath the material of his pants.

"Nice job," I say, stepping back. Thomas is still right there next to me.

Cole bends at the knees a few times, testing out the feel. "It's not bad, I guess."

"You made that?" Thomas asks.

"I sure did," Cole says, ruffling the top of Thomas's hair. "Pretty cool, right?"

Thomas's eyes are wide. "Really cool. Can you make me something?"

Cole is about to answer, but instead he takes a step back and stiffens. It only takes me a second to realize the groaning of the building has stopped, the pink and black glass building stands fully formed before us at the center of the circle. But instead of feeling inviting, there is a force coming off it that I've felt before. Waves of terror pulse out from it, as if a malevolent entity is inside.

Main Control Room Alpha. We've found it. But we aren't the only ones here. Chaos is inside, waiting for us. There is no doubt in my mind.

"I think you should make me a weapon," Thomas says. He sounds so grown up in that moment, and I wish desperately that none of this had ever happened. That I wasn't in a situation where I would consider having to make him something to protect himself.

I squat back down. "What kind of weapon do you want?"

Thomas seems to consider this. "Maybe an ax." His voice is uncertain, no doubt remembering back at our house in Florida when we'd found my parents' ax. He'd almost killed me with it back then. But that was then.

"An ax sounds perfect," I say. Whatever is ahead, weapons for all of us is a really good idea.

xl

HUDSON AND TAYLOR JOIN US. COLE and I craft weapons, pulling from the surrounding structure to create them. Taylor gets a giant bow worthy of the one she lost in the labyrinth. Hudson gets something that looks like a Frisbee made of sharp metal that returns to him when he throws it. Cole makes himself a hammer. It's as long as his forearm and has a head as black as ink. But the best part is that when he spins it in a circle in the air, it renders him invisible.

"Nice thinking," I say, balancing the ax I've created in the palm of my hand.

Rex and Amanda join us.

"You found her," Taylor says, nodding her head at Amanda.

Rex puts his arm on Amanda's shoulder. "She was trapped in Refuel Zone Kappa. I went back. I got her out."

Amanda frowns and nods over to where Simone and Damien watch us. "I tried to kill them. I wanted to go back. But the world gate kept me away."

Maybe intentionally, I think. Maybe so more of us would be

here, now, at the end.

"How'd you get here?" Cole asks. He keeps an eye on Simone and Damien and clutches his hammer solidly, ready to attack.

Rex points to his temple. "The heads-up display. It alerted us that we could transport to a new simulation. That the old simulation would be shutting down."

This must have been when Iva opened the simulation up wide.

"So we went," Amanda says. "And now it seems like I'll get my chance for revenge."

I don't think seeking revenge on Simone and Damien is our biggest concern at the moment. It's Chaos that we need to worry about.

Cole and I make weapons for Rex and his twin, double daggers for Amanda and a long straight sword for Rex. Then Rex enables something via his heads-up display. Invisible armor pools over him, molding to his body. Either he brought it from the other simulation or he found it here. Maybe he has help from the gods also.

Harsh words float to my ears, and I look over to see Owen and Abigail arguing with each other. If I wasn't seeing it, I wouldn't believe it. It's got to be the first time I've seen her stand up to him and not agree with his every word and action. I try to listen in, but their words are muted though the anger on their faces is not.

"We're wasting time," Taylor says.

She's right. It's time to move.

I look down at Thomas. "Do not leave my side. No matter what. Okay?"

He nods. "Why would I?"

"You wouldn't," I say. "But I don't know what's going to happen in there. Just make sure you stay right next to me, always. Promise."

"I promise," Thomas says.

I look to the others. I don't have to say what I'm thinking. Look out for my brother.

Taylor nods, her eyes fierce. She knows what it's like to lose a brother. She won't let that happen to me. Then we start forward toward the control room.

The waves of terror increase the closer we get. It starts out as a force, like air that is trying to push me backward, but soon I'm shaking. Not a huge amount, but like I've been shocked and I'm trying to put it behind me.

This is such a bad idea. All we're going to find inside is death.

No. That's not me thinking. It's what this simulation wants me to think. It's Chaos trying to get into my mind. I don't have room for him in there. I push the thoughts away.

But no sooner are they gone, a new thought begins to form. Pia is inside, and I know the second we walk through the door, she is going to grab Thomas and kill him. I will watch him die.

No. That's not real either. Pia is dead. Chaos used her until she wasn't of any use to him anymore. And Thomas is not going to die.

One after another, with every step we take, the thoughts that pour through my mind get worse. Thomas dies. Cole dies. Hudson and Taylor die. Even the thought of Owen dying inside doesn't fill me with relief. Chaos is a common enemy. Owen and I can have our final fight after he is gone.

Finally we stand in front of the glass building. An invisible sun shines down from above, glittering off the pink and black glass windows. There is no door. There is only a huge panel that shimmers in a rainbow of colors.

Owen and Abigail join us. We don't speak. We stand there watching the panel. Then Simone and Damien join. Anger fills me the second she's near. But if anger fills me, it doesn't begin to describe what Rex and Amanda must be going through. Amanda visibly begins to shake, and Rex places a hand on her arm. He whispers something in her ear. I don't know what. I can't worry about it now.

The red-head from the labyrinth joins. A couple others I don't recognize. Over twenty of us stand there at the barrier to the control room. Twenty of us left. It's too many. Or is it enough?

Nobody moves. It wasn't supposed to be like this. But we have to get inside. I have to get inside. I pull up my inventory and I find the pieces of the key. I grab the first piece, and with my heads-up display, I select INTERACT on the panel.

Immediately the panel stops shifting in color and settles on solid red. I transfer the first piece of the key to it and the color shifts to orange. I select the second piece, but before I get the chance to use it, someone else transfers it to the panel. It shifts to yellow. Then the third piece and the panel turns green.

I see how this is going, so I select the final piece and I wait. The fourth piece of the key is transferred and the panel turns blue. It's time to act. I transfer the fifth and final piece of the key to the panel.

Nothing happens. At least not at first. The symbols sit there, in a row, just like I've transferred them. Then they begin to float around on the panel, spreading apart. But the color of the panel doesn't change. And if there is a door to Main Control Room Alpha, it is certainly not revealed.

"My fifth piece doesn't look like that," Owen says.

Abigail shakes her head, her long hair flowing around her. "Mine either."

"Also me," Taylor says.

One by one the truth is revealed. We each got a different code. And I worry about what that means. It could be that only one of them is correct. Only one of us will be able to enter Main Control Room Alpha.

Logic filters into my mind, trying to make sense of the situation. *IF-THEN-ELSE.* If I got a piece of the key, and if it is not the same as anyone else's piece of the key, then . . . I don't know. But we need to find out.

I lean over and whisper to Cole. "Put your fifth piece on there also."

He nods and transfers his piece of the key to the panel. The symbols are definitely different than mine, and they do the same thing, floating apart, but changing nothing. One by one we each transfer our fifth piece of the key to the panel. Abigail. Hudson. Simone. Damien. Everyone else who stands there with us transfers their piece until only Taylor and Owen are left.

Taylor looks directly at Owen. "Same time." She points to the Oculus. "With this thing, I see at least fifty futures where you cheat. And each time you cheat, you die. I kill you. Every. Single. Time. So don't cheat, okay?"

Even Owen is not immune to the power of prophecy. He swallows and says, "Same time."

They both transfer their pieces of the key to the panel. The symbols float into place, shifting the other symbols apart until the entire fifth piece of the key is formed. Then they morph and become a string of symbols I've seen before, outside the volcano, on the box holding the compass.

God. The Home of the Gods.
We've made it here.
We've made it to the end.

The panel changes to purple then it shimmers until it becomes nearly transparent. This is our entrance. Our final stand. If we fail here, we fail for good. There won't be any other chances.

I grab Thomas's hand and we step through.

xli

CHAOS WAITS FOR US, SITTING ON A
golden throne in the center of a great room. In my mind, I've
pictured him exactly like the god I defeated at the end of the labyrinth: withered, thin hair, so weak he can barely open his lips to
speak. It's what I've mentally prepared for. What I find I am not
prepared for at all.

A guy stands up from the throne. He's got light brown hair
capped with a heavy golden crown covered in gemstones. His
skin is tanned and healthy. His muscles strong, showing prom-
inently in his blue T-shirt. He wears jeans and gym shoes. He
can't be any older than we are. He's someone I could have walked
by a million times back in Florida. Gone to school with. Seen on
the beach. At the store. He's strong and stands tall. Confidence
flows off him like water flowing from the zodiac jug.

"I'm so happy you could finally join me," he says, speaking to
all of us. His confidence defines him, but I can't help but wonder
how much of it is an act. There are over twenty of us here now
before him. And whatever side we were on out there, in here, we

are all on the same side: the side opposing Chaos.

Chaos walks away from the throne toward Taylor, and he holds out a hand. "Just so you know, it will be much easier if you hand it over."

He's talking about the Oculus. Just seeing him there demanding it makes fear quake through my body. I hate myself for thinking it, but I am so happy to not be the one holding it.

Taylor crosses her arms. "Not gonna happen."

Chaos laughs. I feel like he could lash out and yank it from her eye socket as fast as a viper, but instead he says, "We can play that way," and turns away. His eyes settle next on Owen. "Your father is gone."

The statement is so simple, as if it is just another event that happened in an otherwise boring day.

Owen's face tenses up and he glares at Chaos. "He's not gone."

Except I think he is. Owen had tried to contact him and it hadn't worked.

Chaos cocks his head. "Believe me or not. It doesn't matter to me." And he turns away.

One by one, he inserts slivers of fear into each of us. He turns to Abigail next and whispers something in her ear. Her eyes go wide and she grabs the cross necklace as if it will give her strength. I don't want him to approach me, but I know I can't hide from it. And like he can hear me thinking, he walks my way.

"Hi, Eden," Chaos says, like he's just some kid I'm meeting at a party. "You know you aren't supposed to be here. You weren't invited."

Deep breath. I can do this. It's just another part of the simulation. Or at least that's what I am going to pretend. But something tells me that this is more real than anything that may have happened thus far in my life. The fate of the world hangs on this moment.

"And yet here I am." I try to sound brave. "I heard there was a prophecy."

"Prophecy," Chaos says, and he rolls his eyes like it's the most absurd thing in the world. "I don't give credence to prophecies."

"You should," Taylor says. "Because in every future I see, Edie kills you. You ready to die, old god?"

"Do I look old to you?" he says.

He doesn't. He also doesn't look ready to die or hand over any kind of power for that matter.

"Your looks don't deceive me," Taylor says. "You forget that I see everything."

Chaos flicks his hand dismissively and turns away from her, back to me. But his face is tense. Nobody wants to hear predictions of their own death.

"Who helped you, Eden?" Chaos asks.

"Edie doesn't need help," Thomas blurts out. I want to will him into silence, but it's too late.

Chaos's eyes drift slowly to my little brother, and then he smiles. "And look, you brought someone you care about with you. Was that really smart? You know I could reprogram him with a simple thought. Is that what you want?"

Anger flashes through me. The ancient snake god had hidden Thomas away, knowing this exact scenario was a possibility. If he was found by Chaos, he could be used against me. And Chaos must have realized this too. So he sent Owen's dad to the data storage banks to find Thomas. To have Pia bring him to the simulation as a backup plan in case I made it this far. Which I have. And I wish more than anything that Thomas was not here with me right now.

"He has nothing to do with this," I say, drawing Chaos's eyes back to my face, away from Thomas's.

Chaos traces a circle in the air with his finger. "Everything is interconnected. It's the way the world works. So tell me, who helped you? How are you here in the simulation? Because as far as I know, entry to the simulation was blocked for you and Cole."

I'm here because Elise, Iva, Zachary, and even Raven all helped me. I'm here because I was not willing to give up. I wasn't going to let the world be destroyed by someone like Owen. But now, with Chaos in front of me, I see that Owen was never the real threat. It was the lingering old gods, still grasping onto the power. Still holding control of the world, unwilling to give it up.

"I was always meant to be here," I say, and I smile. "The prophecy foretold it. You know that. You tried to ignore it. But you can't ignore prophecy."

"I ignore whatever I choose," Chaos says. His voice is filled with confidence which I hope is an act.

Chaos steps back from me and looks to Cole but doesn't say anything to him, though he could have the same conversation if he wanted to. Instead he addresses all of us.

"I am asking you all to leave," Chaos says. He holds up a finger. "And I won't ask twice."

"I'm not going anywhere," Hudson says.

"None of us are." It's Owen. On our side. And for the moment, that is good enough for me.

"This old god is going to lose," Taylor says, and she smiles. "He's going to lose, and it scares him more than anything."

I don't know if she sees this with the Oculus or if she's making it up. The former, I hope.

"I am not going to lose!" Chaos booms, finally losing control just the smallest amount. His voice carries across the entire chamber, making the hanging crystals sway and clink together, a musical manifestation of his anger.

This only makes Taylor's smile grow. "He is."

But before she can say anything else, she cries out in pain and collapses to the ground, pressing her hands on either side of her head. My first reaction is to rush over and help her. But the best thing I can do for her is to stop Chaos.

"Your time is done," I say.

Chaos smiles. "My time is only just starting."

"That's not what the other gods say," I say. "They say you should have left long ago. They say that you agreed to. And if that's true, why are you still here?"

He puts a hand to his chest in mock surprise. "But I'm the only one left. Without me, what will happen to the world? I need to be here. I need to protect it."

Iva pops into existence four feet in front of him. She's half his height and still wears the blindfold, but I think she sees better with it that the rest of us without. "We had an agreement," she says. "You would step down. You would pass on the power. You told us that. You swore it."

Her presence only stirs his confident facade for a moment. Then he says, "Iva, do you believe everything I say?"

Iva laughs, the giggle of a little girl, the power of a god. "I don't believe anything you say. I knew you'd go back on your word before the deal was even made. I expected it. The prophecy foretold it."

"Enough with the prophecy!" he yells, again losing control. Any more of these slips, and he could break down altogether. But in the event that I have deluded myself into thinking Iva has any power of him, he flicks his hand, and Iva is thrown backward against the crystal wall of the chamber. She lands hard and is pinned against the wall, motionless.

Raven appears next in front of Chaos, almost in the exact spot where Iva was. She wears the long yellow dress that brushes on the ground. Hair splayed around her like an aura. Balancing on one leg with the giant lioness beside her. "The prophecy is real. It always has been. It always will be. Your time is done."

Almost they have been watching the entire time, Elise and Zachary appear on either side of Raven. Gamma also appears next to Elise, one hand resting on her shoulder. Her willowy form is like a tall column next to the little girl.

"Why do you have to be such a pain in the ass?" Elise says.

"Language," Gamma says, whispering loudly enough for us all to hear.

Zachary catches my eye and gives me a small nod. They all are here because they knew Chaos would never keep his word.

"Pain in the ass?" Chaos says. "I guess it's what I'm good at. Regardless, this battle doesn't have a place for minor gods." And without another word, Zachary, Elise, Raven, and even her lioness all fly backward like Iva had done.

"I'm here for a contest," Owen says, stepping forward. "And I'm ready."

"Me, too," Cole says. His eyes are fierce. "You aren't going to back down from our challenge, are you?"

Chaos smiles, like he's one of us, though I now know his appearance is a complete deception designed to make us lower our defenses. "A challenge. So be it." He taps his crown. "If you want to defeat me, all you have to do is take my crown."

And so the battle is on.

xlii

ONCE HE SAYS IT, ALL I CAN SEE IS
the crown. I know it may be a trick. That I can't trust everything
I hear has become more than obvious. But deep down, I believe
this to be the real thing. All I need to do is get the crown.

Hudson is off like a flash. He runs toward Chaos. I hold my
breath. Chaos points at Hudson, and he collapses with a scream.
His legs twist under him at angles that shouldn't be possible. He
doesn't get up.

An arrow flies from Taylor's bow. Time almost seems to slow
down as it spirals toward the old god. Then, in what may be the
most perfect shot ever, it strikes him right in the chest, easily
going through his blue T-shirt. But instead of burying itself deep
inside him, it comes out the back and keeps moving, only stopping when it sticks into the crystal wall far on the other side of
the room.

Taylor is not ready to stop. She fires another arrow, then another. They do the same as the first. When she shoots the fourth
arrow, Chaos raises a hand.

"Don't you ever learn?" he says, and he flicks his wrist in a circular motion. The arrow stops in midair and turns, facing Taylor. Then it launches forward. It is coming right for her chest. She barely has time to jump out of the way. I think I almost see her die. Instead of the chest, it catches her in the upper arm, sticking deep in the bone.

Taylor doesn't even fall. She reaches up and snaps the arrow in half.

"I see your death," she says to Chaos. "I see it and I can't wait for it."

Then the other three arrows pull from the wall and come directly for Taylor. One hits her hand and keeps going, pulling her backward and sticking into the wall, holding her there. The other two hit also, one in her side and the other in her lower leg. She struggles to try to free herself.

This is the time to strike, while Chaos is thick in his victory. I clench the ax in my fist, feeling its weight. But Rex and Amanda run forward and attack. Rex swipes out with his sword, but it's pulled from his hand and turned against him, coming right for his side. The blow should kill Rex when it hits, but he only stumbles and gets right back up.

That's right. His armor. The red-head attacks next. Then some of the other kids who've joined our group. There is power in numbers, but Chaos fights them easily, even finding a way to get through the chinks in Rex's armor. At least three kids fall, and they don't rise.

I lean down to Thomas. "Go stand in the back, against the wall." I don't want him anywhere nearby.

He nods and tiptoes backward toward where Zachary and Iva are still pressed against the wall. There is only a handful of us remaining: Cole, Owen, and Abigail, a few others. Abigail holds out the necklace and lightning explodes from it, striking the god.

He extends his arms as the electricity runs through him. But instead of weakening him, I'm reminded of how Abigail got the lightning in the first place.

"Stop!" I shout. The lightning isn't hurting him. It's fueling him. Giving him one more weapon to use against us.

Abigail realizes this too late. She drops the necklace, but the lightning doesn't stop until the necklace sparks a couple times and falls back to her chest. Then it flies from Chaos, bursting like an explosion. Two kids drop instantly. I never knew their names. I never will.

I'm thrown backward, landing hard on my butt. Cole is next to me. He says something, but my ears are ringing and I can't hear him. Then he gets up and vanishes. There is only a blur in the air, like a wave of heat as his hammer circles. His invisibility shield. Owen is heading toward Chaos also, and together they attack. Cole pops back into visibility and swings down with the giant hammer, smashing the old god over the head. Then he vanishes again. Owen holds a sword and swipes out in a stroke that severs an arm.

This is my moment. I run forward. He's right in front of me, staring at the severed arm that lies on the ground twitching. I bury the ax in his chest. Over and over again the three of us attack. Chaos falls to his knees, but he doesn't give up. He pulls on the lightning again and in a blast, we're thrown back. I drop my ax, and I scramble to get it. It's lodged near the leg of the chair. I grab it, then look back to Chaos.

He's standing again, pulling himself back together, healing as we watch. I run forward again. I'll do this as many times as I need to.

It won't work, Zachary Gomez seems to whisper in my mind.

He can't be killed, Iva seems to say.

Can't be killed.

But the prophecy . . . , I think. *It had said I would kill him.*

No. That's not right. Not kill him. It had said I would *defeat* him. And to defeat him, I don't have to kill him. I only have to get the crown.

I throw my ax far across the room, causing the distraction I hope to. Chaos looks over toward it, wondering what I'm aiming for, and when he does, I rush forward.

My fingers wrap around the crown at the same time as Cole and Owen. Chaos snarls in rage, but the crown won't come off of his head.

"It will only come off if I'm dead," he hisses.

Only when he's dead but he can't be killed. It makes no sense. But the harder we pull, the more it sticks.

It's not about the crown, I think. *It never was.* The crown is nothing but a deception. It is about Chaos here, right now, uncontained.

Uncontained. That's it. We can't kill him, but we can contain him and take his place.

I look to Iva. Even though she can't see me, she smiles and nods. Then I pull on my power, and I think of the black glossy pearl I'd retrieved for her from her domain. Markers on memorials for dead gods. Markers . . . or maybe something more. With the power, I deconstruct it and send the bits of data that make it up across the air to me. In my palm I rebuild it. Then, when it is complete, I create a latch and open it.

Chaos lets out a cry of pain that makes my bones vibrate. He howls as if he's being subjected to a fate worse than any death. Then his streams of data pull apart and begin to siphon into the pearl like a gray stream of water drifting through the air. I don't move as I watch it, and only when I'm sure the last byte of data has been placed inside the sphere do I flip the lid closed and latch it. Then I remove the latch, making it once again impenetrable.

Not dead but contained. We've reached the end. We've defeated the last of the old gods. But it's not just me. It's all of us. And I'm not sure what will happen next.

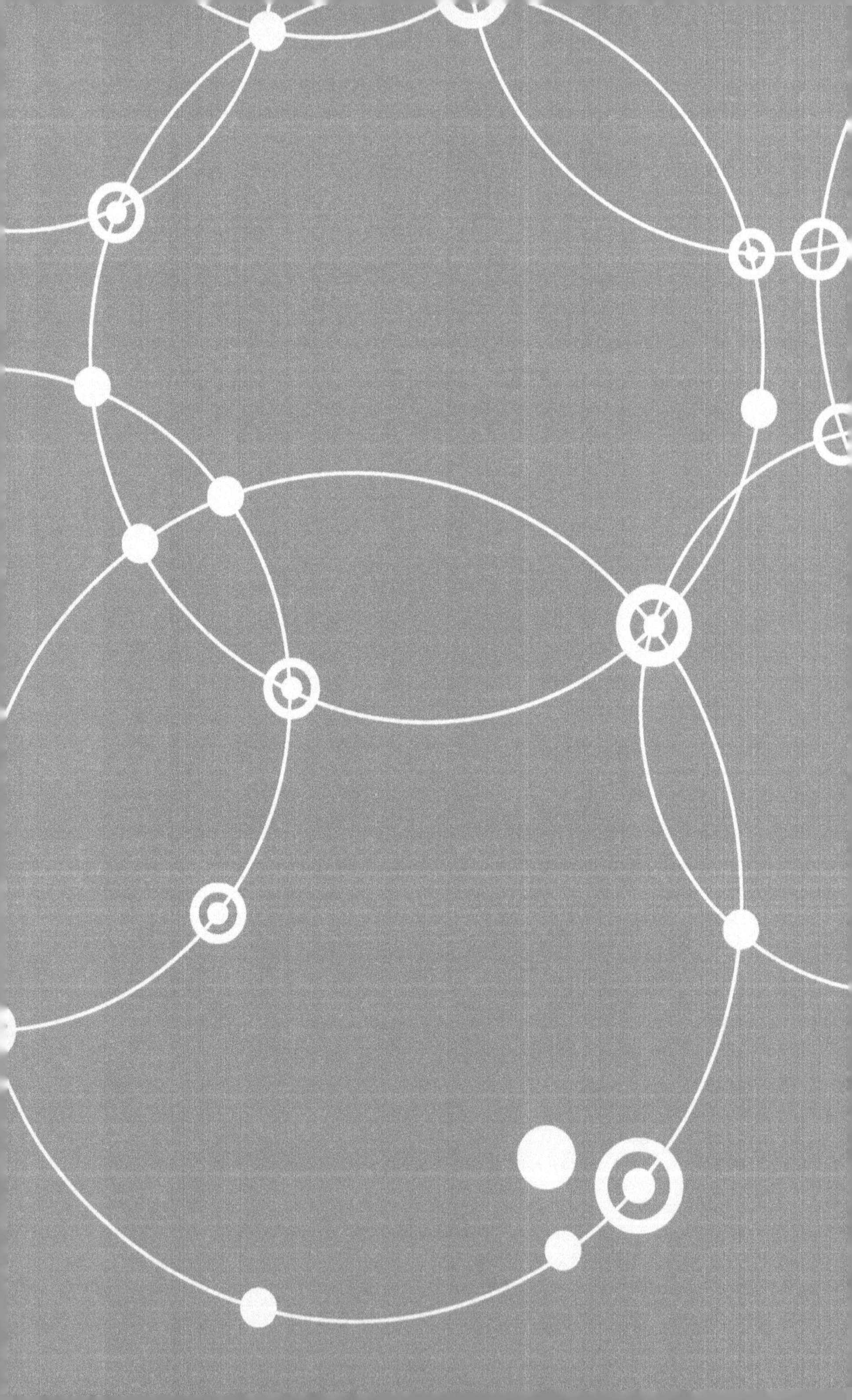

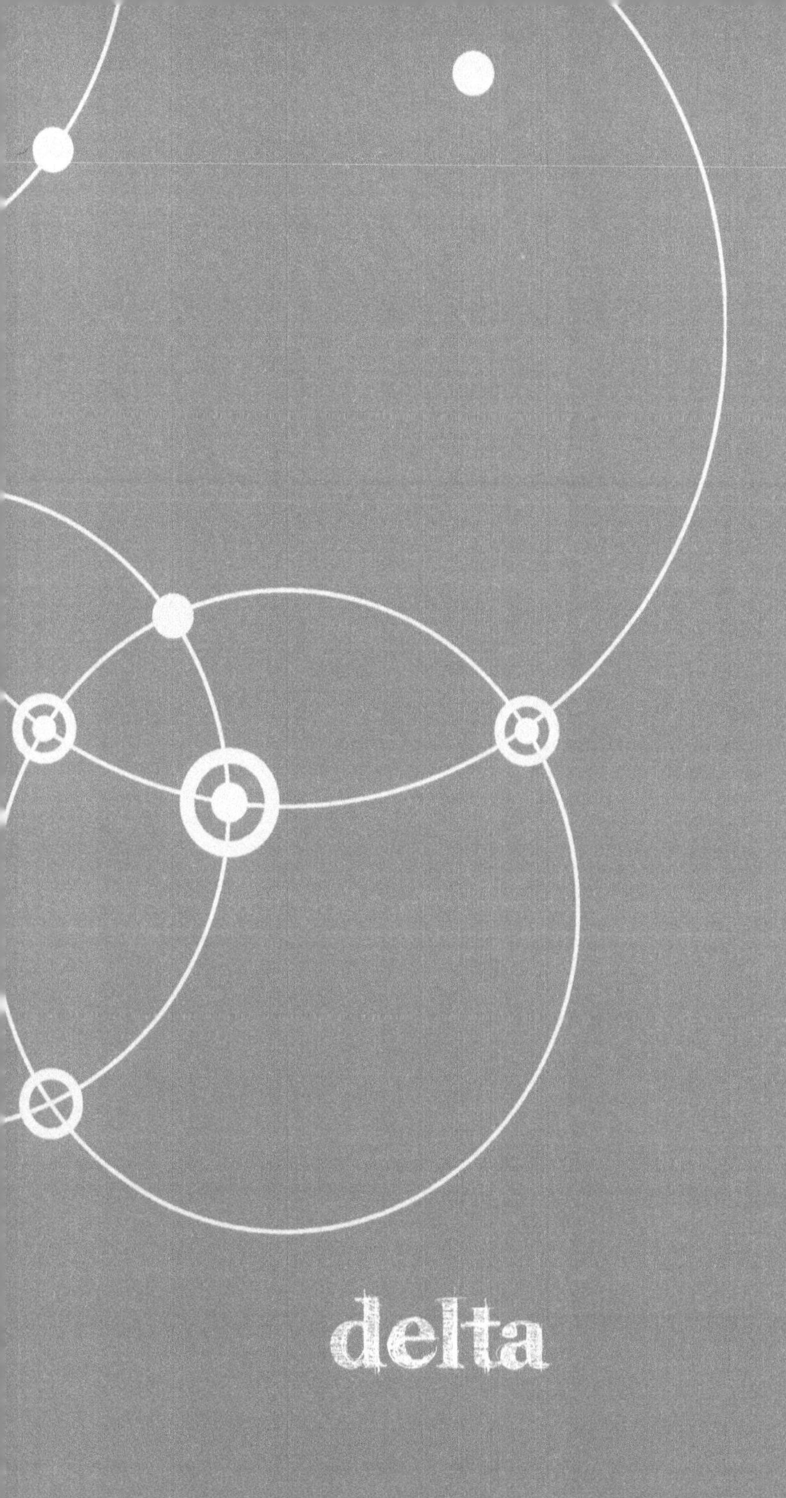
delta

xliii

I HOLD THE PEARL IN MY HAND, UN-
sure what to do with it.

Iva skips up to me, now free from the earlier bonds that held her. "Do you want me to hold it, Eden?" she says in her sing-sing voice, like we haven't just fought a battle that nearly killed us all.

Keep it, Zachary says in my mind. A telepathic bond that no one else knows about.

I shake my head and give Iva a huge smile. I still don't trust her. Not really. I don't trust any of them, not even Zachary. "I got it," I say. I construct a chain out of metal from the world around me, and I attach the pearl on a pendant. I clasp it at the back on my neck and lay it flat against my chest. I, instead of Iva, can be the one to keep it safe. To keep Chaos contained. Then I look to my friends because this is far from over.

Hudson is squatting on the ground next to Taylor, and as Cole and I watch, her skin and muscle is regenerated. It's a power he's had all along, maybe, and never fully understood. And now, with Chaos dead, it can be completely his. He's already healed himself

and is slowly working through the rest of us. Taylor frowns at him like she can't believe she has to lower herself to actually taking his help.

She gets to her feet and mutters something that might be a thank you.

"What?" Hudson says. "You'd rather be walking around with arrows sticking out of you?"

Taylor shrugs. "They didn't hurt."

I know that's a lie. But it is a little bit of normal back in our virtual world.

We're still in the chamber where we entered. The golden throne sits empty. I look up, but instead of levels and levels of computer workstations and terminals like I'd pictured Main Control Room Alpha in my mind, all I see is a huge atrium that reaches up to the very top of the pink and black glass building.

Like the world is coming alive, sunshine moves across the sky outside and light moves through the windows, creating beams of color that bounce around and light up the crystals that hang from the pedestals.

"Where's the control room?" I ask. We've done everything we were supposed to do. I'm ready for this to be over.

Zachary walks over with Raven limping at his side. Following them is Elise. She's holding a giant mug of something. Eggnog I'm willing to bet. She takes a long sip and then grins, a mustache of the stuff on her upper lip.

"This is the control room," Raven says.

I shake my head and motion around at everything, which is nothing. "This isn't a control room," I say.

"Are you sure?" Raven says. "What does your logic say about it?"

Logic. I piece through what I have. We are here, in what I thought was Main Control Room Alpha. We've defeated the final old god and trapped him. He was in control before. He was here. And now we are here. We are all here.

But there isn't a control room. And there is supposed to be.

But there's not.

No control room.

That's the only answer.

"There is no control room," I say.

Iva and Elise both burst out into a stream of giggles. Then Elise says, "You're thinking too logically."

I've never thought there could be too much logic. Logic answers everything. But I'm also missing something.

Maybe she's right. Maybe I am thinking too logically. Everything is being controlled . . . just not in the way I thought.

"Oh, I get it," Hudson says. "This is the control room. Right here. We're in it."

He's wrong . . . I think.

"Good," Raven says. "And . . . ?"

"And . . . we're all here. We're all in control," Abigail says. She tosses her hair around, instantly making it fall into place in perfect waves despite everything we've been through, like she has some magical control of it.

Like she can manipulate it the same way I use the power to manipulate bits and pieces of the virtual world. Like she has control.

"Man, you guys are smart," Zachary says. "No one of you is in control. All of you are. You each have different abilities. Different ways to shape reality. That's what the world needs. Lots of gods, not just one or two. And not some ancient relics that can't even remember what day of the week it is. Fresh. New. And plural."

"Like a council," I say. Not one person in control, but people who can work together to make sure the world thrives.

Work together or fight each other, I think. Because no matter what has just happened, I will never be on the same side as Owen.

Or Simone. Damien. And yet they're here. Part of the future.

"It's like a pantheon," Thomas says, grabbing my hand. "Remember Mom talking about a pantheon, Edie?"

The word floats out there, just beyond my memory. But Hudson immediately understands.

"A pantheon is a group of gods," Hudson says. "And we're the new gods."

The new gods. Just like the old gods had been. A new generation to replace the ones that were no longer worthy.

Raven beams at Hudson, a little too much. Kind of like she wants to spend time with him now that this is all over. "Exactly. The world had old gods, but they'd run it into ruin. Now it has you. And it's time to make things right."

Make things right. But where to begin?

xliv

I WALK A SLOW CIRCLE AROUND THE
room, acting like I'm studying every detail. Really, I'm trying to
get my thoughts in order. Halfway across the room, I spin to face
Iva, Elise, Raven, and Zachary.

"Where do you guys fit into this?" I ask. Zachary always re-
ferred to himself as a minor god.

He takes a step toward me, causing a frown to form instantly
on Cole's face. Zachary places a hand on his chest. "We're minor
gods. You guys are the major gods. Minor. Major."

Taylor's frown matches Cole's though for a different reason.
"And that means what? You listen to us? You do what we say?"

Iva giggles. "Of course not. Where would the fun in that be?"
And without another word, she and Elise join hands and vanish.

The current game of the gods may be over, but I have no doubt
there will be more in the future, especially with those two around.

"So," Taylor says to Zachary. "You promised me—"

Zachary holds up a hand. "I did. And I am good for my word."
Then he disappears and five long seconds go by. Taylor looks like

she's ready to strangle someone. But when he reappears with Adam at his side, everything changes.

Taylor's face is unlike I've ever seen it before. Her eyes are wide as she rushes over to her twin and grabs him so tightly I worry she'll cut off his circulation. I can't help the tears that well up in my eyes. They speak in low tones that I don't try to listen in on. Then Zachary walks over to me and grabs both of my hands. Behind him, Cole clears his throat loudly.

"Don't worry," Zachary says. "We're on the same side."

"What side is that?" Cole asks.

Zachary doesn't bother looking at Cole. He only keeps his eyes on me. "The side that's going to get the world back in order." Then he leans forward and plants a kiss on my cheek.

This is about as much as Cole can take. "Are we done here yet?" he asks.

Zachary lets go of my hands and steps back. "Done? You haven't even started. And I haven't either. Before I got here, I'd almost found the warehouse with the destroyers. And once I do . . . Well, I'll fill you guys in on that when it happens."

Then he, too, disappears right in front of my eyes.

Raven limps up to Hudson and presses a hand on his chest. "I like you," she says. "You were immune to my powers."

Hudson's face turns about as red as the inside of a watermelon. "Yeah . . . well . . . ," he starts.

"Come visit me anytime," she says. "You know where to find me."

The image of her domain with the animals around her forms in my mind. It had existed in the virtual world, in Simulation Avine, and yet I'm sure it is a reflection of her reality, too.

Hudson shrugs and tries to act like he's all cool with it. "Maybe I will," he says.

I'm willing to bet a week doesn't go by before he takes her up on the offer.

Then Raven turns into her namesake bird and flies away, leaving only Gamma, tall and willowy. She steps forward.

"I'd like to offer my services," she says, bowing to all of us.

I want to tell her not to bow to me, that I'm just some normal kid from Florida, not some god. But the words remain unspoken.

"With what?" Owen says. Of all of us, he looks the most comfortable with our newfound divine power.

Gamma smiles. "I'm an excellent chef. I love to bake, a different recipe every Friday. No one can match my abilities at making eggnog. I clean. I run errands."

And I offer sound advice, she says directly in my mind. I look to her, wondering if I'm the only one who heard her. Her eyes are fixed only on me. She spoke to Elise telepathically back when we'd visited Elise's cloud zone. And here . . . maybe she's willing to do the same for me.

The image of the giant snake returns to me. Ancient gods still remain, as in plural. And I can't help but wonder if Gamma is just like him. Maybe I'm stupid to keep one of the ancient gods near me. But I also wonder if I have much choice. At least if Gamma is nearby, I'll know where she is, too.

I'll take all the advice I can get, I think.

Gamma smiles, like she's heard me. And maybe she has.

"Sure," I say, shrugging like it's no big deal. "I like eggnog."

Gamma clasps her hands together and smiles. "Good. Then it's settled." Then she walks away and slips around a corner of the room whose walls form as she goes.

That leaves the rest of us. The ones who have survived. At our feet lay those who fell during the battle, but some remain. Those I know are Cole, Taylor, Hudson, Abigail, Owen. Adam, newly restored from the dead. There's Rex and Amanda though I hardly know them. Simone. Damien. There's the red-headed girl from the labyrinth. A couple other kids I'd seen there and seen in Simulation Avine. In total, there are fourteen of us, not including Thomas.

"Fourteen," Hudson says, breaking the silence that has filled the chamber. "You know there were fourteen Olympians back in Greek mythology."

"Probably a coincidence," Taylor says.

Hudson shrugs. "Probably."

"Yeah, well what are we supposed to do now?" Taylor says.

Hudson decides we need some kind of council chamber, like a place we all meet to discuss things, so he, Rex, and Amanda start work on that.

I have a few things to do, none of which I want to do with everyone watching.

I pull materials from the surrounding area, but here, in this control room, I have at my fingertips materials from all the worlds, not just those in the immediate vicinity. I construct four walls and a roof, simple in design, hardly even noteworthy. Then I make a door and pull Thomas inside. Once we're inside, I increase the space, not taking away from the immediate area around me but from the overall unlimited space of the world. I add more and more space until I have enough for Thomas and me to move around comfortable.

Then I find my parents.

They're been stored away, in the banks of people. Billions of them, filed away. But everything is stored logically, and I'm able to find them easily. I pull their storage into a local area and then I reanimate it here, in this place.

I shake as they take form. What if something is wrong? What if everything has changed? But nothing has changed. The second they are complete, I am certain of this.

"Mom? Dad?" I say, and I rush over, letting them pull me into their arms. Thomas immediately runs over to us also, and we hold on like we never plan to let go again. It's only after at least a minute that maybe they realize everything is not as it should be.

Dad pulls back from the hug. "Where are we?" he asks, shaking his head, trying to make sense of what he sees.

Mom cocks her head. "The ship . . . It was going down."

That is their last memory. Digging too deep. Being pulled under, into the crack in the earth, the place that separated their reality from the world of the gods.

"You guys have missed a lot," I say. And then I hug them again. We have an eternity to catch up. For now, I don't want to ever let them out of my sight again.

There's a knock on the door as Cole walks in, and immediately my heart sinks. I have my parents and Thomas. He has no one. Not even Pia.

I extend my hand, inviting him over to me. And when our hands meet, I interlock my fingers with his.

Dad raises an eyebrow. "Who's this?"

"This is Cole," I say. "We've been through a lot together." And like my parents, I know I never want to let Cole out of my sight either.

"Cole?" Dad says. "Where did you guys meet?"

I can't help but laugh. But I guess the story has to start somewhere.

Slowly, bit by bit, Cole and I fill in my parents and Thomas on everything that's happened, from the world turning upside down to the labyrinth and Simulation Avine. As I talk, I pull on the power, adding elements to the room around me.

I start with the walls, turning them into pink and black crystal on three sides. On the far side, I create sand and the ocean, a lot like Iva's domain. I add space as I need to, and each time something new appears, Mom and Dad look a bit more skeptical. I still haven't managed to get out the reality of my future. But Thomas takes care of this for me.

"Edie and Cole are gods," Thomas says.

If I think Mom and Dad are going to be surprised, I'm completely wrong. They only nod and make suggestions about how the room around me should look.

No, not room. Domain. This is my domain, and I plan to make it exactly how I want.

Then Hudson knocks on the door. When I open it, his eyes go wide.

"I thought I'd been busy," he says. "But I guess I'm not the only one."

"Guess not," I say. And I introduce him to my parents. Then he suggests a council meeting. He doesn't tell Cole and me we have to attend. He doesn't try to take charge. It is a suggestion, but a good one. But before I leave, I reach to my pocket. The apple seeds I acquired in Iva's domain are still there, transcending the boundary of the simulation. I bend down, dig a small hole with my hands, and plant them. Then we leave my parents and Thomas there and head back into the main chamber.

xlv

HUDSON RUNS AHEAD BUT COLE STOPS
me once we're outside my newly constructed domain. Without
a word, he lowers his head and we kiss. I press him against the
crystal wall and lean in close to him, needing to feel him next to
me. Even if everything else is in disorder, Cole is still here. Solid.
Real. And ready to face the future with me.

He runs his hands over my back and pulls me close. I reach up
and run my hands through his thick dark hair, holding his face to
mine. Warmth runs through me, and I let the kiss last well over a
minute. Maybe two. Who's counting anyway?

Finally I pull back because reality is tugging at me. But I lean
close and place my lips against his ear.

"I'm glad you're here with me," I whisper, barely audible.

He puts his lips to my ear and whispers back, "Don't leave me,
okay?"

I answer with a single kiss, sweet and full of my intent. I have
no plans to leave Cole. Not now. Not ever. Then I pull back from
him and we continue forward until we find the newly constructed

council chamber.

Owen and Abigail are the last to arrive. We sit around a round table, fourteen chairs. Hudson clears his throat and says something like, "So I guess we should figure out what—"

But the rest gets lost because Owen cuts him off. "We need a leader," Owen says.

Unspoken, but oh so obvious, is that he thinks he should be that leader. I don't want to work with Owen on anything, but I know deep down that I'm going to have to. We're all going to have to work together.

"Maybe we should talk about restoring the world first," Taylor says. "Last I saw, there weren't any people there."

It is a good place to start. But so is cleaning up the world. And the reality of what we face slams into me. We have so much work to do. Whatever happens, whatever we decide, it won't happen instantly.

"Alright," Hudson says. "Who has ideas? How about we go around the room and everyone gets five minutes?"

Owen scowls. "Nobody put you in charge."

But Abigail places a hand on his arm, and some sort of calming seems to wash over him, like she's using her power on him and he's completely unaware.

I stand up, scooting my chair back. "I'll go first," I say. Then I lay out my plans for reshaping the world.

I start with the plan to repair the crack under the ocean floor. To reseal the barrier between the world of the gods and the human world. And after that, I continue on, refilling the ocean, repairing infrastructure, making the place livable again. I'm sure I'm overlooking obvious things, making mistakes. But I'm also not going to sit back and let everyone else decide. Every single one of us will make mistakes. I might as well be the first.

ABOUT THE AUTHOR

P. J. (TRICIA) HOOVER WANTED TO be a Jedi, but when that didn't work out, she became an electrical engineer instead. After a fifteen year bout designing computer chips for a living, P. J. started creating worlds of her own. She's the award-winning author of *The Hidden Code*, a *Da Vinci Code*-style young adult adventure with a kick-butt heroine, and *Tut: The Story of My Immortal Life*, featuring a fourteen-year-old King Tut who's stuck in middle school. When not writing, P. J. spends time practicing kung fu, solving Rubik's cubes, and watching Star Trek. For more information about P. J. (Tricia) Hoover, please visit her website www.pjhoover.com.